Songs of
Summer

Also by Jane L. Rosen

~~~~

Seven Summer Weekends
On Fire Island
A Shoe Story
Eliza Starts a Rumor
Nine Women, One Dress

Songs of Summer

Summer

Jane L. Rosen

BERKLEY
NEW YORK

BERKLEY
An imprint of Penguin Random House LLC
1745 Broadway, New York, NY 10019
penguinrandomhouse.com

Title page art: Headphones © Melodiana Studio / Shutterstock
Book design by Alison Cnockaert

Library of Congress Cataloging-in-Publication Data

Names: Rosen, Jane L., author.
Title: Songs of summer / Jane L. Rosen.
Description: First edition. | New York: Berkley, 2025.
Identifiers: LCCN 2024044137 (print) | LCCN 2024044138 (ebook) |
ISBN 9780593818787 (trade paperback) | ISBN 9780593818794 (hardcover) |
ISBN 9780593818800 (ebook)
Subjects: LCGFT: Domestic fiction. | Novels.
Classification: LCC PS3618.O83145 S66 2025 (print) |
LCC PS3618.O83145 (ebook) | DDC 813/.6—dc23/eng/20240924
LC record available at https://lccn.loc.gov/2024044137
LC ebook record available at https://lccn.loc.gov/2024044138

First Edition: May 2025

Printed in the United States of America
1st Printing

The authorized representative in the EU for product safety and compliance is
Penguin Random House Ireland, Morrison Chambers, 32 Nassau Street,
Dublin D02 YH68, Ireland, https://eu-contact.penguin.ie.

This is for you, Daddy.

—Stevie Nicks

———

In loving memory of my dad, Seymour Levenbaum

SEPTEMBER 22, 1922–SEPTEMBER 22, 1976

If music be the food of love, play on.
—William Shakespeare

Songs of
Summer

Maggie May

♩ ♫ ♪

MAGGIE MAY WHEELER had moved into the house with the big willow tree out back a few months before her tenth birthday. She didn't want to leave the Main Street apartment over the record shop in Chagrin Falls, Ohio, where she had spent the first decade of her life. She adored living over her parents' store, loved going down the back stairs with her dad every morning before school to prepare to open. There, Maggie would sit on the stool behind the cash register eating an English muffin with peanut butter dripping from its nooks and crannies. She'd watch as the morning sun caused the words painted on the front window—MAGGIE MAY RECORDS—to dance across the hardwood floor while her dad, Hank Wheeler, got down to business.

Hank would methodically begin each day by opening the boxes from the day before. He liked to check out the new albums in the calm of the morning, contemplating the track list, the cover art, and the liner notes, before gently placing the record on the turntable and dropping the needle to play. The store carried every genre, so it was anyone's guess whether Maggie would begin her day to the sound of Out-Kast singing "Hey Ya!" or Aretha Franklin calling for "Respect."

"Can I have this dance, Maggie May?" her dad would ask when the rhythm moved him, and the two would spin or twist or twirl until Maggie's mom came down to scoot her off to school.

Maggie's mom and dad were older than the other kids' parents, but it didn't bother Maggie. She hadn't even realized it until she was waiting in line at the start of second grade. Jill Rose's mother studied Jenny Wheeler's loose gray curls and remarked, "How nice that your grandma brought you on the first day."

Maggie looked from Jill's mom, with her miniskirt and shiny black hair, to the moms in front and behind her, and back to her own, and noted, for the first time, the difference in age between them. She asked her mom about it on the way home, and on that night, her parents sat her down and told her that she was adopted.

Soon afterward, Hank and Jenny Wheeler became fixated on the idea that it was unconventional for a child to live above a record store and spend so much time with adults. They became obsessed with giving Maggie a conventional upbringing in a house with neighbors and a backyard. Her parents wanted her to play outdoors with other kids, to spend her free time with the OutKast generation instead of Aretha's, they'd explained. *That*, she understood. But even so, Maggie always associated the move with learning she was adopted.

Maggie was devastated by the thought of leaving the apartment over the record store, but not wanting to upset her parents, she didn't object. For reasons she couldn't explain, she had been on her best behavior since learning the big news, as if her mom and dad might give her back if she misbehaved. It was an absurd thought. Both Jenny and Henry adored their girl more than anything in the world, and she knew it.

From her bedroom window over the shop, Maggie could see beyond the treetops as far as the train station. She could tell when the 6:07 from Akron came in behind schedule and could count the alarms when the local firehouse had a call. Once, she saw the biggest bully in her class, Kimberly Kahn (nickname—Genghis), drop her ice cream cone on the sidewalk and burst into tears. After that, Maggie never feared Kimberly Kahn again.

None of this would be visible from the three-bedroom Victorian or colonial or ranch with neighbors and a yard that her parents were constantly combing the real estate section of the paper in search of. Nothing felt more boring to Maggie than neighbors and a backyard.

It was nearly a year later that Maggie first climbed the willow tree in the backyard of the prewar Victorian she now reluctantly called home and spotted a neighboring kid that looked to be about her age. With her long ponytail tucked under her Rock and Roll Hall of Fame baseball cap and her overalls' pockets stuffed with candy, she called out to him.

"Hello down there!"

"Hello up there," the boy bellowed back, without missing a beat. "Want to see my turtle?"

She stepped onto a lower branch that extended over the back fence into the boy's yard, then fearlessly slid down it, landing with a thud on the other side. The boy, Jason Miller, looked at her like she was the coolest girl he had ever laid eyes on, even before she unloaded her pockets. Odds were, she was.

"Fun Dip?" she asked, adding "It's Razz Apple!"

"That's my favorite flavor!" he gushed.

"Mine too!"

Maggie split the sticks, handing one to Jason, and from that day on, the two were inseparable.

Maggie and Jason waited at the bus stop together, where Maggie had once pummeled Emmett Pitler for hitting Jason with a rock-filled snowball. They waited for each other after school, when Maggie's mom would shuttle them over to the record store to do their homework and help close: straightening the albums so they wouldn't warp and making sure that customers didn't accidentally put back Led Zeppelin under Z or Rod Stewart under R. Maggie's dad would pay them in 45s and they would spend hours playing Name That Tune with their bounty on rainy weekends. Jason always lost but was just happy to be with Maggie. He was always happiest with Maggie.

Maggie and Jason's birthdays were two days apart, May third and May fifth, so they made a tradition out of celebrating together on the fourth. They went all out with themes and decorations and music and food, especially the cake. For their tenth, the theme was May the Fourth Be with You (Jason's brilliant idea); for their eleventh, Battle of the Boy Bands; and for their twelfth, *High School Musical*. By their thirteenth birthdays, Maggie declared that they were too old for backyard parties. Their parents organized a big family dinner instead. The "big" part referred to Jason's side of the equation.

Jason Miller was sandwiched between two sisters and

lived across the street from a whole other Miller clan, an aunt and uncle, who had five kids. Maggie's dad would spend hours before their birthday parties pairing each guest to a record that matched their personality. Maggie would meticulously wrap the albums in the glossy gift wrap her mom had designed for the store—bright yellow paper covered in 45s with Maggie May Records printed on their tiny labels. Handing out the personalized party favors was Maggie's favorite part of her birthday.

On the night of their thirteenth, Maggie and Jason climbed up the willow tree. (They spent so much time there that their dads had built a platform around the trunk for them to hang out on.) Maggie brought out two pens, a notebook, and a Ziploc bag.

"What age do you think is really grown up? Twenty-one?" she asked Jason.

"No way. I have a cousin who's twenty-one, and he got a marble stuck up his nose on his last birthday."

Maggie laughed. "What about twenty-five? That seems old."

"I say thirty. Why do you want to know?"

"OK, thirty it is. Here."

She handed him a piece of paper, a pen, and an envelope. Maggie loved games. Jason did not. He rolled his eyes.

"It's not a game. Not really. We're writing letters to our future selves. I read about it in *Seventeen* magazine. Put down everything you hope to be by the time you're thirty on your sheet and then seal it in the envelope. I'm gonna do the same thing, and when we're thirty, we'll come up here and read them out loud!"

He rolled his eyes again, but leaned back against the trunk and began. They both took the task very seriously, and nearly an hour later she put their envelopes in the Ziploc, sealed it tight, and wrote:

DO NOT OPEN UNTIL MAY 2025

Maggie shoved it into the hollow of the tree, Boo Radley style, and neither of them thought much about the contents of their letters again.

Put Your Records On

♩♫♪

May 4, 2025

Maggie

MAGGIE MAY WHEELER pressed the last strip of Scotch tape onto the vintage yellow Maggie May Records wrapping paper just as the reindeer bells rang on the front door of her record shop. She looked up and smiled as Jason strolled in. A matching smile lit his face.

"Hey, thirtieth birthday girl!" he proclaimed.

"Hey, thirtieth birthday boy," she responded.

Jason looked around the store to double-check that it was empty before giving Maggie a sweet birthday kiss.

Maggie and Jason had been sleeping together since Halloween, but they were still the only ones who knew about it. It wasn't a planned thing, or even something they'd discussed casually; it was just something that had happened. The fact that they were dressed at the time as Ken and Barbie (wigs and all) had helped her feel bold enough to make the first move, though if Maggie were being completely honest, she would have to admit that it was less about their costumes and more about Jennifer Alexander endlessly flirting with Jason at the party they were at. She had even asked him to sing a duet for karaoke. Suddenly, while watching the two crooning "Islands in the Stream," the possibility of losing Jason, and losing his family, became too much for Maggie to bear. When he dropped her off that night, with the help of some liquid courage, she leaned over and kissed him, really kissed him, and after his initial shock, he kissed her back.

That first time was a frenetic, alcohol-fueled combination of hookup and head trip. Breaking through twenty years of platonic friendship was intense, though they seemed to be in tune. Clearly, they had both been curious over the years about what it would be like for them to fool around, but acting on it felt a bit surreal. Plus, they had kept the wigs on.

The next morning, in her natural brown curls, Maggie had no idea what Jason was thinking.

She slipped out from under the covers, grimaced at the sight of last night's crumpled Barbie costume, and grabbed a Case Western sweatshirt from the back of Jason's desk chair. The two were nearly the same size, both slim and fit, so it barely covered her bum. She scooted to the kitchen, holding the side of her head. She needed coffee.

While the Keurig brewed, so did she.

She knew the next move was up to her. Everything between Maggie and Jason was always up to her. It wasn't that Jason was wishy-washy; he just always put her first.

The thought made her laugh. What could be better than dating your best friend who always puts you first? She weighed the options, from never again to a split-level ranch with 2.5 kids and a golden retriever named Ringo, and decided to keep her mouth shut for now.

Later that day, at a boozy brunch with Jason's family, his

sister got right to the heart of the matter with Maggie and Jason.

"What did you go as for Halloween?" she asked, adding, "If you two are still dressing as a couple, neither of you will ever meet someone else."

Maggie had no interest in meeting someone else, and even less interest in a solo Halloween costume. They had already discussed reprising their sixteen-year-old Elvis and Priscilla getups for next year. She pictured herself going alone as Priscilla. No one would even know who she was.

She downed the mimosa she had been sipping and decided to bring up the issue on the ride home.

"Do you think it's true, what your sister said?"

"No. Jennifer Alexander had no problem moving in on me at the party last night."

"Ya, and because of it, I jumped you in the front seat of your car."

"I knew it—you were jealous."

"It wasn't really jealousy. It's just, I don't know, I don't care to share you with anyone else."

"I get that. Me neither."

They braked at a crosswalk for a family of five to cross the street.

"Did you like it—you know, last night?" he mumbled, blushing awkwardly.

"Yes," she laughed, "did you?"

"Absolutely. It may be weird to do it again, though."

"Maybe," she lamented.

"Want to come over and find out?" Jason proposed, flashing his best boyish grin.

They laughed until the car behind them beeped.

While it was a little weird making love to her best friend in the light of day, it was also very sweet, which only brought up a bigger question.

Namely, were they now boyfriend and girlfriend?

Seven months later, when their birthdays rolled around, they were still sleeping together, though Maggie had never done so entirely sober. The one time they attempted it, Maggie found herself laughing every time Jason touched her. She claimed she was feeling ticklish, but he didn't buy it, and it sparked their first lovers' quarrel. That's what Maggie kept calling it, in the hopes of making Jason laugh enough to let it go, but he only moped harder. Beyond that, they were still sneaking around in secret and hadn't made it official in any way whatsoever.

And now Maggie wondered what they were waiting for.

~~~~

BOTH MAGGIE AND Jason had moved back home right after college graduation, Maggie to help her then-ailing parents in the store, Jason to save money by living at home during grad school at Case Western, where he was now a professor of ethics. When Maggie's parents passed away a few years later—her mother from the same heart disease that had prevented her from carrying children, her father six months later from a different kind of broken heart—Jason and his family were with her every step of the way. There was no doubt in Maggie's mind that they were her family now. It was one reason she never mailed in the 23andMe kit she'd ordered one night at three in the morning, when curiosity about the family origins she had never paid much attention to got the better of her. That, and remembering the tears of relief that had poured down her mother's face all those years ago, after Maggie learned she was adopted.

Always intuitive, always empathetic, young Maggie had touched her mother's cheek in response to her offer to help find her birth mother and comforted her by saying, "You're my only mom. I'm good." And Jenny was still her only mom, in memory at least. Maggie had no intention of revisiting that question now that she was gone.

On the morning of May fourth, Jason looked at Maggie as she carried in the pile of perfectly wrapped albums she'd put together and asked, "What did we get everyone?"

Maggie was excited to flip through the stack, excited to be with family again on their birthdays and to show off how well she knew everyone by nailing each gift.

"Wanna guess?"

"You know I don't want to guess."

"You may as well give in now." Maggie smirked, but as much as Jason still wasn't a game player, he could never resist Maggie, who would turn anything into a friendly competition if she could.

"Fine, I'll try."

She boosted herself onto the countertop like a gymnast and ruffled Jason's perfectly coiffed hair before planting another quick kiss on his lips. She wondered, if they were ever to settle down together, whether their kids would be fair-skinned with silky straight hair and matching brown eyes like Jason's, or olive-toned with violet eyes and brown curls like her own. She hoped they'd look like her. It wasn't that Maggie didn't think Jason was cute; he was certainly cute, especially when dressed in his little tweed professor jacket. And she wasn't feeling her biological clock ticking or anything like that. It was just a side effect of being adopted. She yearned to see herself in someone else.

Jason feigned eagerness.

"Hit me," he said, slapping his hand on the counter like a Vegas card player.

"OK, record number one, The Cars, *Shake It Up?*"

"That's easy, Cousin Bobby, the wannabe race car driver."

"Good job! The Kinks—*Soap Opera?*"

"My drama queen sister—the older one."

"Yup! James Brown. *Sex Machine?*"

"Me?" Jason laughed, adding, "That's a good way to break it to my family that we're sleeping together."

Maggie tossed that one aside with a big smile and a "Kidding!"

Since they still presented as best friends, never kissing or holding hands in public, and certainly never in front of his family, she couldn't imagine the reaction that revelation would bring. Well, she could imagine. Jason's father would be over the moon, fast-forwarding to their wedding and declaring Maggie would finally be his daughter. Jason's sisters would burst into happy tears, and his mom, "Sheila the worrier," would pull them aside separately and warn them of all the potential negatives of their coupling. And there were negatives. If either were to want something different in the end, they could very possibly lose their best friend and, for Maggie, the only family she had left.

Maggie held up the next record. "*James Bond 007: 13 Original Themes?*"

"Ah. My dad will love that!" Jason declared.

Maggie's face lit up. Jason stood and pulled her off the counter for a hug.

"Mags. You know my family loves you more than they

love me, right? No need to impress them—plus, this is our celebration, not theirs."

"Well, you know I like giving more than receiving. And they've all been so good to me."

It was true. Ever since they were kids, Jason's family had welcomed Maggie as if she were their own flesh and blood, and Maggie, as the only child of two older parents, ate up the daily chaos of the Miller house, even if she loved jumping the back fence and going home afterward even more. She relished the quiet familiarity of her own home: Joni Mitchell singing "Big Yellow Taxi" on the turntable, her mom preparing dinner in the kitchen, three plates set at the table, four eyes staring at their greatest gift, asking about her day or her dreams or even just how she liked the turkey tetrazzini.

Don't it always seem to go, that you don't know what you've got till it's gone?

It had been four years since she'd lost her parents, and it still felt very fresh to her; you could see it in her eyes. Birthdays and holidays were brutal.

"Where did you go?" Jason waved a hand in front of her face. She smiled.

"C'mon. You can quiz me on the rest in the car. We're already late, and you know what that means."

She did. The only seats left at the table would be between his great-aunt Lauren and great-uncle Mike. Lauren was a close talker and Mike did this thing where he grasped your hand when making a point, leaving you unable to lift your fork to your mouth. He made a lot of points. Jason had sat next to him last year and barely got three bites in. He ate two bowls of cereal when he got home. Maggie hurried, packing up the gifts.

Birthday

♩ ♫ ♪

Maggie and Jason

IF EVERY BIRTHDAY had been painful for Maggie since her parents had passed, this milestone felt particularly crippling. Not wanting to cause a scene or dampen Jason's thirtieth, she kept her sorrow to herself. Or so she thought.

"What's wrong?" Jason asked her while she was making herself busy in his parents' kitchen for the fifth time that day. She avoided his eyes, but he knew what was wrong anyway. He had always been in tune with her every emotion. Her mother used to say that if Maggie was cut, Jason would bleed. He didn't wait for an answer.

"I miss them too. I'm so sorry, Mags." He wrapped his arms around her, but she quickly broke away.

"It's not only that."

He knew again.

"I'm your family, Maggie. And my family is your family. That's not going to change."

Jason was that friend who let you talk about the same thing seven thousand million times. This was the seven thousand millionth and one.

"For now, we are family. But one day you will meet someone and fall crazy in love, and I will be that girl that used to live behind you. I will lose a whole other family."

"That will never happen."

"It will. You're a good catch. No woman will stand for this"—she motioned to the space between them—"even after we stop sleeping together."

"Well, what if I already fell for that girl twenty years ago?"

"Stop." She smiled, gently shoving him away.

"I'm serious. You're my family, Maggie, and you're my girl."

"For the time being." She dramatically sighed, teasing him now. She hated being vulnerable, always had. Being adopted didn't help, and her parents' deaths compounded her fear of walking without a map. She did everything she could to protect what was left of her resilience, which for her meant keeping everything as it was.

"How long till your sister mentions fixing you up with that woman from her office again, or till Jennifer Alexander asks you to sing karaoke again? Next time it will be '*Voulez-vous coucher avec moi*.'" She laughed, quoting the '70s Patti LaBelle hit that they used to sing all the time as kids until they learned what it meant.

He grabbed her hand to lead her to the dining room. "C'mon, let's tell them!"

"What are we going to tell them? That we're sleeping together? That's just . . . icky," she laughed.

"We can sing it—in French!"

"Very funny."

"Seriously, let's tell them that we're trying things out—romantically. That we are now girlfriend and boyfriend."

He blushed when he said it.

"Please. They'll have the wedding venue booked by morning."

Jason stopped in his tracks. "That's fair. At least come inside and stop hiding in the kitchen."

She agreed, and somewhere between opening presents and blowing out the candles on their shared birthday cake, Jason quietly reminded Maggie of their childhood pact. In a minute, she was out the door, headed to the willow tree in the backyard of her old house. She sold it after her parents had passed, and she moved back to the apartment on top of the record store. Even though the letters had been her big idea at the time, she had totally forgotten about them.

Maggie hopped the fence as easily as she had at twelve and proudly hightailed it up the trunk while the new owners, frequent patrons of the record store, waved from the kitchen window and Jason laughed from below.

"Are you coming?" she hollered, gloating a little bit.

"Just bring it down," he said.

"No can do." She rattled the ancient Ziploc bag.

He gave up and followed her. Why should today be any different?

"Should we say anything, or just open them?" Maggie asked, handing Jason his envelope.

"I don't know. How about 'Happy birthday, Maggie'? Whatever it says in here, I could not be happier with how things have turned out."

He corrected himself, realizing that both her parents were gone. "How we have turned out, I mean."

"Me too." She leaned over and kissed him quickly on the lips.

"You go first," she instructed him.

"No, you go first!" he countered.

"Odds or evens?"

He couldn't help but laugh. "Odds."

"Once, twice, three, shoot," they sang in unison.

Jason held out three fingers and Maggie two. Maggie took the loss like a champ and began.

> *"Dear Old Maggie,"*

"Old Maggie! That's harsh," she scolded her thirteen-year-old self before continuing.

> *"Happy thirtieth birthday! Congrats on being the Ohio State Lip Syncing champion six years in a row."*

"Is that even a thing?" Jason asked.

"I don't think so, but it should be!"

Maggie continued:

> *"You live back over the record store with your husband, Justin Bieber."*

They both laughed.

> *". . . and your twins. A boy and a girl. Joplin and Jagger."*

"Hmm. Those names are in now," she bragged.

"A trendsetter married to a pop star!"

> *"You run the store while your parents help care for*
> *the twins and we all still spend birthdays with Jason*
> *and his family."*

She looked up and smiled at him.

"Finally—I thought you forgot about me."

"Never!"

Maggie's face dropped as she looked at the next line.

"What?" Jason asked. "What? Tell me, you have me married to one of those Spice Girls, Orange Spice, and now you're uncontrollably jealous?"

"It's Ginger Spice," said Maggie. "When it comes to music, you may be the most clueless millennial on the planet . . . with a girlfriend who owns a record store, no less."

"Oooh. You're my girlfriend now? Is that an official confirmation?" He reached over and tickled her around her waist.

"Please, Jason, you know I'm your girlfriend."

Maggie began folding her letter away, but Jason wasn't having it.

"No way, Maggie. Read the rest."

She opened it back up.

> *". . . and we all still spend birthdays with Jason and*
> *his family, and my birth mother, who I found when I*
> *was twenty and who is pretty great."*

"Wow," said Jason. "You never even talk about your birth mother; do you think about her?"

Maggie took a deep cleansing breath before admitting, "Lately, every day."

"Lately, every day?" Jason questioned, scooting closer, putting his arm around her. "Maybe you should talk about it. Or do something about it."

"Maybe." She took a beat, wiggling out from under his arm. "Read yours!" she said, while folding her letter back up, signaling a hard stop to the conversation. So Jason did as he was told.

"Dear Jason—"

"Yours is better already," she interrupted with a smile.

*"Congrats on being the youngest baseball player
signed to the majors."*

Maggie smirked. Jason didn't even make varsity ball in high school. He smiled, too, and proudly noted, "At least I was confident!"

His letter went on to talk about being captain of the debate team, which he had been, and going to his dad's alma mater, Ohio State, for undergrad, which he did. And one thing that gave Maggie pause.

"There are pins covering your map!"

One wall of Jason's childhood bedroom was covered in a map of the world. He had a constant itch to travel and discover new places, a sharp contrast to Maggie, who had little interest in venturing beyond Chagrin Falls. Aside from his travels his junior year abroad, Jason had yet to pin many spots. Her thoughts on the matter were interrupted by Jason's seventeen-year-old postscript.

> *"P.S. I will be married to my best friend in the world,*
> *Maggie May Wheeler, and we will raise our family*
> *over Maggie May Records so they will grow up to be*
> *as cool as their mom."*

"Oh my God, Jason. That is the cutest thing!"

She wiggled back under his arm.

"We should do it," he said, just above a whisper.

"Do what?" she asked.

"We should get engaged."

She slid back out, faced him.

"Stop kidding around."

"I'm not! Hear me out. If we come out as dating, my whole family, and possibly the entire town, will obsess over us getting married, like we've talked about. This way we cut them off at the chase! We can be engaged in peace without everyone speculating where it's going."

Maggie laughed. "A long engagement—it's actually not a terrible idea."

Jason spun around and reached down into the crag of the tree. He pulled out a Mad Libs filled with every expletive they had known at twelve, a purple Princess Diana Beanie Baby they had been convinced would be worth a small fortune one day (it wasn't), and a mixed bag of plastic figurines from McDonald's Happy Meals. He felt around in the dark to the corners until his hand grazed upon what he was looking for. He held it up like a prize, a small jewelry box that she immediately recognized.

"Remember these?"

"Of course I do. Our mood rings."

Jason fumbled with the box and took one out. He got

down on one knee, took a deep breath, and with a nervous expression asked:

"Maggie, I can't imagine loving anyone more than I love you. Will you marry me?"

He slipped one of the mood rings on her finger and gave her an encouraging smile.

"I don't know," she said. "I was kind of hoping for a Ring Pop!"

He placed both hands on her face and looked into her eyes.

"Maggie, I'm completely serious."

"Jason. You can't ask me to marry you because you predicted it when you were thirteen . . . or because it's easier than telling your family we've been sleeping together!"

"That's not why," he insisted. "It's always been you, and I want us to be family—officially and forever."

His first attempt to take charge of the direction of their lives was certainly a humdinger. She loved Jason—of course she did—and couldn't imagine life without him and his family. But they had said they were boyfriend and girlfriend for the first time only minutes ago. Now he was proposing! This was a leap she hadn't anticipated, and she wasn't much of a leaper.

"Give me a minute," she said, as sweetly as she could. Jason's face turned beet red. She hurried her thoughts, out of empathy for his obvious embarrassment. It turned out to be true that if Jason was cut, Maggie would bleed too.

"How about we secretly get engaged to be engaged?" she suggested.

"Until I can get you a proper diamond?"

"Well, that would be nice, but I need a little time to figure some things out before announcing it to the world."

Now he looked dejected. She couldn't take it and blurted out the softest thing that came to mind.

"I want to find my birth mother first," she said, quickly realizing it was the truth. "It feels like a puzzle piece that's missing. I can't get married with a piece of me missing!" She smiled at him, hoping he would understand and smile back.

He did.

"I get it," he said. "You want to know where you come from before you decide where you're going."

The conversation had taken some unpredictable twists and turns, but Jason looked visibly relieved. Maggie wondered if he had perhaps gone further than he'd meant to and welcomed the delay to give them both a bit more time to process the idea. She opened the jewelry box and wiggled the other ring onto Jason's pinky to seal the engaged-to-be-engaged deal. They both looked down at their fingers and did their best to assess the color in the dark.

"Mine's green!" Maggie exclaimed.

"Mine looks green too. I'll google it unless you remember."

"I only remember that blackest black was down and depressed and darkest blue was love."

Jason pulled out his phone and searched.

"This is nice—green is calm, comfortable, and content!"

"I love that for us," Maggie gushed.

"Me too."

And they sat up in the willow tree in silence for a good long while. Contemplative, calm, comfortable, and content.

I See the Moon

♩♫♪

Beatrix

BEATRIX SILVER STROLLED along Middle Path, a ten-foot-wide tree-lined gravel walk that ran the length of the Kenyon College campus. She had been walking that same path since she'd first arrived there as a freshman over thirty years before. Now a tenured English professor and a world-renowned expert on Henry James, she still marveled at its beauty.

Kenyon College, in the small town of Gambier, Ohio, was everything one would imagine of a two-hundred-year-old liberal arts campus. Tall trees and gothic architecture towered above idealistic young minds. Walking through the grounds never got old, whether it was a spring day like today or, at other times of year, crossing the snow or fallen leaves.

A casual end-of-semester get-together was being hosted that night for the English Department at the dean's house on Wiggins Street. Bea usually looked forward to these potluck events, a chance to socialize with faculty and show off her mother's famous chocolate cake recipe, but baking it last night had thrown her into a hysterical fit of tears. So much so that she worried the cake would taste salty.

She had remembered that it was her daughter's thirtieth birthday, and she hadn't laid eyes on her since she had brought her into the world. This wasn't something she usually cried about—not since the child was a baby or a toddler or a little girl—but something about this very adult milestone set her off.

Three decades ago, Beatrix Silver had given birth in a hospital a few towns away from school. She hadn't even realized she was pregnant until well into her second trimester, when her best friend came to visit from New York City and saw her naked. By then, she was about five months along with a small but rather distinct baby bump. Bea hadn't noticed either the change in her figure or the fact that she hadn't gotten her period since the summer. She was often irregular, and her weight had fluctuated throughout college.

She was like a girl on one of those Phil shows (Doctor or Donahue) who goes to the bathroom with a stomachache and comes out with a baby.

Her friend had insisted she call her mom, who promised not to tell her dad and arrived in Gambier the next day. Bea had never even been to the gynecologist until her mother took her then. The doctor, a warm woman with cold hands, told them all they needed to know about the adoption process in Ohio. Neither Bea nor her mother raised the possibility of keeping the baby. The father was not in the picture whatsoever and really, at twenty, Bea was just a baby herself.

The pregnancy reopened wounds she was still recovering from, compounding her regret, and fueling her anger over the circumstances of the baby's conception. It was easier, at the time, to blame what had happened on everyone but herself.

Bea hid the remainder of her pregnancy behind big flannels and leggings and glasses of ginger ale that she passed off as gin and tonics. The warm weather made her belly harder to hide, but she had managed. It helped that her boobs had gotten so large that they extended out farther than her baby bump, distracting anyone who looked at her twice.

Her mother returned to the college a week before her due date, camping out across the street at the Kenyon Inn. Beatrix went there every afternoon after class and fell asleep beside her mother in the four-poster bed while her classmates were out celebrating the end of their four years in Gambier.

The first cramps of labor started a few days later in the middle of the night. Bea slipped quietly from her dorm room and headed to the Inn. She stood at the front door knocking like a loon, not caring who she woke as long as someone let her in to see her mommy. She still called her that at the time, making it all the more absurd that she would soon become one herself.

At the hospital, her mother filled out the paperwork.

"What is your address at school?" her mom had asked.

"Just put our home address," Bea had replied.

"No, your school address is better," her mother had insisted.

She remembered the day like it was yesterday. The antiseptic smell of the hospital room, the pain, the pushing, the pressure inside her that felt like a freight train barreling through a pinhole. She couldn't believe how barbaric the whole thing was.

Early the next morning, a six-pound, three-ounce lavender-eyed girl with a tuft of dark hair like Bea's entered the world. The nurses tucked her next to Bea in her bed, giving her a chance to meet her child. For the first time during the whole ordeal, Bea fantasized about keeping her.

Not knowing what to do, and still in quite a bit of shock, Bea broke into a lullaby that her grandmother used to sing called "I See the Moon, and the Moon Sees Me."

When she got to the second verse, the magnitude of what was happening sank in.

> Once I had a heart, it was good as new.
> I gave this heart from me to you.
> Take care of it, like I have done.
> 'Cause you have two now, and I have none.

Her baby girl had already got ahold of her heart, and soon she would disappear with it. Bea thought some more about changing her mind, about keeping her, and gingerly brought it up when her mother entered the room.

"Do you want to hold her, Mommy?"

Her mother reached her hands under the baby's bottom and scooped up the tiny pink package. Holding the infant in front of her like a football, Caroline Silver stared from her granddaughter's lavender eyes to her daughter's brown ones.

"Does she look like me, you know, when I was born?" Bea asked.

"A little, I think."

"Too bad we can't keep her," Bea mumbled, passively challenging the plan, waiting to gauge her mother's reaction. As was typical of her mother's British upbringing, she remained unemotional and reserved. If her father were there, he may have been halfway out the door with the baby by now. Maybe she had confided in the wrong parent.

But when the social worker came in a few minutes later, Bea signed the papers like she had agreed to, without a word to the contrary.

It was only when she was back in the city, with post-partum hormones fueling her pain and regret, that she truly confronted her feelings.

"You did what was right by her; you were a good mother," Caroline insisted, wiping away Bea's tears. "There will be other babies, Beatrix, and they'll be born under far better circumstances. I'm sure of it."

But Beatrix never had another baby. And the song that she sang in the hospital, the one her grandmother had sung to her growing up, became their song.

Bea would look up at the night sky, wherever she was, picture her baby girl looking up at the same moon, and sing.

I see the moon, and the moon sees me,
The moon sees somebody I want to see.
God bless the moon, and God bless me.
And God bless the somebody I want to see.

Years later, when she was feeling particularly worried about her future or reflective about her past, Bea asked her mother about the specifics of the adoption.

"Why didn't you put down our home address?" Bea asked tearfully. "Then she could have found me."

"It was a closed adoption, honey. She's not finding you."

Beatrix cried some more, and her mother softened.

"It was the best decision at the time. You were a child yourself. My child. I was looking out for you. And for the baby."

The decision, seemingly the only logical one at the time, affected everything that came after, starting with the fact that Bea never lived outside of Gambier again.

Whenever she took day trips to other quaint Ohio towns or cities, Bea would look for her daughter. She was convinced that she would recognize her in an instant. Once, at the Rock and Roll Hall of Fame in Cleveland, a group came in on a field trip from a local middle school. "How old are you?" Bea had asked, inappropriately accosting a girl from the group in the bathroom. She was twelve, the same age that her baby would be. She trailed behind the group for the rest of the day, searching their faces for one that resembled her own.

The year her baby was to turn seventeen, Bea began eating her lunch on a bench on Middle Path so that she could watch the tour groups stroll through campus, studying them for some hint of recognition. The year her daughter would be starting college, Bea fantasized she would be in the incoming class at Kenyon, once again studying the faces of every girl in her lecture hall.

She went through all the steps one can take to find a child. While the agency was long gone, she registered at the Ohio Adoption Subsidies and Children and Family Services and checked back with them regularly.

And that's how it went for years until 2007, when a private company in San Francisco began offering autosomal DNA testing for ancestry and genealogical tracing. Beatrix didn't think twice before ordering her kit, spitting into the enclosed vial until her mouth went dry, and sending it back, hoping beyond hope it would be the answer to her prayers.

In the end, she got the opposite result. Unlike her husband, a fellow academic, whose Asian heritage meant that he barely turned up a single connection on the service, Bea was abounding in family. Being a quarter Ashkenazi Jew and a quarter Sephardic, she discovered she had sixteen hundred known relatives. She found second cousins in Israel, a few more relatives from her mom's side in England, and was duly surprised that a girl she'd graduated college with turned out to be a distant cousin. But 23andMe never came up with a match for a child, and though she checked back often, by 2014, when her daughter would have been an adult, she had to admit to herself that if her child knew she was adopted, she clearly didn't want to be found.

In a last-ditch effort at tracking her down, Bea even encouraged her friend, an author on Fire Island, the place where she had met her child's father and gotten pregnant by him, to include the story of the adopted child in the book he was writing—names, birthdates, and all. But it had been over a decade since the novel was published, and nothing had come of that either.

Still, Bea never strayed from that school address, and in the back of her mind she knew it was because her baby girl would always know where to find her.

In the end, she was right.

TRACK 4

Smile

♩♫♪

Maggie

MAGGIE CHECKED HER email, as she did every morning when she woke up, but usually not in this panicked, heart-racing way. She had since reached the two-to-three-week mark when the genealogy results were due to arrive. *Would today be the day?*

It was. Her results were in.

She clicked on the message with shaky hands and bated breath.

Maggie Wheeler: 50% English, 12.5% Ashkenazi Jew, 12.5% Sephardic Jew/Arabian Peninsula, and then a spattering of German, Italian, Irish, and even Nordic.

She ran to Jason, who was sitting at her kitchen table over the record shop grading final papers.

"I'm a quarter Jewish!" she yelled, placing her laptop with the news atop his stack.

"*Mazel tov!*" he responded. They both laughed too hard, nervous about the rest of the revelations.

"You look, I can't." She sat down next to him and tapped on the computer.

"OK, I got you."

"Click on DNA relatives." She was in agony, burying her head in her arms.

And there it was.

Beatrix Silver. Mother. 50% DNA shared. He rested his hand on hers.

"Your birth mother's name is Beatrix Silver. She was born in 1974." He took a beat to let it sink in before revealing the punchline.

"She lives in Gambier, Ohio."

"Oh my God. All my parents knew about her was that she was a local college girl."

"Kenyon College."

She turned the computer toward her and googled "Beatrice Silver, Kenyon College."

"Ugh, nothing."

"You spelled her name wrong. It's 'Beatrix' with an 'x.'"

"Like Beatrix Potter; that's weird."

"It is. Maybe you should forget the whole thing," he deadpanned.

She laughed and tried again: Beatrix Silver, Kenyon College.

And there she was.

Professor of English. Expertise in English and American literature with a concentration in Henry James.

And Maggie May Wheeler's birth mother.

It didn't say that last part, but on closer inspection of the thumbnail photo, it may as well have—they shared the same beautiful smile.

Maggie took a screenshot of Beatrix's picture and spent the next ten minutes zooming in and out, concentrating on each feature of the woman's face and comparing it to her own. There was no doubt that their coloring was the same, aside from their eyes—Maggie's were violet-blue, Beatrix's brown. Maggie had always wondered where her olive skin tone originated—though she never imagined it to be from the Arabian Peninsula. She studied Beatrix's nose, her eyes, the texture of her hair. She guessed people called her Bea. Beatrix was a mouthful.

She wondered about her nature. Her own mother was the most loving woman that Maggie had ever met. Being the beneficiary of her warmth on the daily had been a beautiful thing. Maggie never felt she was a particularly warm person herself, and she often wondered, growing up, if it was hereditary. When she'd first decided to take the test, it was about learning the facts. Learning more about herself and where she came from. Learning what her mother looked like (check), learning that she wasn't in jail (check), and maybe learning the genetic markers that she hadn't even looked at yet.

Even with all those checks, she was surprised to find that she suddenly desperately wanted to catch at least a glimpse of her birth mother. She wasn't sure whether she wanted to formally introduce herself, or ask some of the big questions that plagued her: Did you hold me when I was born or turn your head? Did you grieve for me or never look back? But she wanted to see her in the flesh.

"Let's go!" Maggie shouted, standing up and pouring Jason's hot coffee down the sink. "Let's go to Kenyon. Let's find her."

Jason walked over to her, resting his hands on her shoulders. "It's Sunday. Let's take the day. Google her a bit. And go tomorrow. We'll have a better chance of finding her on campus on a weekday."

Maggie watched the last of Jason's coffee make its way down the drain.

"I'm sorry I dumped your coffee." She burst into misdirected tears. Jason tried to comfort her, pulling her into him, but she stiffened. Maggie had never been good at letting anyone perform that role.

When Jason had previously called her out on this behavior, she'd defended it casually with, "I'm just not a hugger," chalking it up to only child syndrome. But sometimes she thought it went deeper than that. She hated to blame her parents for anything, especially since they were gone, but she wished she'd known she'd been adopted from the get-go. Not finding out until second grade fueled a distrust toward others that made her feel she could only count on herself.

"I think I want to be alone for a little," she sighed, ignoring his dejected expression.

She took her computer downstairs to the store, where the sun shone through the front window, reminding her of her dad and their early mornings together. It was funny, she noted, how she never even thought of looking for her biological father. When she thought of her mother, *a local college girl*, as her parents had described her, she pictured her carrying Maggie in her womb, going to classes with a secret in her belly. She wondered if she would reach down under her desk and rest her hand lovingly over the place where her baby girl was growing inside her, or if she never thought of her as anything but a disaster—the worst thing that had ever happened to her. Her gut told her it was the latter. That's how Maggie herself would have felt in that situation at least. As for her biological father, she considered him as not much more than an accidental sperm donor. There's a reason they call it birth mother and biological father. Her birth mother carried her. The guy just ejaculated. He may not even know of her existence.

By the end of the day, Maggie knew all the internet had to offer on Beatrix Silver. For starters, Beatrix was the only one (besides Maggie) in her immediate family who had had their DNA analyzed by 23andMe, though other family members may have opted out of the DNA Relative feature, like Maggie intended to do as soon as she finished reading her lackluster report. Aside from a first cousin in LA she found only distant relatives. She did a general Google search. Beatrix Silver had donated to Kamala Harris's campaign for president and to the annual fundraiser for BalletMet of Columbus, whose website showed a photo of her at their fall gala dressed in a white pantsuit and heels. She looked shorter than Maggie and bustier. She didn't seem to have any social media presence, which Maggie knew was common among professors who didn't want to share personal info with students. Thinking of academics and their privacy reminded her of her favorite website in college: *Rate My Professors*, a platform inviting student feedback on a scale of 1 to 5 and including a brutally honest comment section. She never signed up for a class in college without checking it first.

Maggie held her breath as she typed in "Beatrix Silver, Kenyon College." Giving her baby up for adoption she could forgive, but there was little Maggie despised more than an unforgiving, C+ grading professor.

Beatrix Silver, Kenyon College

GRADE: 4.7

Pretty great!

100 percent would take her class again.

Get ready to read.

Caring.

Tough grader.

Participation matters.

Thoughtful. Engaging.

Love her popular cultural references, especially her literary analysis of Buffy the Vampire Slayer.

Returns emails quickly.

Maggie felt comfortable around academics from her time hanging out with Jason and his colleagues. Sometimes she found them a bit pompous, throwing big words into every sentence and ready to debate anything and everything, though Jason was the least pretentious person she knew. Maggie was intelligent and always did well in school, but she wasn't as cerebral as that crew.

Maybe she should send Professor Silver an email.

Dear Mom,

I'll get right to the point—oops, I already did.

The sound of her laughter was drowned out by the jingling of the reindeer bells that her mother had attached to the front door before her final Christmas. Maggie had never taken them down.

Saved by the bell, Maggie thought, until the nosiest and most famously nitpicky customer in all of Chagrin Falls entered the shop. What if her mother was like that chick?

She wouldn't email Beatrix; she would drive to Gambier in the morning and check her out in person.

Little Lies

♩♫♪

Maggie and Jason

MAGGIE WOKE UP at dawn and changed six times before she and Jason started out on the two-hour drive to Gambier. In the end, she decided, it didn't matter what she wore. She would not meet her mother on that day; Jason needed to vet her first. She would wait to spring this news on him until the last leg of the ride.

"J?" she said in a saccharine-coated plea as they exited I-71. "Can I ask you a favor?"

He looked at her quizzically. She had been staring out the window since they left Main Street, and conversation had been limited to a couple of yes and no answers and a grunt or two. Jason had let it slide. This could not be easy for her.

"Of course," he answered, patting her knee.

"You may not like it. It's possibly unethical."

"Worse than when you made me steal two pieces of Bazooka Joe from the candy bins at the Popcorn Shop?"

She laughed. "Yes, worse than that."

"Lay it on me."

"I want you to meet Beatrix on your own. Maybe say you are thinking of applying for a job."

"She's in the English Department. I'm in Philosophy and Ethics. It makes no sense."

She must have looked deflated because he reconsidered.

"She's a Henry James expert, right? How about I say I'm writing a dissertation on ethical judgment through the lens of Henry James and would love to ask her some questions?"

"I have zero idea what that means, but it sounds perfect."

"Perfectly unethical," he grunted.

~~~~~

THE KENYON CAMPUS was small and easy to navigate. They had both been there once before, on a college counselor–led trip during the winter of their junior year of high school. All they remembered was the gorgeous new gym and how beautiful the lawns and halls looked in the snow. It wasn't lost on either of them, as they thought about it now, that they may have walked right by Maggie's birth mother.

"It looks different in the spring, doesn't it?" Maggie remarked, trying to make normal conversation when she really felt like vomiting.

"Still so beautiful, though," Jason responded.

She could picture him in this old-school/old-timey academic life, living in the bubble of a college campus, wearing vests, smoking a pipe, and making jokes in Latin. Case Western, with its modern buildings and abstract sculptures, had a much different vibe. Professors there commuted from all over the place, and its proximity to Cleveland gave it a more urban feel.

She stopped in front of a campus map, her eyes panning

from the YOU ARE HERE mark to the academic buildings, searching for one named Waite House.

"It's over there," she said, pointing to the left before putting her hand to her stomach.

"What's the matter?" Jason asked.

"My stomach hurts. Probably IBS rooted in generational trauma. All my Jewish friends in college had weak stomachs when they were nervous."

"You're nuts, you know that?" He wrapped his arms around her for a hug. This time, she took the comfort. She needed it.

They made their way to the English Quad, where Waite House and Beatrix Silver's office were located. Before pulling open the heavy wooden door, Jason paused.

"Are you ready?"

"Not at all. I think I should wait out here."

"Really?"

"Yes. You know me better than anyone. Just go in there and figure out if I would want this woman in my life."

She held up her mood ring; it was black. He laughed.

"I need a little more than that."

"If you meet her and she sucks, nothing lost, no drama! I'm doing so well right now. I just got that business improvement loan. I'm coming to terms with losing my parents, a little bit at least. We are engaged to be engaged."

"Though we haven't told anyone," Jason pointed out. "If a tree falls in the forest and no one hears it . . ."

Maggie smiled. He may be the most patient man in all of Ohio, but even Maggie was not sure why she still wanted their quasi-engagement to remain quasi.

"I know. I think I've been waiting for this. Like you said,

I need to know where I come from before I decide where I'm going."

"OK, then, I'm heading in."

He ruffled her hair and motioned to a bench where she could plant herself.

~~~~~

WHILE IT WAS true that Jason was particularly inept at lying, he wasn't a bad actor. When he and Maggie had auditioned for *Romeo and Juliet* in high school, he got Romeo, and she got the fourth handmaiden.

He stood outside of the door marked BEATRIX SILVER, fluttered his lips like he learned in drama club, and got into character. One more flutter, and he rapped his knuckles on the door.

"Come in!" a gravelly baritone voice bellowed, leaving Jason to wonder if Maggie's mom had a two-pack-a-day habit. That wouldn't bode well for anyone.

A towering man in a bow tie rose from behind the desk to greet him.

Jason looked down from the desk placard that read BEATRIX SILVER to the man behind the desk and back again. The man laughed and reached out his hand.

"Dave Weinstein. My office is being painted; you're looking for Professor Silver, I presume?"

"I am."

Jason looked around the small office, taking it in. At Case, some professors went all out personalizing their studies, filling their bookshelves and walls with photographs, important works, and memorabilia, while some didn't reveal a clue as to who they were. Beatrix was somewhere in the middle. Her walls held her diploma, a couple of awards, and a few black-and-white photos. Her shelves were, unsurprisingly, filled with volumes and volumes of literature. A wedding photo sat on the corner of her desk. It looked recent. The wall to his left was covered in cork and filled with fliers and events, both past and future.

"Do you have an appointment?"

"No, no," he improvised, "I'm an old student. Just stopping in to say hello."

"Oh, that's a shame. You just missed her. She turned in her final grades and she's heading east for a wedding, I believe." As he said it, he motioned to the bulletin board.

Jason noticed what looked like a wedding invitation. He inched toward it to get a better look.

"Would you like to leave a note?" the man asked.

"Um, I'll be in the area again in the fall. I'll stop back then."

"I'm afraid that won't work either. Professor Silver is traveling abroad in the fall to England. She's chairing the Kenyon-Exeter program for the year. Lucky gal!"

"Yes, very."

"Did you go?"

"I didn't."

"Too bad. You missed a great opportunity."

It was clearly time to leave, but he needed a better look at that invitation.

"On second thought, I'll write a note," Jason blurted out, reaching for a pen before purposefully flinging the whole cup of them off the desk. "Sorry, sorry."

Startled, the man bent to collect the scattered pens. With one quick swoop of the hand, while the professor was playing

Pick-Up Sticks, Jason swiped the invitation from the bulletin board and shoved it in his pocket. He was amazed by how quickly he went from liar to thief.

"I'll just email her," he flip-flopped.

And back to liar.

Maybe they would hold up a bank on the way home, profit from his crooked turn.

"As you wish," the man responded, adding, "Have a good summer."

"You too," Jason called back to him, halfway out the door.

In My Life

♩♫♪

Beatrix

BEATRIX LOOKED IN awe at her husband, Paul, sitting in the next airline seat. Not because, after a year of marital bliss, they were still in the honeymoon phase, or that she found him adorable, or that she was excited to finally be showing him her favorite place in the world, the town she had grown up in on Fire Island. And not because she had basically given up on finding true love or even tethering herself to anything more substantial than an African violet when this sweet man had walked into her office in a panic looking for directions.

"I'm trying to find Hayes Hall. I have my first lecture there at ten."

It was 10:05. Apparently, a couple of students had recognized that he was a newbie and hazed him by sending him the wrong way across campus.

"I'd better show you the way," she had suggested, taking pity on him.

The next day Bea found a note taped to her office door inviting her to dinner as a thank-you for saving him. She had sworn off dating colleagues after a stint with an American history professor who had written a book about twentieth-century spies had soured years before. She left that relationship with a broken heart and an abundance of knowledge she had little use for, though when she faced a lull in conversation at cocktail parties, she often played, "Guess what Harry Houdini, Marlene Dietrich, Cary Grant, and Julia Child have in common?" (The answer: they were all spies.)

Outside the faculty, pickings were slim in Gambier, so she agreed to dinner.

Who would have thought that a mathematics professor and an English professor would have such chemistry? It was instantaneous, and six months later, they were married right on campus. As romantic as that sounded, her awe on the airplane was not inspired by finding true love at fifty. That was unusual, yes, but they were heading to a wedding where both the bride and the groom were of the same generation.

The reason Beatrix looked at Paul in such wonder, as they sat buckled into their coach seats on the Delta Airbus, was his unfailing ability to nap anytime, anywhere. Chances were her husband (she still pinched herself when saying that) would sleep the entire two-hour flight from John Glenn Airport to JFK, leaving her alone with her thoughts and his complimentary bag of Chex Mix.

Even if Bea had been a napper, she was far too excited to sleep. Her childhood best friend, her summer sister, was getting married to the local ferry captain, and she was the matron of honor. They had all grown up together, in the summers at least, in a tiny beach town as part of the same friend group. There, most experienced their first loves, or first times, or at least their first kisses. She remembered the night her best friend Renee, the beauty queen, had kissed the shy boy who worked the ferry boats. (His first kiss, not hers.)

Bea had yet to really hook up with anyone at the time, and when she finally did, with a lifeguard named Chase Logan, it would have a very different ending. Renee was now set to marry that shy boy from the ferry boats, a second marriage for them both, while Beatrix and Chase's brief romance had devastated her life at the time.

And there lay the problem with her beautiful Fire Island memories: she always landed on the Big Bad Thing.

Growing up, Beatrix probably heard the refrain "Take your sister with you" more than any other parental request. As the '80s rolled into the '90s, Bea's sister, Veronica, though nearly four years her junior, was fully integrated into the older kids' friend group. Long milky-white legs, long auburn hair, Julia Roberts smile—by the time she was a sophomore in high school, Veronica was getting much more attention from the boys than her collegiate sister. Shorter than V, and the sole recipient of their Russian ancestors' ample bosoms and strong thighs, Beatrix, with her warm smile and beachy brown curls, was often labeled cute. Soon Bea's directive changed from dragging her sister along to being called by her friends to come and collect her. Add in Veronica's practically nonexistent tolerance for alcohol, and Beatrix found herself in the guardian role more than she wished.

She remembered one such occasion, Bea was rubbing Veronica's back while Renee held her hair as Veronica threw up into the upstairs toilet as a random house party raged below. Veronica had slouched back against the bathroom wall and wiped the vomit from her lips with the back of her hand.

"Can I tell you guys a secret? I did it with Danny Zuko tonight."

That wasn't his real name—obviously—but a nickname all the girls gave to a dark-haired lothario with a cleft chin like John Travolta's, who was also particularly fond of summer loving. It bugged the other girls the way Veronica tore through "their" guys. And even though Bea, more sidekick than siren, never stood a chance with someone like Danny Zuko, it bothered her just the same.

"You should really think about how you will feel the next morning, before you do stuff like that, V," Beatrix said crossly.

"I'll feel fine in the morning," Veronica insisted. "Same as Danny Zuko."

Whether she really meant it or just didn't feel like being lectured by her older sister, who knew? Bea remembered waffling between judgment and jealousy at the time—until Veronica's next question, which elicited embarrassment and anger.

"When did you lose your virginity?" Veronica asked Bea, with a hint of payback for what she must have felt was Bea's holier-than-thou attitude.

"I don't kiss and tell like you do," Beatrix fibbed. It wasn't all a lie. The first half of the sentence was painfully true. Boys liked Bea, but they liked her as a friend. In contrast, those same boys only wanted to get into V's pants. Everyone chose Veronica, and she used her sex appeal like a power trip. Until one day the following summer when a lifeguard named Chase Logan, whose unofficial motto was "Savin' lives and breakin' hearts, dude," called out to Beatrix from his perch in the sand.

"Hey, Bea!" he yelled.

Beatrix was shocked that he even knew her name. She approached the chair feeling unusually confident, sporting the two-toned Norma Kamali bathing suit her mom had treated her to for spring break in Acapulco. Her mother had been duly surprised and excited that Bea wanted to partake in the collegiate tradition of sun and debauchery. Both her parents, Caroline and Shep, were very social creatures and known to be the life of every party. While Veronica seemed cut from the same cloth, Bea was much more reserved.

She walked right up to Chase and said hello.

"You're reading *The Fountainhead*? Cool," he shot back with an approving look. Bea smiled, shocked that he was interested in literature. By the time she found out that he only knew the book because Robbie, the jerk-faced waiter in *Dirty Dancing*, waved it in Baby's face to justify his ego, she had already lost her virginity to Chase. It was a big deal. She had been the only one of her friends who was still a virgin.

Suddenly they were an item, and it was Beatrix, not Veronica, who was nestled on the couch at house parties, making out with the hottest lifeguard on the beach. She hadn't realized until then how jealous she had been of her sister. It made her feel awful: she knew that jealousy was the most divisive emotion, especially within a family.

She wondered if Veronica would still have that effect on her today. She thought not, but couldn't imagine an occasion, aside from her father's eventual passing, when they would be in the same room together to find out. With any luck, Shep Silver would outlive them all.

Now, as they reached a cruising altitude of 35,000 feet, Bea opened Paul's Chex Mix, slipped on the airline headphones, and flicked through the zillion choices of in-flight entertainment, searching for something light to get her out of her head.

Veronica

♩♫♪

Veronica

"I DON'T GET why you are going. I never even heard you mention these people before."

Veronica (Silver) Morgan looked up over her suitcase and grimaced at her husband. It was an absurd thing to say. Veronica may not have detailed her sordid past to Larry over their twenty-year marriage, but he certainly knew plenty about it. And if he wasn't listening, which was often the case, there was a *New York Times* bestselling novel that included enough barely disguised detail about Veronica to raise eyebrows. The tell-all of sorts, chronicling one summer in the small beach town back East where Veronica and her sister Beatrix had come of age, didn't cause as big a stir as when Charles Webb turned Pasadena upside down with his "fictional" account of a recent graduate's affair with Mrs. Robinson. But it got people talking—especially the ones from their little sliver of sand who had always wondered what had come between the two Silver sisters, whose rift had become fodder for small-town gossip.

Larry knew Veronica wasn't an angel before he married

her. He used to joke that her fiery red hair was sourced from the fire in her belly. But years later, when the local writer's book had made quite a point of sullying her reputation, he learned more than he had previously imagined. So did Veronica. The author, her dad's neighbor at the beach, let her read a chapter or two in advance and asked permission not to change her (maiden) name. "It's the least you could do for your sister," he said. Shocked that the reason her sister didn't speak to her was revealed in its pages, she agreed. She had hoped that the sacrifice would encourage Bea to forgive and forget. It did not.

Veronica knew she had hurt and betrayed Beatrix in the worst way possible, but until then, she didn't know the repercussions of her betrayal. She signed the author's release, only asking that he change the name of her town and her husband's line of work. The author moved them to Palo Alto and wrote that her husband had made his fortune in tech when in truth they lived in LA, where he had got in early with crypto.

The discussion had reminded her of the sidewalk game she and her sister would play at the beach, back when they were young and still thick as thieves.

"V my name is Veronica and my husband's name is Vance and we come from Venice where we sell vaginas." They would fall to the ground laughing.

It may have been the last time they'd laughed like that together, certainly the last time they laughed like that together on the subject of Veronica's vagina.

She moved to the bathroom to pack up her makeup and toiletries. Larry followed.

"I'm going to miss you," he said, pouting.

"Well then, you will know how I have felt for most of our marriage."

She stopped to look at herself in the magnified mirror. Just last week she had noticed the appearance of jowls. They were ever so slight, but they were there, on either side of her mouth, threatening a perpetual droop. You couldn't get filler for jowls. No dermabrasion or Fraxel or cream made from the womb of an octopus would counter the gravitational pull of time. Veronica's usual expectation of being the prettiest woman in the room would not hold up well with jowls. Jowls were next-level aging. She was not ready for next-level aging.

She finally answered her husband, as best as she could.

"You don't get it, Larry. All these years I've felt like a pariah at the beach, and they've finally included me. I am invited to Renee and Jake's wedding and I'm going, with or without you."

"That last part is funny, V, because I don't remember you inviting me to come with you," Larry quipped.

She stopped packing up her toiletries and asked, "Larry, would you like to come with me to Fire Island to stay at my dad's house and attend a wedding on a boat?"

She knew it was an empty invitation. Among other things, Larry got seasick on a float in their pool.

He rolled his eyes. "You know how busy I am at work right now."

"That's what I thought," she scoffed. Larry was always busy at work these days.

"What about the kids?" he tried.

"The kids? They'll reach out if their debit card balance gets low. Beyond transferring money, you should be fine."

She was being sarcastic, but it wasn't far from the truth. Like most parents of college-age kids, the only way she got hers to call her was by emptying their accounts or changing the Netflix password. Her daughter was OK enough, an emerging filmmaker who still said "I love you" before hanging up the phone, but her son hadn't offered her a kind word in years. He was emerging, too, she feared, an emerging a-hole.

Veronica's role as a mother, the one she previously touted as the job of a lifetime, was barely a walk-on part anymore. Her status as a wife felt equally nonexistent. V had no idea what she would do with the rest of her life. She didn't play golf or tennis or cards. She had no hobbies beyond stealing a Marlboro Light from the pool boy every week and sneaking out behind her prized rosebushes and forsythia to smoke it.

"Will your spinster sister be there?"

"That's not nice, Larry. And she is no longer a spinster."

"It's funny to me that you jump to defend that woman when she blew off our wedding and never met our children."

For a long time, Veronica had considered that last part unforgivable, but their mother's death had left a void that only her sister could fill.

"Blood is thicker than crypto," she retorted, proud of her comeback.

Even though she might not speak to Bea, she would still walk through fire for her. She was pretty sure the reverse was true as well. That familial obligation to go to bat for a sibling had been drilled into them by their parents. Despite all the trouble they'd had, remnants of that early training still existed.

Maybe this invitation, given that the bride was Bea's best friend, meant that her sister was ready to talk. To forgive. Hope springs eternal, Veronica thought, before wondering if she was reading too much into the situation. Her stomach filled with knots as she placed the last packing cube in her Louis Vuitton suitcase and zipped it shut.

Rock the Boat

♩♪♪

Maggie

JASON QUIZZED MAGGIE when he dropped her off at the airport like a dad sending his kid on her first solo flight. Truth was, the Wheelers weren't big travelers, partly on account of being tethered to the store. And even as an adult, Maggie preferred to stay close to home. She sometimes worried she was holding Jason back in that department. If he were to write another letter to himself—a Dear Jason at Fifty—his desire to travel would probably still be top of mind, along with a coveted doctorate of ethics degree from the University of Leeds in England. She'd seen an application for the program once on his work computer. When she'd asked him about it, he explained it was a pre-Maggie dream. I thought you said you could barely remember anything pre-Maggie, she noted.

"It was before we went from friends to lovers," he whispered, as if there were someone else there to hear. She knew he felt funny keeping their relationship a secret. Any secret felt ethically questionable to him, even before they were sleeping together. Now that they were pre-engaged, the idea seemed even more egregious. It was a good thing she was going it alone this weekend. If she didn't find her birth mother before the wedding, she might have to crash it, since it was the only place she knew Beatrix would be for certain. Jason, with his finely tuned conscience, would make a lousy wedding crasher.

"I know we are on the way to the airport, but you can still change your mind."

"I'm sticking with the plan. If I don't find her before Saturday at dusk, I will be on the beach on Fire Island, eavesdropping on a wedding. I even brought a dress."

"Just saying, she will be back in her office in Gambier in a year. You've waited this long."

"You know me. I can't wait a year. I would practically hold my breath till then. All forward movement in my life would come to a standstill."

"Fine." He reached his hand into his backpack, digging around for something.

"Here, I printed out the Fire Island Ferries schedule for you." This made Maggie laugh.

"You didn't have to do that. I have it on my phone."

"What if your phone dies?"

"When was the last time I let my phone die?"

"I don't remember."

"Correct, because it never happens."

Maggie was one of those people who charged her phone when it hit 80 percent and filled her gas tank at the halfway mark. She took the paper with a smile. Jason was sad that his summer school gig prevented him from coming with her, so the least she could do was humor him with his silly precautions.

"You should be boarding by eleven," he added. "Did you decide how you're getting from the airport to the ferry?"

"I'm gonna Uber. It will be pricey, but the train seems complicated."

"You got this," he encouraged, before wrapping her in his arms and kissing her sweetly on the top of her head.

As she pulled her bag through the revolving door, she witnessed another couple passionately kissing goodbye. Her first inclination when saying goodbye to Jason, or hello, was still to fist-bump or high-five. She thought of the lame goodbye kiss they'd shared and decided on a redo, continuing, full circle, until she was back outside again.

His car pulled away just as she called out his name, leaving her dejected. She shook it off and continued on her adventure.

And some six hours later, she was standing at the Fire Island Ferries terminal just as her birth mother probably had countless times before. Between the fabulous weather forecast, and what she had learned about the carless thirty-two-mile barrier island, it promised to be a beautiful long weekend. As the departure time approached and the crowd thickened, Maggie couldn't help but search the faces for one that looked like her own.

The wedding was in four days' time, though if this small town was anything like the one she hailed from, she would probably cross paths with her birth mother before then. She pulled up Bea's photo on her phone and took yet another good look at her.

The plan was to settle into the room she'd booked in town before trying to find Beatrix, first getting a feel for her before possibly introducing herself. Maggie was still dead set on not pursuing things any further unless she believed it would be a drama-free, value-added relationship.

Part of her wanted to find her birth mother and make a smart decision about whether to let her into her life, but she knew that another part of her was using this as a stall tactic. Accepting—or refusing—Jason's proposal would dramatically redefine their relationship. If she wasn't willing to move forward, then wasn't she just holding both of them back?

She vowed to use her downtime to think about their future as well.

Maggie's stomach rumbled, interrupting her thoughts. She realized that the meager flight snack she had bought on the airplane didn't cut it. She waited in line at the snack counter, where every single person in front of her ordered clam chowder. When in Rome.

Her first bite was delicious—possibly best ever. She hoped it was a sign that she had made the right choice to come here.

"All Aboard Bay Harbor," the captain crooned.

Maggie boarded the ferry and picked a seat up top, happy to have her face in the sun and the wind in her hair. She slid onto the bench and leaned her elbow over the side rail, enjoying the view of families and friends of all persuasions boarding the boat. She watched as the last passenger stepped aboard. The crew shut the doors and the whirr of the engine sounded. They were off, or so she thought. Seconds later, a stretch limousine pulled into the parking lot, beeping its horn just as the ferry was about to pull away from the dock. The limo driver, a large man with a larger voice, stepped out and bellowed with a sense of urgency:

"Hold the boat!"

The man sitting to Maggie's left laughed, causing her to

look his way. He grinned, acknowledging her with an explanation.

"They don't hold the boat for anyone."

A leggy redhead stepped out of the car and waved up to the captain as if she were not just anyone.

The captain held the boat, the limo driver retrieved her luggage, and the woman paraded onto the deck like she was boarding the *Queen Mary* instead of the Fire Island ferry.

"Veronica Silver, as I live and breathe," the man to Maggie's left declared.

Silver!

It wasn't a very common name—Silver—according to the three-day Google trip that Maggie had embarked on after learning her birth mother's name. The surname Silver ranked around 1600th in popularity in the United States; Wheeler, in comparison, ranked 243rd. But from what Maggie could tell during her brief research as a newly anointed member of the tribe, there were many Jews named Silver. Veronica Silver could very well be related to her mother, though she didn't look to be.

"It's not Silver anymore," the man on the other side of her neighbor corrected. "She's married to some West Coast crypto tycoon."

The man seated next to the man seated next to him loud-whispered, "Oh my God, she must be here for the wedding. I can't believe they invited her. On a boat, no less."

Did everyone know everyone around here? Was it possible that this place was even smaller than Chagrin Falls?

The hairs on the back of Maggie's neck stood on end. More than that, they throbbed, as if they were screaming, "Danger—abort mission!"

Said danger rose from the stairs below, smiling coyly at whomever she passed. Some smiled back, others seemed to avoid eye contact.

Veronica Silver Something-or-other sat down on the bench in front of Maggie, causing a plume of Chanel No. 5 to do battle with the fresh sea air. The woman reached into her monogrammed LV tote and pulled out a silk scarf that even Maggie's humble eyes knew to be Hermès and tied it over her head with ease. Maggie prayed she wasn't a close relative and, if she were, that her mother would not be as . . . fancy. Maggie had a style of her own, but her bohemian record store owner vibe mostly came from the thrift shops she frequented in Cleveland. She saw no resemblance between herself, with her dark curls and olive complexion, and this fair-skinned redhead.

Within seconds, her chatty seatmate said hello to the woman in front of him.

"Veronica Silver, it's been a long time, but I would recognize that carrot top anywhere!"

Maggie wondered if he was making a move. If he were, he should have gone with something sexier than *carrot top*. The name brought back images of that unruly comic from the '90s. Veronica turned back, resting her arm over her seat as if parallel parking, and blinded them with the huge emerald-cut diamond on her finger.

Her face showed no sign of recognition. The chatty man got that too.

"Mitch Grabow? We were in youth group together. Picture me with braces and a big 'fro."

Veronica's expression remained the same. He soldiered on.

"I pulled a fishing hook out of your knee once. Remember that?"

"I do," she acquiesced. "It left a scar."

A small laugh escaped Maggie's lips, and she blushed from her obvious eavesdropping. There was no doubt that Veronica Silver was a piece of work.

"Here for any special reason?" he asked, clearly indulging in another kind of phishing.

"A wedding on this very ferry, I believe," she responded.

"Yup, the wedding of the century. I'll be there too."

She smiled the phoniest smile Maggie had ever seen.

"Is Beatrix in town for it?" he asked.

Damn it—close relative, Maggie thought.

It seemed an innocent question, but the looks of bewilderment she saw on the faces of those around her made her wonder.

"I wouldn't know. My sister and I are not that close. But you already knew that."

"Oh God," Maggie mumbled, under her breath, but loud enough for them both to glance her way. She looked to her phone as if it held the cause for her alarm, turned her body toward the bay, and considered jumping. She was a strong swimmer. If this was indeed her mother's sister, she feared she would have little in common with her long-lost family, plus, talk about messy! Maggie's plan to suss things out before admitting who she was felt smarter than ever.

As the ferry entered the basin on the other side of the bay, Maggie panned the crowd looking for her birth mother. Her throat tightened, her heart raced, and her eyes watered at the possibility of seeing her for the first time. The feelings surprised her. She was not a highly emotional person. Her parents had raised her that way, never really arguing and fostering a low-maintenance, "it is what it is" sort of attitude.

She could tell from the brief trip on the ferry that her Auntie Veronica was the definition of high maintenance. She wondered whether Beatrix was the same.

Maggie held back a little, allowing the other travelers to depart before her. She was keen to see who was waiting for Veronica at the dock. Surprisingly, it was no one.

The tiny town was straight-up adorable. Barefoot people meeting passengers, kissing them hello, and placing their belongings on wooden wagons. Kids shouting, "Lemonade here!" and others hawking friendship bracelets and painted shells. The lack of cars was immediately evident, as was the abundance of bicycles.

Veronica headed for the only commercial building in sight, with a big sign on top that read BAYVIEW MARKET. She had a confusing energy about her, like a swan, elegant on the surface, but paddling like crazy underneath, to keep herself afloat. Maggie followed her, careful to stay ten steps behind. She watched as Veronica entered, raised her oversized Chanel sunnies, eyed the teenage girls at the register, and smiled. Maggie had a feeling she was hoping for a bigger welcome on Fire Island than she had thus far received—which was zero until Veronica arrived at the deli counter, where the three guys behind it all stepped around to greet her. A round of "It's been forever"–type sentiments was followed by hugs and kisses. Maggie stood in the far aisle, taking it all in. She noticed that Veronica was one of those huggers who led with her breasts. Maggie, on the other hand, always awkwardly caved her chest inward in that situation, taking more of a headfirst approach.

The guys seemed thrilled to see her. A fourth put down his meat cleaver and called out "Veronica Silver!" in a bellowing voice that filled the store. Across the aisle, a middle-aged woman in cutoff jeans, Ray-Bans, and the newly anointed Kenyon College mascot—an owl—on her baseball cap, clearly heard the "announcement." She visibly startled and dropped her container of eggs flat out on the floor as if her hands had stopped working.

Maggie gasped and the woman looked up to see where the gasp had come from, cocking her head to the side. Maggie herself was famously a head cocker. Her father used to call it her puppy-dog face. She froze at the sight of the woman, who looked both familiar and like a complete stranger.

An uncanny feeling came over her.

She knew she had just seen her mother.

Maybe a glimpse of her was enough. Maybe she could go home now. Maggie quickly memorized her familiar coloring and the texture of her hair peeking out from her telling baseball cap. The woman's lips, now curved downward, reminded Maggie of her own. But mostly there was something about her essence that felt known to her. She considered helping her pick up her eggs, to get a closer look, but the woman turned and ran.

Maggie didn't follow her but stepped out the front door of the store just in time to see her jump on a bike and pedal off. She watched her for a minute, until tears unexpectedly blurred her vision. Seeing her mother, seeing her in the flesh mere minutes after her arrival, tugged at feelings she didn't even know existed. She wiped her eyes and did a little emotional exorcism to calm herself. When she did so, cautious Maggie screamed: sit back down on the bench by the ferry and wait for the next boat back to the mainland.

She bravely headed to the register instead and asked the

girls there if they could point her toward her hotel in Ocean Beach. They seemed to grimace when she mentioned where she was staying. She thought to ask them why, but it felt pointless. She had prepaid for the room. She grabbed something to eat, adjusted her expectations, and went on her way.

Ironic

♩♫♪

Matt

MATT TUCKER EMPTIED the last items from his suitcase, including the seersucker suit he was instructed to wear when giving his mother away at her wedding. It was a lot to unpack—figuratively, more than literally.

In a shocking turn of events that no one could have predicted, least of all Matt, his mother, Renee, and his closest childhood friend's father, Jake, were getting married. They had begun keeping company the winter before, when no one was around to catch them doing so. Jake Finley, the local ferry captain, had lived on the island year-round all his life. Until about a year and half ago, when Renee had some sort of midlife crisis, she had only ever lived on the island on summer weekends and a week or two in August.

Renee had been an uber-successful Manhattan divorce attorney until an irritatingly spoiled couple who couldn't agree on the custody of their two-hundred-year-old bonsai tree pushed her over the edge. She quit her job and took a remote position at a New York City nonprofit called Her Justice, concentrating on underserved women who needed help with matrimonial law. Renee had been souring on the corporate grind for years and was financially comfortable—from that same corporate grind—so taking the job did not come as a surprise to Matt. The surprise had come when she sold his childhood home, a three-bedroom condo on the Upper East Side, and moved into their summer place on Fire Island full-time. To some this may have sounded like no big deal, but it was very much the opposite.

Living on Fire Island in the winter is not for the faint of heart, and while Matt's mom was a killer in the courtroom, she wasn't the most capable in the domestic arena. The super had spent so much time in their apartment that, as a toddler, Matt had learned to say his name before "daddy." Renee's plan had all the hallmarks of an impending disaster, and as her only child, Matt did his best to convince her it was a poor, if not insane, idea. He began with a list of obvious things she would need to do without: her weekly manicure, her monthly hair color, the frozen yogurt at Bloomingdale's, not to mention her favorite doorman, who placed a single cup of coffee from the corner deli in the elevator for her every morning and who assisted her with hard things, like turning off the flashlight on her iPhone.

Convinced that the move was a colossal mistake, Matt found that, as per usual, it was difficult to argue with his mother, the litigator. Still, he did everything in his power, short of pulling out the deed to the Fire Island home, which had been transferred to him during his parents' divorce, and evicting her.

Eventually he gave up.

Truth be told, you would be hard-pressed to find a summer resident who didn't daydream about living on the island year-round at one time or another, though you'd be much harder pressed to find one who actually attempted it. Matt, who was currently living a somewhat nomadic lifestyle as a concert reporter for *Rolling Stone*, made the trip to check on Renee a couple of times over the winter, bundled up on the lone morning ferry, as its captain, the one whom he eventually found out was sleeping with his mother, navigated the patches of floating ice on the bay. When the bay truly froze over, the ferry stopped running altogether, leaving Renee stranded or at the mercy of residents with off-season car permits. To protect the fragility of the island, only 145 winter car permits were distributed yearly. Turnover for said permits, prompted by death or relocation, were rare.

Truth was, the image of Renee driving a four-wheeler down the beach to the Fire Island Inlet Bridge to the west, or the Smith Point Bridge to the east, was hard to conjure. Often feeling like his mother's guardian since the divorce, Matt was not unhappy about the driving permit limitation.

The off-season vibe of the island was completely different from what they were used to. The few times Matt had visited Renee in the winter, he had to admit that he marveled at the sight of the low winter sun, the high ocean waves, and the herd of deer dressed in their winter grays. Calls from his mother, who now reported sightings of seals bathing in that low winter sun with the same enthusiasm she once reserved for spotting Paul McCartney at Nobu, were surprising as well.

The most obvious difference between the winter and the summer was the people. Specifically, the lack of them. While the island's summer population could swell to over twenty thousand on a busy weekend, in the off-season it would be four hundred tops, dusted across the thirty-two-mile-long island like powdered sugar on a loaf of pound cake.

Renee's social life, which had previously consisted of frequenting see-and-be-seen-in restaurants and hit Broadway shows, was now "filled" with potluck dinners at the firehouse and fish tacos at the bar of CJ's—the one restaurant that remained open year-round. The community was tight, though. Renee claimed she was less lonely now than she had been postdivorce in Manhattan.

Even so, Matt figured that after one winter, she would come to her senses and move back to the city.

He hadn't counted on the Hallmark version, in which she secretly fell for the ornery ferry captain. And he certainly didn't count on her falling in love with the father of the first girl he himself had ever truly loved, his oldest friend, Dylan.

Dylan and Matt had "dated" for two summers when they were teenagers after being inseparable for the fifteen summers prior. They had never fully consummated their relationship back then, though not for lack of trying. On the few occasions that their trips to the island lined up as adults, their interest in carnal pursuits did not. One or the other was invariably in the throes of a serious relationship, and one year, Dylan had a bad case of mononucleosis. Somewhere along the way, like many best friends, they made a pact to get married if they were both still single at thirty. Dylan was about to turn thirty and Matt was a year behind her. This would have been that summer, their summer, not the summer of his mom and the ferry captain.

Matt never forgot their pact, even though he and Dylan never spoke about it, and she had a memory like an elephant, so he was pretty sure she remembered it too. Given that they would soon be stepsiblings, the notion now felt insane, complicated, and kind of gross. Matt had zero desire to go down that road. He hoped Dylan felt similarly and was worried about them not being on the same page.

They'd had a few phone calls in recent weeks to report on, digest, laugh, and on one occasion, burst into tears (his) over the whip-fast trajectory of their parents' relationship. Besides that, their usual communication over the years had dwindled to texting birthday wishes, remember when's, and random memes of dogs surfing.

With the pact in mind, Matt checked Dylan's social media, hoping for an update on her relationship status. Dylan was a big poster—usually of sea life and such. A mermaid at heart and a marine biologist by profession, she was never far from the water. When she had a steady guy, and for a brief stint, a girl, there was always evidence on her feed. Lately: nothing. His concern changed course when he looked out his bedroom window to see his mom's oldest friend, Bea, looking panicked as she tossed her bike in their front yard, her feet barely touching the ground as she flew into their house.

Up on the Roof

♩♫♪

Renee

"DID YOU GET the eggs?" Renee Tucker, the bride-to-be, asked her oldest friend despite witnessing her dramatic entrance.

"I dropped the eggs," Bea managed.

"Oh, that must have been embarrassing. Was it the last dozen?"

"Did you invite my sister to the wedding?"

"What? Of course not!"

"Well, she's here, with a hanging bag."

There was little reason to come to Fire Island with a hanging bag unless it was to attend a wedding.

"That can't be. Sit down." Renee pulled out a chair and poured Bea a glass of water.

"I think I could use something stronger."

Matt came bounding down the stairs to say hello. It was obvious from the look on their faces and the way Bea had rushed in that something was up. Still, his and Bea's visits hadn't aligned in years, and he was delighted to see her.

"Matty!" Bea stood, clearly trying to refocus and match his enthusiasm.

"It's just Matt now," his mother corrected.

"I know, I know. Your mom sends me all your articles. I share them with my students sometimes. You are the perfect answer to the question, 'What am I going to do with an English major?'"

Her hands were shaking.

Renee poured her a glass of wine. She took a large gulp and fell back into a state of panic.

"I'll kill my father if he set me up like this."

"Bea thinks she saw Veronica in the market."

"I don't *think* I saw her. She's here. My whole chakra is off."

"I didn't know you were a yogi," Matt remarked, one eyebrow raised.

"I'm not. But I know I'm off-balance, and I know she's here. She'll be minutes behind me unless she stops to hook up with one of the market guys in the stockroom—again." Bea couldn't resist this cheap shot.

Matt blushed and smirked.

She added, "Sorry, Matty. My sister brings out the worst in me."

Renee nodded in agreement, before asking Matt, "Did you hear anything from Shep about Veronica coming?"

"I didn't, but we could see everything from the roof."

"I'm not going on the roof four days before my wedding," Renee protested.

"Yes, you are," Bea ordered.

Bea absconded with the bottle of wine. Renee and Matt followed, and for a hot minute it felt as though the absurdity of them climbing out on the roof like three incorrigible teenagers would override the sister drama. It didn't.

Matt grabbed his binoculars and instructed his mother

and her friend on the best way out the window (flip onto your stomach so that your hands can hold the sill and wiggle out), and the best angle to sit (at the top of the roof slope), and ran a little drill on what to do when someone looked in their direction (lie flat, don't move). It was obvious that he and, most likely, his best friend—and soon-to-be stepsister—Dylan did this often as kids.

"Where was I when you guys were hanging out on the roof?" Renee asked, grabbing the wine bottle from Bea and taking a big swig.

"I don't know," he said, motioning to Bea by cocking his head, "but her parents rarely wore swimsuits in their pool."

They all laughed, perched together on the highest point of the roof like three birds on a wire. Until they saw her.

The three of them watched in silence as Veronica Silver sashayed down the block wheeling her Louis Vuitton suitcase and matching garment bag.

"I'm shocked she didn't bat her blue eyes and get someone from the market to scoot her over in a golf cart," Renee couldn't resist saying. Realizing she wasn't helping the situation, she pivoted. "Maybe she's changed."

Veronica seemed to look in their direction.

"Lay flat," Matt barked with authority. They did.

"If she comes to your wedding, I swear I'm going to have her thrown overboard," said Bea.

"She's not coming to the wedding," Renee assured her.

Matt surveyed the scene. "You can sit up now if you want. The coast is clear," he said.

They watched Veronica arrive at the house diagonally across the street. With her back to them, she knocked on the door.

"Why is she knocking?" asked Renee. "It's her house."

"Neither of us thinks of it as our house," said Bea.

The estranged sisters had grown up in a different, smaller house from the one their parents later built catty-corner to Renee's. Their childhood home was now inhabited by Ben and Addison Morse and their two daughters: a sweet family of four. Ben had been married to Renee's other best friend, Julia, who had tragically passed away years earlier. Renee and Julia had been summer sisters, just as she and Bea had been when they were young. It was hard to believe how long ago it was that Julia died—over twelve years now—but that was a whole other story.

Bea grabbed the binoculars from Matt as Shep opened the front door and greeted his younger daughter with open arms. It was obvious from his expression and reaction that her arrival was not a surprise to him. Bea's face contorted in anger.

"He set me up."

"Matty, can you maybe go over there and do some investigative reporting?" his mom asked.

"Sure." Matt looked at the two women. "You should come inside, though."

"I'm not going anywhere till this is cleared up," Bea insisted.

Her eyes were crazy and her tone erratic. *Crazy* and *erratic* were not words one would normally use to describe Beatrix Silver. The roof may have been a bad idea, thought Matt, sharing a concerned look with Renee as he climbed back through the window.

Bea lay back down, staring at the clouds. Renee sensed she should leave her be—maybe give her time to come to her senses. She wondered if Bea was playing out in her head the thirty-year-old incident that had first come between her and Veronica, or the many unfortunate interactions—and missed interactions—that had since fueled their great divide. When they were young, Renee, as an only child, would sometimes feel jealous of Bea having a younger sister who worshipped her. She remembered Veronica as a sweet little kid, just happy to be included with the two older girls. She was always willing to be Skipper when they played Barbies or take the weird white-flavored Freeze Pop when there were only two blue raspberry or watermelon left. Things began to sour when Veronica became a teenager, until they famously imploded.

Renee knew the story by heart, as did most everyone on the island. Back in the summer of 1995, Beatrix had lost her virginity to the notorious lifeguard Chase Logan, and proceeded to fall head over heels. In her mind, it was much more than a summer fling between a college coed and a hot lifeguard. By the time July rolled into August, Bea was fantasizing about spending her life with Chase. She was sure it was true love. A couple of years older and wiser, Renee had warned her at the time that she was getting carried away, but she didn't listen. She lay in bed at night dreaming of having his blond-haired, blue-eyed beach babies and raising them on Fire Island. She pictured herself teaching at the island's only school, Woodhull Elementary, which served about forty kids from all over the island, while Chase did off-season construction for one of the local contractors. She imagined them having the perfect life, one that could only be dreamed up in the mind of a young woman in love for the first time, happy to ignore that there were more red flags with this lifeguard than you saw on the roughest day on the ocean.

As the August days waned, leaving everyone scratching

their heads over where the summer had gone, Beatrix had decided she wanted to give Chase something special to remind him of her over the winter. They hadn't yet had that long-distance relationship conversation that she had heard couples have at summer's end, and she figured that gifting him a token of her affection would be a good segue to "the talk." She went to town to buy him a surfboard pendant on a leather rope, which had become the hot accessory on the island. The artist who created them, a New York City schoolteacher named Kenny Goodman, had recently opened a little shop that was quickly dubbed the Cartier of Fire Island. A constant presence at the beach and a man who knew everything and everyone, Kenny helped her choose one of his silver surfboard charms with a heart carved into it.

"I'd like to inscribe it," she said.

"OK, to whom?" he asked.

When she told him, he looked at her funny and tried to dissuade her from having "B.S. ♥ C.L." carved onto the face of the charm.

"It's not returnable when you do that," he warned. They went back and forth about it until Kenny gave in. The interaction was odd, Bea thought, but she had no idea why.

She wrote a beautiful card filled with her feelings and dreams for them both and set out to find Chase at the big end-of-year bonfire on the beach.

"Haven't seen him," his best friend told her.

"He went home," the one kid who didn't know the real deal informed her.

She practically skipped to his house in the next town. She was so excited to give him the necklace.

Ocean Beach was even more of a bungalow colony than

Bay Harbor, with many of its small beach cottages dating back to the 1930s. Chase spent his summers in one such cottage with his mom and older brother. It was his grandmother's house, but she'd been living in a nursing home on the mainland, close to where Chase and his family lived in the off-season.

Bea let herself in, which was common local practice, and headed right to his bedroom.

Beatrix was the last one to know that her sister was screwing her boyfriend. Yes, even Kenny Goodman had gotten word of the betrayal. She threw the necklace at him and ran from the house in tears. She never had the chance to confront her sister in person, because Veronica stayed away until Beatrix went back to college a few days later.

And that was officially the end of Bea and V.

What's Going On

♩♪♪

Matt

UNLIKE VERONICA, MATT had no problem walking right into Shep's house. Shep was more of a grandfather to him than his own blood relations, and he knew Shep felt like Matt was family too.

"Matty boy!" he exclaimed, bringing him in for a hug.

While Matt would often stop into Shep's house or his other neighbor, Ben's, immediately on arriving on the island, he hadn't this time. Truth was, after Dylan, Shep and Ben were Matt's closest friends here. Age was irrelevant on Fire Island, where Matt's bonds with Shep, a retired nonagenarian, and Ben, who was pushing fifty, didn't seem odd.

Both Shep, Bay Harbor's literal Greatest of All Time, and Ben, a sportswriter and author now with two kids of his own, had had a big effect on Matt's path in life. He might not even have become a journalist if it weren't for Ben's mentorship.

Veronica swept down the stairs. Matt had little memory of meeting her in the past, but her reputation seemed on the money.

"I took the bedroom on the left," she said.

Shep grimaced.

"That's where Bea usually stays."

"First come first served, no?"

"She's here somewhere," he stammered, gesturing at Bea's bags, which were still sitting by the door.

"Want me to take her bags up?" Matt offered.

"Thank you, son."

He mouthed—the bedroom on the right—followed by a wink. Shep had his hands full. Matt felt badly for him, even though he knew in every ounce of his being that this was Shep's own doing. Matt had gotten into more trouble beside this old man over the years than with his buddies from high school and his fraternity brothers combined.

"This is Renee's son, Matt. I taught him everything he knows."

He should have added "about baseball"—but Matt let it slide. Everyone let everything slide with Shep, though whatever he had done to orchestrate this present catastrophe might prove to be the exception to that rule.

"I want to say hello to your mom, to thank her for inviting me to the wedding. I was so touched. Is she in the house?"

"Not exactly," Matt answered, amusing only himself.

Veronica busied herself on her phone and Matt took the opportunity to quietly confront Shep.

"What did you do?"

"Between you, me, and the lamppost, I sent her my invite." Seeing Matt's reaction, he added, "What? It didn't say nontransferable!"

It amazed Matt that, at ninety-three, this man showed no signs of mellowing. Shep continued:

"I did what had to be done. And I'd do it again."

"Beatrix won't come down from my roof."

He peeked out the window.

"That's not like her," he said, before ordering Veronica to apologize to her sister.

"What did I do now?" Veronica asked, apparently in all innocence.

"It's not what you did *now*, it's what you did *then*."

"You know what, *no*! I've apologized, Daddy. Aside from the fact that she has plenty to apologize to me for, I've spent my whole life apologizing to her. I have written letters, left messages. I text every year on her birthday. Crickets. I was a kid. But even so, it's not all my fault. The pregnancy was not my fault. The fact that she never had other children, not my fault. That she never got past me sleeping with some stupid lifeguard who everyone and their mother slept with—again, not my fault."

"Whose mothers slept with him?" Shep asked with a boyish grin.

"Daddy, stop."

She looked at Matt, angling for his sympathy.

"She blames everything on me. If she tripped over something in Ohio and stubbed her toe, I swear she would yell out, *Veronica!*"

Matt just smiled. It was a lot.

Everyone thought when Shep and Caroline constructed the big house across the street from the one they raised their daughters in, the sisters would make up and fill it with their own families. But they made every effort never to visit in the same month, let alone on the same weekend. For sure, people thought losing their mom, Caroline, a dozen years earlier would unite the two sisters, but they took care of all the arrangements, and their father, by text, with little physical interaction. It was well known that this division in their family was the biggest disappointment in both Caroline and Shep's lives, and the one thing Shep wanted to fix while he was still able.

"Please. Just once more, for me. She won't come down off the roof," Shep pleaded.

"That's mature. Where's her husband? Can't he get her down?"

"He went to visit some relatives on Long Island. He's not back till the weekend."

"That's too long," Matt joked, trying to lighten things up. No one laughed.

"Please, baby," Shep pleaded with his fiery daughter.

"Fine. I'll do it for you," Veronica conceded.

She stormed out of the house, with Shep and Matt following behind her.

Should I Stay or Should I Go

♩♫♪

Maggie

SO FAR, MAGGIE was pretty sure this entire adventure was a colossal mistake. Her primary criterion in deciding whether or not to introduce herself to her birth mother—assessing whether she would be a positive addition to her life—was looking highly unpromising. If Beatrix was the woman she'd seen at the market, she seemed completely undone. Maggie despised undone. She needed a second look. From the little she had witnessed, there were more theatrics surrounding these people than you'd find on a Broadway stage. Not that she'd ever seen a Broadway stage.

The "Inn" that Maggie had paid for in full up front was equally disappointing. Its description on the website, which included mention of a delightful sea breeze wafting in from the bedroom window, was clearly written by someone who had never inhaled there, let alone slept there. Maggie breathed in a potpourri of stale cigarettes and mold. The photos proved misleading as well and must have been taken decades earlier. She pushed away thoughts of what may have gone down on the queen bed that barely fit in the tiny room, and she removed the bedspread, using as few fingers as possible and shoving it out of sight. The pièce de résistance, the shared bathroom down the hall, made her want to cry. If she were going to make it through her stay, she needed to spend as much time away from the "Inn" as possible. She had noticed bikes chained outside. She went down to the desk to inquire about borrowing one in order to traverse the car-free island.

"You can't ride in town," the old-timer behind the counter explained. "But you can ride anywhere through the towns to our east and west."

The home of the betrothed couple seemed like a good place to start. Maggie pulled the wedding invitation Jason had snagged from Beatrix's office out of her backpack.

"Do you possibly know where Renee Tucker or Jake Finley live?"

"The bride and groom! Not exactly."

"But you know them?"

"Everyone knows them. Jake Finley is the ferry captain, and when she was young, Renee was the island's unofficial beauty queen. She's still quite beautiful. It's a surprising match—right out of the wife's romance novels."

The man noticed Maggie's blank expression.

"You know, big-city lawyer throws it all away and moves full-time to a summer island, where she falls in love with a local. I have an old Bay Harbor Directory with a map around here somewhere. Give me a minute."

She was soon pedaling east.

As Maggie rode from Ocean Beach to Bay Harbor, she noticed the sidewalks change from traditional concrete to fancy pavers. The houses looked fancier too, bigger and with more space between them. It was obvious that Bay Harbor was the posher of the two towns. Maggie did not consider herself posh, and between the ritzy aunt on the boat and the upmarket town they hailed from, she worried even more about fitting in.

She passed the market and the ferry terminal she had arrived at, the marina, and eventually the playground where the "innkeeper" had instructed her to hang a right.

She heard them before she saw them.

"Come down off that roof immediately," an old man's voice demanded.

Maggie intuitively followed the shouting. She knew, she just knew. She pulled the bike over on the corner and took cover behind a juniper bush to bear witness to the family reunion from hell.

"What is V doing here? How could you set me up like this—again!"

The woman, the same woman from the market, clearly Beatrix Silver, her birth mother, was screaming from the roof.

Whatever went on between these two must have been a Britney and Jamie Lynn Spears–level feud.

"I was invited this time, Bea. And I'm sorry I slept with your stupid fucking boyfriend thirty stupid fucking years ago!" Veronica yelled up at her sister.

And there it was. A million thoughts blew through Maggie's mind, from *Is that stupid fucking boyfriend from thirty years ago my father?* to *RUN!!!!* But she couldn't pull herself away. It was like reality TV, live.

The old man (her grandfather?) lightly punched her aunt in the arm, and she took it like a champ. She calmed down, a little, and turned to face her father.

"Daddy, do you remember when I arranged the baby naming at the synagogue for when Bea would be here?"

"I do."

"And do you remember that she found out and left on a water taxi ten minutes before my boat arrived?"

"Please, Veronica," he begged, hand to his heart.

"Beatrix. I'm truly sorry. Please come down from there. You're going to give Daddy a heart attack."

Beatrix stood tall, precariously so, and Maggie thought, hoped, that she would head back through the open window. But she didn't. She stood even taller and in a gut-wrenching voice screamed at the top of her lungs:

"You ruined my life!"

Veronica wasn't having it. It seemed she had already given what she could with her last apologetic plea. She stood equally tall, and shouted equally gut-wrenchingly:

"What life?"

And with that, the old man grabbed his chest and fell to the ground, just as Veronica had prophesied.

Peace Train

♩ ♫ ♪

Beatrix

SHEP'S NEIGHBOR BEN, his wife Addison, and their old dog Sally stormed into Shep's house to find Beatrix, Veronica, Matt, and Renee holding a vigil in the living room while the town doctor examined Shep in his bedroom. Bea's face reddened at their arrival, wondering if they had witnessed her and her sister hissing at each other like two feral cats. Bea had known Ben for years but had met his new wife only a couple of times. The whole incident was so unlike her and, Bea imagined, Addison must think she had completely lost it. She *had* lost it, but certainly not completely. What made it worse was that she had been so excited to spend this time on the island with Paul when he returned from visiting his relatives, and to be such a big part of Renee's happy ending. When she saw her sister and she pictured how they now would all be relegated to bit parts on *The Veronica Show*, she'd snapped. Obviously, she now wished she could do it all over again, given the outcome. Veronica's face, on the other hand, seemed to show no remorse, though Bea guessed her lack of expression was most likely cosmetic, not apathetic.

"What happened?" Ben asked in an offensive accusatory tone.

"Beatrix gave him a heart attack," Veronica said drily.

"Fuck you, Veronica."

"Good comeback, Bea. What is it you teach? English literature? Is that how Shakespeare would have put it?"

"Would you prefer I quote *Macbeth*? 'Go away, rump-fed runion slut!'"

Ben stared them both down.

"He can probably hear you fighting from his bedroom," he said. "Haven't you both done enough?"

Neither answered him. Bea was fond of Ben, but it sometimes annoyed her that he and Matt acted like they knew what was best for her dad better than she did, and V probably felt similarly. There was, however, no denying that Shep's neighbors, Matt and Ben, spent more time with him than his daughters did, both in the city and at the beach.

Ben continued to lecture them.

"There were so many times, as far back as when your mother was alive, that I thought to call you two myself and give you a piece of my mind, and I never did. I don't care who did what to whom—your dad suffers from it terribly, and you know what, your mom passed suffering from it too. Why can't you just suck it up, play nice the few times you see each other, and then talk behind each other's backs, like a normal family?"

The sisters shot each other a look from their long-shuttered treasure chest of expressions. It was their "We've gone too far" look, one they had perfected decades before when they recognized they were pushing one or the other parent to the brink and should immediately cease and desist.

It was funny to Bea that they could still communicate silently like that after so many years of not doing so.

The bottom line was, their dad was old, very old, and no one lives forever. Whether it was today—which from the comforting fact that neither an ambulance nor, God forbid, a helicopter had been summoned yet, made her think her dad was fine—or one day in the future, Shep would not be around forever. V would then be her only family. Except for her husband, Paul.

"Paul. I should text Paul, tell him to come back sooner," she said out loud, changing the subject.

As she did, Matt pulled Ben aside and whispered in his ear. Ben's shoulders relaxed, and a small smile crossed his lips before he pressed them together to extinguish it. Bea caught it all. Her gut was already telling her that her dad was faking his condition to manipulate his daughters, and that little exchange between them all but confirmed it.

Ben went to Shep's bedroom door and knocked, inching it open to peek inside before entering. Neither Bea nor V had been allowed to come in. This gave Bea more pause.

Ben's wife, Addison, tried to soften his words.

"He's just upset. He loves Shep like a father."

"So do we," Veronica responded acerbically, amusing Bea. Veronica, saying and doing whatever she wanted, had always tickled her sister. She was funny—until Bea was on the receiving end of her narcissistic behavior.

Ben's dog, Sally, lay waiting outside Shep's bedroom door, triggering images of their childhood dog, Fluffy.

"Remember how much Fluffy loved Dad?" Bea said, tossing the memory to Veronica like a peace offering. She bit. (Veronica, not Fluffy.)

"Remember how he would take her on those long walks after dinner in the city—until we found him out?"

They both laughed. Veronica turned to Addison to explain.

"Shep would only walk the little white dog after dark. He said it was embarrassing to be seen with her. Then one night he had the flu and our mother sent us to walk Fluffy after dinner."

Bea jumped in for the punchline.

"We got as far as MacDougal Street and Fluffy refused to budge, planting herself in front of the door of the Old Rabbit Club Bar. Veronica pushed the door open, and a bunch of drunks yelled 'Fluffy!'"

The three women laughed, nervously, until Ben came out wearing the same sour expression he'd walked in with.

"He's going to be fine. Dr. Jim will tell you more, but he said no more stress."

Relief flooded the sisters' faces, and they both promised to toe the line.

The doctor followed.

"My guess is that Shep had a panic attack, though he may be dehydrated. He's refusing to go the hospital, but his vitals are normal, so I'm not overly concerned. Someone should go to the store and get Pedialyte. He will probably refuse to drink it, so pour it in a glass with some ice and tell him it's a sports drink. He needs electrolytes."

"I'll go," Matt volunteered, desperate to get out of there.

"Did anything stressful precede the incident?" the doctor asked.

"Possibly," V said.

"Yes," Bea admitted.

"Well, you are two grown women. I don't need to lecture you."

Both Bea and V flashed an eerily similar case-in-point look at Ben, before both swearing on all that was righteous and good to behave.

And for that night, they both did.

A Bar Song (Tipsy)

♩♫♪

Maggie

MAGGIE PEDALED BACK to Ocean Beach, her legs moving as fast as the tears that streamed down her cheeks.

In all her thirty years, she had never felt so far from home. She missed Jason. She missed her own bed and the record store and her own bathroom. She really missed her own bathroom.

But that's not why she was crying.

The truth was, although she rarely let herself go there, Maggie didn't just miss her mother, she desperately missed having a mother. She missed talking to that one person in the world who cared about every little detail in her life, in her day, in her heart. And while she had billed this trip as nothing more than a fact-finding mission, she had fantasized that those facts would be conducive to finding something more.

When Maggie pictured meeting her birth mother and possibly her birth family, a PowerPoint presentation of possibilities had flooded her brain. Her mother standing on a rooftop screaming down at her sister to go fuck herself was not in the deck.

Suddenly she felt infinitely disappointed.

She crumpled onto the musty bed in her hotel room, curling up into as small a ball as possible—uber-aware of every point where her body touched the seedy bedding. If she were to abandon her plan, by tomorrow night she could be back home in her own bed. She was certain that was the best decision. There was nothing for her here.

Maggie dozed off, then woke up in a sweat and looked at her phone.

Jason was still in class, but she was desperate to hear his voice, so she called his cell anyway.

His nerdy message, which usually made her cringe a bit—*It's Jason, you know what to do*—now tugged at her heart, reopening the watershed. Everything she was feeling, including the fact that she never wanted to leave his side again, spilled out into his voicemail. She knew it would break him to hear her like that, but she felt better after saying it all out loud.

She washed up in the sink in the hallway, threw on jeans and a coat of lip gloss, and hit the town in search of a comfortable seat at a bar for dinner. Hearing the unmistakable sound of Miles Davis escaping from a restaurant a few blocks away, the Salty Pelican, she ventured in.

The bar was empty, aside from a weatherworn bartender and a cute guy around her age with a subtle hipster aesthetic. He looked like he could be one of those dudes chilling on a hammock in an Airbnb ad. She sat two seats away from him on a barstool.

"Nice tune, Chase," the Airbnb model with good taste in music remarked to the bartender. And even though she was intent on leaving the island the next day, no matter how much of a waste of money the trip had turned out to be, Maggie marveled at the fact that her birth mother may have sat in this exact bar and flirted with this exact bartender, though she hoped she had better taste in men than this guy. It was a mean thing to say, or even to think, but he reeked of has-been.

She ordered a much-needed vodka soda and busied herself perusing the menu. She had eaten little all day. Her stomach had been acting up, and today's scene had put a whole new spin on the phrase *inherited trauma*.

"Do I know you?" the bartender asked. "You look very familiar."

"I've never been here before," Maggie assured him.

He set down her vodka soda and continued to stare at her quizzically.

Airbnb boy clearly interpreted it as lust, but Maggie didn't get that sense at all.

"A little young even for you, Chase," he declared, adding, "Watch out for this old horndog," in Maggie's direction. She laughed at the implausibility, but flashed her faux engagement ring, just in case.

"I'm engaged," she said, exaggerating the truth just a little. Engaged to be engaged didn't sound like as much of a roadblock.

"Congratulations," said the Airbnb model, reaching out his hand in introduction. "I'm Matt."

"Maggie May Wheeler," she said while shaking back.

"So did your parents like the Faces or the Beatles?" he asked.

Both wrote songs featuring Maggie May.

Maggie laughed, "Faces, and I'm impressed. Most people say Rod Stewart, not his old band."

The bartender was still hovering. It was strange to Maggie, but he seemed harmless enough. Matt kindly included him in the conversation since it was clear he wasn't going anywhere.

"'Maggie May' came out in '72 and Stewart went solo in '75," he informed the bartender before turning his attention back to Maggie. "I'm a reporter for *Rolling Stone*."

"Whoa—that is so badass. I sell *Rolling Stone* at my store, Maggie May Records. It's in a small town in the Midwest."

The bartender piped in with "*Just a small-town girl, living in a lonely world.*"

They both laughed, more at him than with him. But it was OK because he clearly didn't catch on. Maggie felt badly about it anyway and pulled out the standard ordering question.

"What's good here?"

"I'm a big fan of the chicken fingers," the bartender replied. "But don't go by me. I've never grown up."

Matt laughed. "I didn't know you were so self-aware, Chase. I'll have the fish tacos," adding for Maggie's benefit, "They're arguably the best on the island."

"Make it two then, please." She smiled, handing back the menu.

"Blackened or fried?"

"Hmm, that's a tough one," Maggie groaned.

"Want to do one and one, and we can share?" Matt offered.

"Sure, sounds good," she answered, impressed by the boldness of the suggestion.

The bartender headed to the kitchen.

Matt slid onto the seat next to her as if it were the most

natural thing in the world. Maggie didn't mind. After all, they were sharing dinner. Being without Jason on this crazy journey was starting to get to her. Not that this guy reminded her of Jason. They were opposites, physically. Airbnb guy had cropped light brown hair with ginger highlights and the perfect amount of grub on his face. Jason was more prepster than hipster, with the smoothest skin and dark brown hair cut in basically the same bowl-like style that he'd had as a kid. She loved that about him. Maggie wasn't big on change, another reason to be true to herself and get out on the first ferry in the morning. *She was self-aware too!*

"My dream is to own a record store. *That* is so badass!" Matt marveled, interrupting her thoughts.

"I know nothing else. It was my parents' store. I grew up in it."

"Sounds like bliss."

"It was," Maggie says, with more than a hint of melancholy, which embarrassed her. She shook it off.

"How did you get into music journalism?"

"It's kind of a funny story. The quick version is my parents got divorced when I was sixteen and my mom started dating this drummer in a heavy metal band. She dragged me on tour with him on weekends and vacations, and I started writing about it for my high school newspaper. My teacher turned one of my pieces in to *Rolling Stone* and they published me . . . at seventeen."

"How Cameron Crowe of you."

"Indeed. I've seen *Almost Famous* a zillion times—the best."

"For me it's *Say Anything*—you know, the boom box scene."

"Sorry, but that may be the cheesiest music scene in movie history."

"Try the most iconic music scene in movie history," she said, sulking a little.

"Please, that dude—"

"Lloyd Dobler," she interrupted.

"Excuse me, Lloyd Dobler, making a total fool of himself for that girl. So cheesy!"

"Try so romantic! If you love someone, you don't care about making a total fool of yourself."

Matt rolled his eyes. "OK, chill. It's not like I dissed the greatest record store story of all time."

"If you diss *High Fidelity*, I swear I'm not sharing tacos with you."

Matt spun around on his stool and puffed his chest out like a rooster. He was wearing the same Pretenders T-shirt that Catherine Zeta-Jones's character wore in the movie. They both laughed—really laughed. And then they laughed some more at how much they were laughing.

The bartender returned with their place settings and awkwardly waited for them to stop laughing. Which made them laugh even more.

Maggie thought about how good it felt to let go like that. It was the kind of comic relief that was so deep, it pushed any tension up and out.

"Your food will be out in a few minutes," the bartender announced when they finally quieted. They both smiled and nodded, but he remained standing there with them like a third wheel. In all fairness, he and Maggie's new companion had started out on an equal footing.

He turned to Matt. "Ready for the big wedding day?"

Matt shook his head and rolled his eyes simultaneously.

"Oh, are you engaged too?" Maggie asked.

"No, my mom is getting married."

Could it be *the* wedding? she wondered. Things were suddenly getting more interesting. She dug deeper.

"So, you don't like who your mother's marrying, I presume?"

"Tacos almost ready, Chase?" Matt asked the bartender, clearly not wanting to answer in front of him. Maggie got it. She was from a small town too.

"I'll check," he said, and obliged.

"No. I like him plenty. I've known him my whole life. It's his daughter, Dylan."

"You don't like his daughter?"

"No, I love his daughter."

"She doesn't love you?"

"She loves me," he laughed at her impatience. "It's just, we had one of those 'If we're both single when we're thirty' pacts and . . ."

Maggie's mind went from recon to romance.

"Well, you couldn't have picked a better person to sit next to—I'm dating my childhood best friend!"

"You mean your fiancé?"

"Yes, yes. My fiancé. I just got used to dating him," she giggled nervously. "You should go for it. It's the best for so many reasons; it's like a guarantee! There are no games; you can totally be yourself around them. You know each other better than anyone else, no surprises either. Oh, and their families—you already feel like a part of them, which is a real plus, for me at least, and for you too, I presume, given the circumstances."

"Slow down," he teased, "I have the opposite problem. I'm worried she will want to get romantic, and I think it's a mistake—you know, because we will be like actual family after this weekend."

"Oh, I get it. Well, that's great too! You will always have her as your family. You'll never lose touch, and when you marry someone else, they won't be jealous or intimidated by her because she's your sister."

"You've really thought this through."

"I guess I have," she laughed.

"You make good points. Let's just hope she feels the same." He took another sip of his drink before asking, "So, what brings you to our little island?"

Maggie contemplated her answer. She was already certain she wanted no part of the crazy messy family she had witnessed earlier, but she was curious about whether this guy knew her birth mother, and if "his" wedding was the same one Beatrix was attending.

"Is your mom's wedding on board a ferryboat?" she asked, clearly piquing his curiosity.

"Yessss," he answered in that tentative way one does when waiting for the other shoe to drop.

Certain she was leaving the next day, she went for it.

"I'm here to find my birth mother, Beatrix Silver."

From his expression, you would think a boot had dropped, and one of those heavy ones, like a size 11 Doc Marten.

"Whoa. Bea is your mother?"

"My birth mother."

"Have you met her?'

"No, but I saw her in action today and it put a hard stop

to my journey. It was . . . messy, to say it politely. I'm not into messy."

"You saw that scene today, in Bay Harbor?" Matt asked.

"I did. Were you there?"

"Unfortunately, yes. It's one of the reasons I'm sitting here at the bar alone. I needed to decompress."

"Do you know if the old guy is OK?"

She was pretty sure the old guy was her grandfather but didn't allow herself to really think about that.

"Shep? Yes, he's fine."

"Was it a heart attack?"

"No—it was more of an . . . episode, I'd say."

"Like a mental episode?"

"No. More like a soap opera episode. He was faking."

"Faking? So, he's crazy too?"

"Certifiable, but he's the only one who really qualifies. Beatrix was just having a bad day."

"I'll say," Maggie joked, though she didn't find any of it remotely funny.

"Shep and Beatrix Silver are two of my favorite people in the entire world, for real. Shep is the GOAT."

It was a big statement—from a complete stranger. A complete stranger with extra points for wearing her favorite Pretenders T-shirt.

Chase returned with the fish tacos. He placed them down and pulled a piece of paper with his phone number written on it from his pocket, handing it to Maggie.

"If you need anything while you're here."

"Oh my God!" Matt jumped off his stool while swatting the paper from her hand like it was on fire.

"What the hell, Matt? Just being neighborly."

"Maggie, I have to show you something," he declared in a panicked tone. He must have realized that he was now acting crazy because he recalibrated his intensity and took it down a notch.

"Do you trust me?" he continued.

"Oddly, yes," she laughed.

"Can you wrap these up to go for us?" he asked as Maggie made a quick detour to the ladies' room. As she did, she heard Matt continue with, "And Chase, I'm not sure what you're thinking, but trust me too, this girl is off-limits."

Behind the closed stall door Maggie did a deep dive into Matt Tucker's social media. He was easy to locate.

Matt Tucker Roving Reporter Rolling Stone

In between pictures of concerts and bylines were personal shots like a loving post dedicated to his mom for Mother's Day and a recent picture of his pet cat, Houdini, with a sweet message about his passing. Even though her gut had told her Matt was harmless just from chatting with him, she was thankful that the internet confirmed it.

She fought the urge to express condolences for Houdini when she confidently hopped on the back of his bike.

Glory Days

♩♫♪

Chase Logan

THERE WAS A reason that the bartender, Chase Logan, was drawn to the olive-skinned, dark-haired girl at the bar—and it certainly wasn't just because she was pretty. His days of picking up women had seriously receded over the years, not unlike his hairline. He had gone from fighting off the hot ones to taking home a straggler or two, to barely receiving a look in his direction that didn't come with a request for a beverage.

He stared at the girl because she looked familiar. And not yesterday familiar. Thirty years ago familiar, which of course was not possible, because she didn't look to be over thirty years old now.

Something about her reminded him of a young Beatrix Silver. He knew that there was a girl walking the earth who possibly looked like Bea, who also possibly looked like him. Which this one didn't, he thought, until he looked in her eyes and saw his own. She had the drop-dead gorgeous violet-blue eyes that he and many in his family were known for.

Chase hadn't known that he had fathered a child until a

few years ago, when a friend told him about a book called *On Fire Island* with a character fitting his description. Plus, the local author barely disguised his name, calling him Logan Chase instead of Chase Logan.

He was made to look like a real chump in the book, but truth be told, it was an accurate description of him in his twenties. He wasn't proud of what went down that summer thirty years ago. He knew it wasn't cool that he'd been sleeping with Bea and her sister, but he never imagined the chain reaction it would set off.

Thinking about it now, he wouldn't be surprised if he had fathered a child or two. He'd been a real jackass when he was younger about using condoms, and he'd suffered unwelcome repercussions from that choice on more than one occasion. It was the reason he steered clear of those ancestry kits—he had nightmares that a mob of millennials would show up at his doorstep chanting, "Papa, can I borrow the car?" or in his case, his bike, now that he lived on the island full-time.

Over the course of a few summers, from the age of about sixteen to twenty-five, the Manhattan girls couldn't get enough of the handsome lifeguard with the killer abs and shy smile. The funny thing about it was that he wasn't shy at all. It was just that half of the time he had no idea what these sophisticated city kids who summered on Fire Island were talking about. He kept his mouth shut out of fear of embarrassing himself.

From the lifeguard stand on the beach, he could see them, lying on their blankets reading, or at least holding a book. And not just that one book that was assigned for summer homework; they seemed to like reading.

They were all educated at private or selective public high

schools, and they would make jokes and remark on things Chase had no clue about. They watched foreign films, and frequented museums and Broadway shows. The only time Chase had been to the Theater District was when a cousin took him to the city to see a peep show. The topless woman on the other side of the glass had spun around a few times and shimmied at the end. Not quite a crowd-raising finale, but memorable all the same.

But Beatrix Silver was different. Beatrix listened to what he had to say and didn't turn every conversation they had into some intellectual debate. She laughed at his jokes and didn't act as if she were slumming, like the other girls Chase had bedded over those prime summers of his youth. Though *bedded* was a misnomer—since his MO was to bring them down to the beach with a blanket and a bottle of five-dollar Boone's Farm wine. It wasn't until years later, when one of those women returned and ordered a drink from him, recalling their pairing from her perspective, that he realized he was the one who was often being used.

"Look at the hot lifeguard I screwed on the beach this summer!" echoed proudly through prep school halls each September, the sexual equivalent of boasting about winning a blue ribbon at the Hampton Classic.

If he were being honest with himself, he knew it had been different with Bea than with the others. Bea had cared for him, and he didn't know what to do with that at the time. It may have been the reason that, when the opportunity arose, he'd slept with her sister. It wasn't a hard thing to do. Sleeping with Veronica Silver was a common notch on many a lifeguard's belt. It was both easy, and the easy way out.

Bea was heading back to her fancy liberal arts school to

read big books and philosophize about the state of humanity, as Chase imagined. She had already snagged his best lifeguard sweatshirt and mentioned him visiting during something called the Fall Harvest Festival. She'd talked on and on about the football game and hayride and hard cider and some harvest moon dance he would need to bring a sports jacket for. He didn't have a sports jacket. Chase liked Bea but knew that, without his surfboard and the lifeguard status, he wouldn't survive such things—let alone a lifetime of them. He needed to break it off. He wasn't much of a communicator, so he slept with her sister instead of having the tough talk.

Now, the hair on the back of his neck stood on end as he watched the young woman at the bar cock her head to the side like a puppy, which came rushing back to him as an expression of Bea's that summer. Not to mention the freckled olive skin and dark curls. Between those and her eyes, it felt like a sure thing, though he wished he had hard proof.

Indiana Jones:
The Main Theme

♩ ♫ ♪

Matt

USUALLY, THE FEELING of giving a pretty girl a ride home on the back of his bike with her hands wrapped around his waist made Matt feel valiant. Tonight, he felt like Indiana Jones, returning home with the Holy Grail.

He had single-handedly found Bea's long-lost daughter, Shep's granddaughter, and in some sick twist of fate, prevented her father, the infamous lifeguard who came between the Silver sisters thirty years before, from possibly making a move on her.

He stopped in front of the baseball field and climbed off the bike to fill Maggie in. He wanted to get in and out of his house unnoticed by his mother, the consummate interrogator, and Jake, whose own house was filled to the brim with visiting wedding guests. He still wasn't used to passing the burly ferry captain in the halls of his home. He wondered if he ever would be. It didn't much matter. Renee and Jake were set to make Jake's home their full-time digs after the wedding, leaving Matt to officially take ownership of this home that he'd grown up spending summers in. He'd only recently begun questioning how he'd fill it.

"I'll lock up my bike on the side. Follow in my footsteps as close as possible, so we get in and out unnoticed," he instructed Maggie.

The moonlight caught the mischievous twinkle in her eye—like they were going on a raid at sleepaway camp. He felt bad, as if he had hinted at an adventure, when in truth she was probably going to be really freaked out by what he was about to show her.

"The second step from the top squeaks like a mouse on steroids, so be sure to skip that one," he added before entering.

They made it into the house silently, aside from the creak of the screen door. Maggie paused at the entrance to his bedroom, flashing back to parental warnings of bad men promising puppies and candy, no doubt. Matt recognized her trepidation and whispered:

"I know this is weird, but don't worry. My mother is in the next room, so you can always scream."

She laughed, and he put his finger to his lips, reminding her to be quiet. She followed him in through his bedroom door and he shut it behind them.

"Sit," he said, directing her to the one chair in the room. He pulled a book off his shelf and held it up for her to see. *On Fire Island*.

"You've never read this, right?"

"No," she uttered, obviously confused.

"My neighbor across the street wrote this book about the summer after his wife passed away."

"That's so sad."

"Yes, it was brutal, but that's not the point. There's a chapter in here about you, when you were born, the circumstances, and how your mother feels about it."

"My birth mother," she corrected.

"Your birth mother," Matt repeated respectfully.

"This is insane. Why did the author do that?" she asked.

"Well, it's a good story, and I think your mo—your birth mother thought publishing it for the world to see might lead to you finding her. Which I guess it did, 'cause you were about to jump ship, but here you are."

He flipped through the book, found what he was looking for, and held it out for Maggie to take.

"Here, it's not going to be easy to read, but if I were you, I'd want to know—chapter thirty-seven, 'Bea's Secret.'"

She took it in silence.

Matt watched her intently; it was too interesting not to. At first, a joyful expression sat on her lips as she read about her mother.

"She sounds less crazy here," she commented. "Is that why you wanted me to read this?"

"Just read," he said with a gentle smile.

"Ohhhh"—she looked up at Matt—"Veronica stole her boyfriend."

"I know." He couldn't help but chuckle at her repeating the contents back to him, as if he, and everyone he knew, didn't know the story.

"He was the hottest guy on the beach—a lifeguard."

"Yes."

Matt worried that she would figure out that the bartender from tonight was the lifeguard and have another legitimate reason to run. Had she caught his name at the bar? If so, she may have put two and two together. He knew he would have to tell her eventually, but she'd come here to find her mother, whom Matt was certain she would be proud of. The two-timing lifeguard who had impregnated her, not so much. He loved his mother's friend Bea and adored Bea's father, Shep, and this girl seemed like a dream. He really wanted this to work out for them all.

"Oh my God."

"What?"

She got off the chair and sat on the floor next to Matt so that he could see over her shoulder what part she was reading.

"She didn't know she was pregnant with me till the fifth month."

"I know," he said again.

She began reading the conversation between her mother and their neighbor aloud, straight from the book. It was surreal.

> "The baby was born about two weeks before gradu-
> ation. My mom flew down in advance. 'Bea is de-
> pressed,' she told my dad. She gave birth at a
> birthing center in Mt. Vernon to a beautiful baby
> girl. Six pounds, three ounces, with olive skin and a
> thick patch of black hair like mine."

Maggie started to cry and handed the book to Matt.

"I can't."

"Do you want me to?"

"Please."

Matt took over reading the book aloud to Maggie.

"I know that I made all those choices myself, but I still daydream about what would have happened if Veronica hadn't slept with him. I swear I would have kept that baby and married the lifeguard. I'm not saying we would have lived happily ever after, like I had pictured us doing at the time, but I would have my daughter."

"And you never had kids," he said, sadly pointing out the obvious.

"Nope. And my sister has two, who I don't even know. I just met them at my mother's funeral for like two seconds."

Matt paused. The next part was going to be tough to hear.

"Have you ever thought about finding your daughter?" Ben asked.

"More like have I ever *not* thought about finding her?"

Maggie let out a heartbreaking sob, and Matt fought the urge to close the book. But then he remembered how she planned on giving up and leaving the next day, going home without even meeting Bea—and Shep. He had to prevent that from happening. He continued:

"As luck would have it, the adoption agency burnt down years ago, which didn't much matter because it was a closed adoption."

"DNA tracing?"

"I did 23andMe—no close match. And you know, if she wanted to find me, she would have done it too—so there's that."

"Well, maybe. I mean, closed adoptions were pretty rare, even back then. There's a chance she doesn't even know that she's adopted. How old would she be?"

"She turned twenty-one on May third."

"Oh my God," Maggie cried, putting her hands to her mouth. "This was nine years ago."

"Your hands," Matt observed. "They're shaking so hard."

Maggie looked down and pressed them to her knees, trying to stop them from trembling.

"I haven't eaten all day. I'm so hungry, but also so nauseous."

Matt recognized that the fish tacos that they took home from the Salty Pelican wouldn't do.

"How about I make us some mac and cheese and then we can talk more."

"The powdery Kraft kind?"

"Yes, Kraft—possibly the most comforting food in the world."

"I could swallow that," she said through tears. "Should I come help?"

"Stay here. The last thing we want right now is to have to explain you to my mother."

Matt returned twenty minutes later with two bowls and two spoons to find Maggie sound asleep in the bottom bunk with the book lying on her chest. He removed it, gently placed his hand on her shoulder, and whispered, "Do you want to eat?" She rolled over to face the wall. He didn't have the heart to wake her.

He climbed onto the top bunk, lost in the childhood memory of eating the same mac and cheese from the same bowl in the same bed. It was all part of the beauty of being lucky enough to be able to come home to the house you grew up in. Even though he only ever lived there in the summer, and even though he had lived in the same New York City apartment for most of his life, Fire Island would always be home.

She Drives Me Crazy

♩♪♪

Veronica

VERONICA KNEW HER reputation on the island, and the truth was she didn't much care, except when it came to her sister. Right or wrong, what her sister thought of her had always had a direct correlation to what she thought of herself. At least, as she witnessed yesterday, she could still make Bea laugh. She loved Bea's laugh—especially when she was the source of it. Her goal, for now, was more laughter. She vowed to be easy and entertaining.

With Shep convalescing in his bedroom, Beatrix and Veronica were forced to spend the day in close company. Despite the doctor's diagnosis of a panic attack, as opposed to a heart attack, they both suspected that Shep was tricking them, no doubt with the doctor's aid. Shep had a knack for convincing anyone to be his accomplice. But without proof, they had to go along with the ruse and follow doctor's orders.

Veronica, for one, was grateful for the ceasefire and assumed that Bea was as well. V was no longer the formidable fighter she had once been, and her sister had never been as skilled as she was in sisterly combat. Bea was more of a ghoster. Ultimately, her ghosting tactic was more painful to Veronica than any vitriolic attack she could have unleashed. Even though there were many things in her life that Veronica was unhappy about lately, she still counted her relationship, or lack thereof, with Beatrix as the single greatest failure of her life.

This temporary truce, although quite welcome, was not a solution to their problems. Their mother used to warn them, to no avail, that if you don't address things right away, cracks become craters. In their case, those craters were now the size of the ones on the moon. Things would have to be talked out for there to be any long-term resolution. She wondered if Bea was even interested in that.

Truth be told, if Bea made it clear that she wanted no contact ever again, Veronica might feel a sense of relief. The long years of sending birthday and New Year's messages and compulsively checking her email for Bea's response would be done. As would beating herself up in the middle of the night when her mind ran back to the decades-old inciting incident, or what she remembered of it at least. She was high as a kite half the time back then.

In the years since their mother's death, Veronica had contemplated giving up on Bea multiple times, but her promise to her mom to heal their rift kept her from doing so. Maybe when both her parents were dead, she would stop torturing herself and accept that her sister was living a happy, fulfilled life and had no room in it for Veronica and her baggage.

Yes, she doubted Bea had any genuine interest in reconciling. She blinked back tears at the thought of it.

Veronica had been so happy to receive the wedding invitation, she'd immediately begun dreaming up all the scenarios of seeing Bea again after so long. Her sister cursing her out from her neighbor's roof was not on the agenda. She questioned whether Bea was unraveling, or if it was merely her presence that drove her mad.

It hadn't always been this way. For most of her young life, there was no one V would rather be with than her sister, and Bea seemed to feel the same way. V looked up to Bea, listened to whatever music she did, watched the same shows, and pinned the same images ripped from teen magazines onto her bedroom walls. Sometime before the lifeguard incident, when Veronica had started to come into her own, her body catching up to her long legs, things started to sour between them. Yes, Veronica was experimenting with anything and anyone, and Bea, who was far more conservative and prudish, had no problem letting her know what she thought of her unfettered ways. Even more than hating her for what she did with the lifeguard, Beatrix not liking her really messed with Veronica's self-esteem. She remembered one fight in particular when Bea's retort broke her heart. Bea, the person she had spent her life looking up to, had screamed, "You and I are nothing alike, not one single bit."

Shep's favoring of Bea when they were kids—always joking that V was Caroline's child and Bea was Shep's—didn't help either. He said it was based on appearances, but anyone could see that Bea and Shep had a bond that exceeded physicality. V's shrink thought it was the reason she had so many sexual partners when she was young—she was constantly seeking male approval. Despite this, she never brought his favoritism up to her dad, and now he was too old for her to hurt him with the accusation and make him feel regretful about their relationship. Besides, she didn't know if she believed her shrink's psychobabble on the subject. It was more likely that she was just a horny teenager.

Veronica Silver was never well liked by the other girls or, later, women. Their men were constantly gazing at her, grinning at her, and finding her every word amusing as if she were brilliant. The women who'd heard the stories about her steered clear. It was one of the reasons she had moved clear across the country: to start fresh.

Bea's husband, Paul, would arrive tomorrow, and Veronica had no idea if that would make things better or worse. She wondered what he was like. It went without saying that she had done a Google search on him, but it didn't provide much information beyond the fact that he was a Harvard-educated math professor from Queens, New York. She imagined him as nothing but a stereotypical number nerd, a perfect match for her academic sister.

The two siblings silently knocked about the house, pretending not to wake Shep, even though they were both sure that his ailment was total BS. Shep had that town doctor wrapped around his ninety-three-year-old finger. Regardless, they were both happy for the silence, interrupted only when Shep summoned them—ringing an old bike bell like a lunatic until one of them appeared in his doorway. The first time he did it, Bea leaped out of the way, as if a bike was set to mow her down in the middle of their living room. The two sisters burst into laughter, just like they had when they were children. It gave Veronica hope.

That was it for communication between them until four o'clock, when Bea gleefully announced, "Cocktail time! I'll make us two mojitos!"

Shep had taught Bea how to make cocktails when she was

a kid. When their parents entertained, he would send Veronica around to take orders like a cocktail waitress, and Bea would whip them up. They were ten and six years old: parenting at its finest.

"Make mine a virgin," Veronica responded. She would have liked nothing better than to tie one on with her sister, but she was sober, and there was little in life that meant more to Veronica than her sobriety.

"I'll have one," a voice bellowed from the bedroom.

"Not a chance," Bea mouthed to her sister, laughing.

"Two thumbs down, Daddy," Veronica yelled back.

"One middle finger up!" Shep retorted, leaving them both in hysterics.

There was no doubt Shep was wearing a wide and winning grin after hearing them laughing together. He surely believed that his plan had inspired a ceasefire. It was merely a Band-Aid, though. As with any ceasefire, if nothing is resolved, you revert to war.

When Veronica picked up the empty bowl of chicken soup that one of Shep's lady friends (as he called the gaggle of widows who flocked to him) had brought for dinner, he made a funny request.

"Go ask Ben to get the old movies down from the attic."

"Our old movies are still in Ben's attic? That's weird."

Their mother had been a minimalist and Shep was a hoarder. When they'd moved from the old house to the new one, Shep secretly put half the stuff she had relegated to a dumpster back in their attic. Their old attic. When Ben bought the house from him, Shep ridiculously suggested that half the attic remain his, and Ben didn't bother objecting.

"Yeah, well, it's my house," Shep argued now. He had no patience for explanations.

"It's not your house, Daddy. Ben bought that house from you a dozen years ago."

"Just get the movies. I want to see your mother."

Ben, it turned out, had done this dance before with Shep and was happy to fetch the stack of 16mm reels from his attic along with the old projector. In the end, they turned it into an evening activity and he and his wife, Addison, joined them.

Shep sprawled out on the Eames recliner draped in an afghan that Caroline had crocheted years earlier. He sipped a mug of tea (bourbon) while inhaling the crackly old footage of Homeowners' Games, summer birthdays, camp shows, and beach days.

They all went to sleep that night steeped in memories and melancholy for what could have been. V had little doubt that had been Shep's plan all along. How many moments together had they missed recording due to their long-standing rift? Memories never made; photographs never taken.

And although on that night her sister laughed and cried along with her at all the right moments, bathing in the beauty of the once-happy family of four, Veronica doubted it would make much difference in the light of day.

She was right.

Stay

♩♫♪

Maggie

MAGGIE WOKE UP with swollen eyes, an empty belly, and a feeling of marked confusion until she noticed a Post-it stuck to the bunk bed frame.

> *Picking up Dylan at the ferry, sleepyhead. Will*
> *sneak you out when I get home.*
>
> —Matt

As she sat up, she unintentionally hit her head on the top bunk, muttering curses as she grabbed her cell phone. She was eager to see if Jason had called. It was dead. Ugh. Jason was surely looking for her after that message she'd left, and this house looked like it belonged to Apple users, not Android. She would figure out a way to escape unnoticed and head back to the "Inn" asap.

The book, *On Fire Island*, sat on the dresser next to a melamine *Powerpuff Girls* bowl with the leftover mac and cheese, an old boom box, and a retro vinyl briefcase-style cassette holder. Maggie had had the same one as a kid. She popped it open and ran her finger over the titles: David Bowie, *Golden Years*; *The Best of Talking Heads*; Steely Dan, *Aja*; Peter Gabriel, *So*. She popped the last one in the boom box and played "In Your Eyes," at the volume of a whisper, while she studied a framed picture of Matt with Dylan, she assumed. They looked to be about ten. The girl in the photo was a few inches taller than Matt at the time, and quite beautiful. They both had eyes filled with mischief, huge grins on their faces, long messy hair, sun-kissed skin, and multiple *Rugrats* Band-Aids haphazardly stuck to each of their knees.

She put down the frame and picked up the bowl of cold mac and cheese. Although the food had been sitting out all night, she contemplated eating it anyway. While she heard that the people at Kraft had swapped the bright orange artificial coloring for natural things like paprika and turmeric, she was pretty sure it still contained enough preservatives to survive the apocalypse. It wouldn't have been the first time she had eaten cold mac and cheese for breakfast.

She went for it, standing in front of the window, looking out, thinking of nothing more than the fact that Matt had served it to her with a spoon when she greatly preferred a fork. She remembered sick days as a kid. Her mom would roll a TV into her room, and she would sit in bed looping the straight little macaronis onto the tines of her fork before sliding them off in one bite with her teeth.

Through the window, she saw Matt walking up the block, pulling a wagon with the ferry captain's daughter trailing behind. She looked different than Maggie had imagined. Athletic and beachy, yes, but her long hair in the photo was now cut into an edgy pixie, like a blond Audrey Hepburn. Next to her was a man—tall, also blond, handsome, even from the distance. Maybe Dylan had a boyfriend after all, and Matt would have no need for any hard conversations. Matt looked up toward the window and they briefly caught eyes. He didn't look happy. She wasn't sure why that was. Clearly, the boyfriend's appearance had eradicated Matt's concerns.

When she heard them enter, she turned off the boom box and opened the bedroom door a crack, hoping to catch the introductions. Their excitement upon seeing each other echoed up the stairs.

"Dylan!" Jake shouted upon seeing his baby girl. From the squeal that followed, Maggie guessed there was a lift and a spin involved. "Love the new hair!" a woman's voice, probably Matt's mom, rang out. Maggie inched out of the room and took a step down the staircase to hear better. Just then, Dylan introduced the guy.

"This is Steve," she said, rephrasing it awkwardly, "my boyfriend, Steve."

It is *her boyfriend. I knew it*, Maggie thought. She took one more step to get a bit closer, when the loudest creak she may have ever heard groaned from below her feet. Ugh, the dreaded second step that Matt had warned of—it was just as he had said.

"Did you hear that?" Renee proclaimed.

Maggie stood still, frozen in place, not knowing whether to remain where she was or run back to the cover of Matt's room. She chose the latter. The creak was even louder on the flip side, and she froze again but it was too late. Jake, Renee, Matt, Dylan, and Dylan's boyfriend, Steve, were all staring up at her from below. Renee spoke first.

"Matty! You picked up a girl and brought her home on the weekend of my wedding?"

"Don't be ridiculous, Mom," he answered, offering no further explanation.

She wasn't having it.

"Then who is she?"

"Hi, I'm Maggie May Wheeler," Maggie offered, casually following the trail of her voice down the stairs.

All eyes turned to Matt.

"Yes, this is Maggie. Maggie is my . . . girlfriend. She, um, surprised me last night, made the last ferry."

The silence was deafening. Particularly from Renee, who looked completely shocked and more than a bit annoyed by yet another surprise guest to her wedding. At least that was how Maggie interpreted it.

"Don't worry, I can sit anywhere, Mrs. . . . ."

"You can call her Renee," Matt jumped in, saving her from the fact that she didn't remember her "boyfriend's" last name. Four sets of eyes stared her down with the fifth, Matt's, desperately avoiding hers. She did her best to redirect their attention.

"So, are you as excited to be brother and sister as Matt is?" Maggie asked Dylan.

"I think we might be a bit too old to adopt that title. Don't you, Matty?"

In a state of disbelief, all he could do was nod.

"Dylan, I put you upstairs, but do you want to take the guest house? It's bigger," Renee offered.

"Well, are you guys staying in Matt's room?" Dylan asked, adding with a giggle, "Do you still have those bunk beds?"

"I do," he confessed.

"Are you top or bottom, Maggie?" Steve asked, in what was meant to be a joke, until Maggie turned him into the straight man.

"Depends on the night," she countered, surprising herself with her somewhat risqué humor.

Renee silently mouthed "What the hell?" to her son before following Dylan and her wedding date to the guest house.

As soon as she was out of earshot, Maggie did more than mouth it.

"What the hell, Matt? I wanted to fly under the radar, remember?"

He nudged her arm. "Let's go upstairs and discuss this in private."

Back in the room, Matt closed the door behind them and quietly pleaded, "I'm sorry, I wasn't thinking."

"I think you were thinking—thinking about how you would feel like a dateless loser at the wedding now that Dylan has a plus-one!"

"I'm not that quick, Maggie." His eyes widened, and a smile slid across his face. "But now that you mention it!"

Maggie grunted, clearly unamused. He took it down a notch and apologized again. "I'm seriously very sorry. I didn't think it through."

"I'll say—you could have just stuck with her one-night stand assumption. You're a grown man. What was she gonna do—punish you?"

"OK, but hear me out: by jumping into the girlfriend role, you could come to the wedding and all the festivities and see that Bea is much more than the loon you saw on the roof. The rehearsal dinner is at your grandfather's house! You can really dip your toe in the familial water."

"That's not my toe, Matt, that's like a deep dive—and you want me to lie to everyone? My birth mother? My grandfather?"

"I'll be lying too. To my whole family and Dylan and the rest."

"Well, that's not on me."

"That's fair."

He sat down on the chair and took a beat. "OK, I'm just going to tell the truth."

"What truth?" Maggie asked with more than a note of panic in her voice. "You can't tell them *my* truth!"

He put his head in his hands, gathering his thoughts before giving it his best shot.

"I know Bea. She's been looking for you for thirty years. In the end, she won't care that we lied, she won't care about anything other than having found you. This way, you can spend quality time around her if you want while deciding what to do, and you don't have to stay in that gross hotel."

"How do you know I'm staying in a gross hotel?"

"Are you?"

"Yes," she conceded, before teasing him with: "Was this all part of an elaborate plan to get a date for your mother's wedding? You can tell me. I know going to a wedding alone is torture."

She smiled sweetly, clearly letting him off the hook.

"So, you're in?" He smiled back.

"What choice do I have? I'm in."

His smile grew.

"OK, we need to synchronize our stories—my mother is a lawyer. She will question the shit out of this."

Right on cue, they were interrupted by a loud knock on the door. Maggie fought the urge to yell, "We're not dressed," to give them more time. She was really getting into character.

Renee didn't even wait for them to answer.

"Can I speak with you alone, Matt?"

He began to rise, but Maggie grabbed his hand tightly and settled him back down. She had a feeling that after two minutes of cross-examination, the jig would be up. She must have been right because Matt quickly played along.

"You can ask me anything you want in front of Maggie," he insisted, falling into character as well.

"OK, well, for one thing, who is Maggie?"

"I'm sorry, Mom, she told you, this is Maggie May Wheeler, my girlfriend."

"OK, no offense, Maggie May Wheeler, but when did this happen?"

"We started dating a few months ago, long distance. I guess this romantic wedding of yours inspired me—after how Matt spoke so lovingly about you and your fiancé, I couldn't miss it!"

"She couldn't miss it," Matt repeated awkwardly.

"I imagine you want to move to the guest room, next door?"

"That's not necessary!" Maggie answered too loudly.

"You know how sentimental I am, Mom. We're good here."

"Whatever. Between you and Dylan springing plus-ones on me at the last minute—no offense, Maggie—I have to go redo the seating chart."

She stormed off, leaving them both to breathe a sigh of relief.

A temporary sigh of relief was more accurate.

(Sittin' on) the Dock
of the Bay

♩♪♪

Beatrix

"DAD!" BEATRIX SHOUTED up the stairs. "I'm going to pick up Paul from the ferry! Do you want anything from the market?"

"Yeah, a newspaper and some pickled herring. Not the kind from the jar, the kind—"

"From behind the deli counter . . . I know."

Veronica appeared at the top of the stairs wearing a Missoni sarong over a matching bikini, her oversized Chanel sunglasses now perched atop her head. She looked like she was in the South of France, not the south shore of Long Island, and it irrationally bugged Bea, though not as much as her next request.

"Can you get me an iced coffee, please, with a smidge of almond milk and the sweetener that gives you dementia—not cancer."

"The green one?" Bea asked.

"Yes," Veronica replied with a smile. Bea doused it with one word.

"No."

Veronica stared back, wounded, which only annoyed Bea more. She had no doubt that Veronica knew better. Breathless with anger that she didn't care to explain, Bea walked out.

She biked to the market with a half hour to spare before Paul's boat was due to arrive, trying her damnedest to justify in her mind her irrational fury toward her sister. It was as if V did one thing that irked her and they were back to square one. She admonished herself for it.

Why can't I cut her a little slack, let things bounce off my shoulders like I would for just about anyone else? she wondered.

Inside the market, she ordered comfort food in the form of bacon, egg, and cheese on a roll with ketchup from the deli counter, as she had been doing since she was barely tall enough to see over it. No matter how many of these she ate in Ohio, they never tasted as good as the ones from Bayview. Bea was unsure why this should be, but it was a fact confirmed by numerous BEC enthusiasts. It was the same with their turkey sandwiches. She threw Shep's requests in the basket of her bike and headed to the ferry dock to savor each bite of her breakfast in peace. She had been doing this too— leaving room for a BEC detour—since she was old enough to be sent to the ferry on her own to fetch visitors, which had probably been by the time she'd reached the ripe old age of eight. Sitting at the dock's far end, she swung her legs like a pendulum over the bay.

The simplicity and familiarity of life on Fire Island, along with the closeness she felt to her mother's spirit when she was there, usually rendered Bea recharged and rejuvenated. On this visit, however, everything seemed overshadowed by the presence of Veronica. At this rate she would need a vacation from her vacation.

The worst thing about being around her sister wasn't the reminder of what happened with the lifeguard all those years ago and the domino effect it had had on the trajectory of her life. And it wasn't the series of altercations that followed, widening the crack in her relationship with her sister until it was the size of the Grand Canyon. The worst thing was the uncontrollable jealousy that resurfaced whenever Bea saw V.

For many years, the love Bea had for the fair-skinned red-headed little girl who followed her around like a puppy her whole childhood went a long way to overriding any envy she experienced as Veronica blossomed into the stunner that she was. At first, she took the attention given to Veronica almost as a mother would, with pride. Strangers would stop them and comment on her sister's beauty: *Look at that gorgeous red hair—those colt-like legs! Did you ever think of modeling?* they would ask, with no regard for her older and shorter sister with her humdrum brown curls. It was when the boys her age started noticing Veronica, the same boys who never noticed Bea, that the green-eyed monster first showed its ugly head. As adults, when logically Bea knew she should be able to put the lifeguard incident behind her, the mere fact that V had two beautiful children while she never even got to meet her daughter defied any and all logic. She hoped her envy would dissipate in time, but it always seemed to be lying in wait, just below the surface.

It embarrassed Beatrix immensely to feel jealous of her own sister, and it embarrassed her more to admit it was the first emotion she felt when she saw her. Not talking to her for all these years was about controlling that ugly emotion more than it was about the lifeguard episode and the years of collective lacerations that followed.

Now, as an adult, Bea realized she really couldn't totally blame the inciting incident on Veronica. For starters, Bea should have insisted that the lifeguard use a condom. She had caved after mentioning it once and fallen for his line about pulling out, which, aside from the obvious risk, was a horrible way to have sex, she thought now.

The ferry boat came into view in the distance and Bea's heart skipped a beat. The boat was still at the point where she didn't know if it would veer right, stopping in Ocean View first, or left toward Bay Harbor, and her marriage was still at the point when every second away from Paul felt arduous. It turned left!

She pushed all the bad thoughts from her head and pictured Paul waving to her from the upper deck and seeing the island for the very first time. She'd never picked up a guy of her own from the boat. She'd picked up guys, of course—friends, cousins, friends of cousins, but never *her* guy. It was funny to think that way at her age; it seemed more like something a teenage girl would feel. But Bea adored her husband and lit up at the sight of him with his fit build, shoulder-length hair, youthful smile, and metal-rimmed glasses. He didn't look like any math teacher she had ever known.

Everything would be better once Paul arrived. She was eager to show him around and knew that no matter what happened during the day, they would end up lying next to each other at night.

The boat angled toward Bay Harbor, and Bea stood at the end of the dock, waving her hands over her head in excitement. When it got close, she scanned the upper deck for Paul and saw that a matching smile lit up his face. On his arrival, she held on a little too tight, nuzzling her head into his neck and holding back tears.

"You missed me so much? It's been like a day," he laughed.

"A day that felt like a week," she admitted. She wondered how much of what had transpired wouldn't have happened if he had been with her.

She threw his backpack in her basket and walked her bike next to him—slowly. She was in no rush to get back to the house.

"This is exactly how I imagined it," Paul remarked. "How's your dad?"

"He's fine. The whole thing was either a false alarm or total BS. Most likely total BS."

"You really think he faked a heart attack to guilt you and your sister into behaving?"

"Absolutely. He would probably have an actual heart attack if it would get us to connect again. Last night he played old movies, and I went to sleep thinking about how much I had adored Veronica when she was little. How I would pretend she was my baby when she was an infant and how, as soon as she learned to walk, she would toddle around behind me everywhere I went."

"That's good. It's good to think of her that way. And maybe she's changed, you know. People do."

"She hasn't changed. As I was leaving to pick you up, she asked me to bring her back an iced coffee."

Paul looked baffled. "Is there more to this story—something a bit more egregious?"

"You don't ask someone to pick up an iced coffee here, especially when they are picking up their husband from the boat for the very first time. An iced tea in a bottle, fine. To get an iced coffee, you must go through the whole effort to make it yourself, and then ride home with one hand on your handlebars and the other precariously balancing it. It's a huge imposition. She was testing me. I know it. Trying to see if she had gotten me back to that place where I would drop anything for her."

"Or maybe just jonesing for an iced coffee."

"You don't get it. It's fine."

"I don't. I'm sorry. And I don't get why you let her get to you so much. You have a whole different energy just being on the same coast as her."

"I know. I hate it."

"So cut it out. Think of the good times with her. Tell her you have moved on, that you forgive her. Whatever it takes, and not just for Shep, for you."

She was perceptive enough to see his point of view, that none of it was serving her anymore.

"OK. You're right. I'm going to do it, right away." She took a deep cleansing breath. "I'm done letting her get to me."

She gave him the fifty-cent tour until they reached her block.

"Here we are!" She spun around at the cross section of her street and presented the four corners to Paul like a stewardess pointing to all available exits.

"The ball field, Renee's house, our old house, where that author Ben lives now, and our new house! Voilà!"

"Amazing!"

She hugged him again at the front door. "I'm so happy you're here. I'm not going to let anything, or anyone, ruin it."

"Hola!" Bea cried out as they walked into the house. They found Shep in the kitchen, eating leftovers out of the fridge.

"Ahhh, reinforcements." He closed the refrigerator door and hugged his son-in-law. "Am I glad to see you!" he added, meaning it.

"That seems like the general consensus."

Bea put the pickled herring in the fridge and began slicing the bagels.

"Do you want this now, Daddy?"

"I would love it, thanks, honey."

"I'm guessing you're regretting your little forced reunion about now?" Paul whispered to Shep.

"It will work out," Shep assured him.

With that, Veronica made a grand entrance into the kitchen, now *just* in her bikini. Bea reacted with a monumental eye roll.

"You must be Paul," V cooed, pulling him in for a hug. "You're taller than your pictures."

As had always been her style, Veronica hugged him with her breasts first. It infuriated Bea or, as her students would say, triggered her.

"He won't fuck you, Veronica," she snarled in her sister's ear before making an equally grand exit.

La Mer

♩♫♪

Paul

PAUL SAT ON a beach chair, staring out at the ocean, and wondering if the wife he knew and loved was still inside the f-word-wielding meanie he had witnessed back at the house. Except for the time she'd cut her finger chopping onions, he had never heard her curse like that. Not because she was a prude, but because of her infinite respect for the English language.

With two of his own, Paul was no stranger to sister troubles, though he had always tried his best to steer clear of them. He was still scarred, quite literally, from trying to break *his* older sisters apart during an epic spat over a pair of Jordache jeans in 1989. Even with that, the feud between his wife and Veronica was unlike anything he had ever witnessed between his own siblings.

Bea casually plopped down in a chair next to him while quoting Henry James.

"'Summer afternoon—summer afternoon; to me those have always been the two most beautiful words in the English language.'"

"So, you're OK now?" he asked, hiding a smirk that he knew might set her off again.

"Yes, why?"

"Well, for one thing, I've never known you to have such a strong eye roll game. You could compete with the freshmen in my geometric analysis seminar when I assign weekend homework."

"I'm fine. Good, even."

He thought to ask her what happened to being nice, but decided to leave good and fine alone.

"OK then," Paul remarked instead, picking up the science section of the *Times* and folding it to one-fourth of its size to read on the windy beach. He had a feeling he wouldn't get through a single article. This trip, which had been billed as a relaxing fun time, was not looking promising.

"Want to hear the schedule?" Bea asked.

"Sure, bring it on."

"Today's a beach day. Renee is bringing down a whole setup soon. Tonight, I'll be making my mom's famous paella for the neighbors and out-of-towners, which I was excited about, but will now be annoyed about, no doubt."

"Why?" he asked, already guessing the source of her pending annoyance.

"Because it's so much work, and when my mom would make it when I was growing up, Veronica would cry at the sight of the langoustine eyes and disappear to her room to get out of helping."

"Well, I'll help you. It's nice of you to make a special dinner for Renee and Jake. I look forward to meeting them."

"I hear you talking to me like I'm about to break. You can stop, I'm fine."

"Yes, you said that."

This time, he risked a smile. Luckily, she laughed. He wrapped an arm around her shoulder and pulled her in for a hug, even though the arm of the chair dug into his side as he did so.

"I got you," he reassured her.

"Thanks. I know that."

She perked up.

"Tomorrow night they're showing *Mamma Mia!* on the Bay. Saturday night, the wedding; Sunday, brunch."

Her phone dinged.

"It's Renee. She's sending Matt's girlfriend down with beach blankets—I didn't know he had a girlfriend." She looked at Paul curiously.

"Well, I certainly didn't know." Paul laughed again.

From her seat by the shoreline, Bea caught sight of a young woman struggling with a pile of blankets at the top of the stairs. She jumped up to help her.

"Want me to come?" Paul asked.

"I guess another set of hands would be helpful, sorry."

"It's all good."

The two did a quick dash across the sand, both wishing they had thought to grab their flip-flops.

"We're coming to help," Bea called out when they were just a few feet away. The pile of blankets was blocking the girl's sight line. Bea grabbed the first few to reveal her face. The young woman looked surprised, as though she had never seen the ocean before.

"It's beautiful, right?" Bea smiled, acknowledging the young woman's look of awe.

"It truly is," the woman agreed.

Paul followed, grabbing more than his share of the pile while Bea jubilantly declared, "Follow me—and keep those flip-flops on!"

Bea and Paul ran across the sand like they were traversing hot coals while the girlfriend walked easily behind them. They both plopped down in their chairs for relief. Bea smiled as the young woman caught up to them.

"I'm Maggie," she announced, awkwardly reaching out her hand.

"I'm Paul." He made a feeble attempt to rise back up from the beach chair, leaving Maggie to respond with the requisite "Don't get up."

"And I'm Bea. We live catty-corner to Matt and Renee. First time here?"

"Yes," Maggie answered, still standing, and holding her pile.

"You two are in the same boat," Bea said, motioning to Paul. "Paul has never been to Fire Island either." Bea took a towel from her beach bag and laid it out in the sand. "Have a seat. We need a few seconds to regroup."

She sat, pulling her knees into her chest, and wrapping her arms around them.

"Where are you from, Maggie?" Paul asked.

"Ohio," Maggie responded tentatively, as if she wasn't sure of her answer.

"Wow! Really? We live in Gambier," Bea reported enthusiastically. "We teach at Kenyon College." She pointed to herself, "English lit," and to Paul, "applied mathematics."

"Two professors! That sounds like a good life. I'm happy for you."

The young woman, Maggie, must have realized it was an odd thing to say, as she turned bright red.

"And you?" Paul asked.

She again took a beat to answer.

"I live in a small town outside Cleveland, Chagrin Falls."

"I've heard of that place—they famously drop a popcorn ball on New Year's Eve, right?" Paul asked Maggie.

"A popcorn ball?" Bea questioned.

"Yes! The Popcorn Shop has been dropping an eighty-five-pound ball for, like, seventy-five years," Maggie explained proudly. "It's not Times Square, but it's pretty great."

"How very small-town Ohio," Paul noted.

Talking about her town seemed to break the girl out of her shell. She continued at about three times the pace of her previous revelations.

"We take our traditions very seriously in Chagrin Falls. After Halloween there's a huge pumpkin roll. High school kids swipe hundreds of pumpkins off people's lawns and roll them down Grove Hill. It started as a prank in the sixties and stuck. No one really knows when it will happen. We go all out for Christmas too. The store owners compete for best window decorations, and Santa arrives in the town square in a hot-air balloon. Plus, there's a documentary film festival every October and Art by the Falls in June."

"Let me guess. You work for the Chamber of Commerce?" Paul joked.

"No," she laughed, blushing, "I own a record store—it's a family business."

"Wow! Matt must love that!" Bea surmised.

"I heard record stores are having a resurgence. Kids today are embracing that delicious feeling of peeling the cellophane off the album cover, pulling out the sleeve, and reading the liner notes," Paul said with a sentimental smile.

"They are," Maggie agreed, putting her hands to prayer. She saw Matt in the distance and jumped ten feet in the air before taking off toward him.

"Young love," Paul observed wistfully. "Remember when we couldn't be apart for ten minutes?"

"We still have young love," Beatrix countered.

"Yeah. As long as you don't go postal on your sister and end up in jail. I'm not making conjugal visits and smuggling in copies of the *Paris Review* and those bran muffins you love from Wiggin Street Coffee."

Bea laughed.

"I'm not going to kill Veronica. I still love her, you know. She's still my baby sister."

"You have a funny way of showing it," he said under his breath.

She responded with another dramatic eye roll.

"Just behave this one weekend, for your dad's sake. I know you. If you don't, the guilt will eat away at you for months."

She appeared to be pondering his words again when Matt arrived and greeted Paul. The two couples began laying out a varied collection of blankets and throws that brought to mind exotic destinations like Marrakesh and Jaipur, though they were more likely sourced from mall stores like Anthropologie or Urban Outfitters.

After weighing down their edges with books and sneakers and beach chairs, the four took a big step back to admire their work. It looked beautiful, like a Bedouin beach festival. Jake arrived with two surfboards (yes, he could carry two at one time) and instructed everyone to construct two long mounds of sand. He placed a surfboard on each and voilà—two cocktail tables ready to be covered in snacks and libations.

The whole experience reminded Paul of one of those bonding exercises at freshman orientation that he and Bea were forced to attend. They were once charged with building a tower out of spaghetti, marshmallows, string, and tape. Bea was surprisingly competitive.

Before long, the blankets were peppered with the early arrivals, cousins of Jake's and Renee's, college friends, and a few of her best mates from the law firm she had worked at for twenty-odd years. Renee and Jake had been stingy with the off-island guest list, not wanting to deal with housing and feeding too many nonnatives, but more generous with the local invitations.

Captain Jake and Professor Paul got into a complex discussion about the mathematical metaphors in *Moby Dick*, to which Beatrix couldn't help adding her two cents. The married professors had big plans to coauthor a book about mathematics in literature during their upcoming year abroad.

"We'll both be overseas," Bea explained. "I'm running the Kenyon-Exeter program in Southern England and Paul is taking a sabbatical to research and work on our book."

"Wow. There's enough material on that for a book?" Maggie piped in from the sidelines. The three of them turned their heads to see that the olive-skinned, curly-haired young woman was glued to their conversation, while the others her age were playing kadima and KanJam. Bea kindly widened their circle so that Maggie would feel included. Maggie smiled and shifted her stance.

"Yes, Tolstoy writes about calculus, and both *Ulysses* and *Finnegans Wake* reference geometry. And there's much more," Beatrix explained.

"Bea is a literary virtuoso," Paul boasted, patting his wife's leg proudly.

Veronica had slithered in quietly, taking her place on one of the beach blankets. She had been flying under the radar all day, possibly in deference to her sister, the matron of honor, possibly because Shep had told her the truth about her invitation.

A football flew over their heads and Matt dove for it.

"Why have you been hiding this one from us, Matty?" Jake joked.

Jake still called him Matty, and Matt didn't bother correcting him. It was pointless. Jake did not seem to be one for change.

"I wasn't hiding her. Just wasn't sure she could make it here until the last minute."

"Where did you two meet?" Jake continued.

Matt sat down in the sand next to Maggie while goading her like one of those old couples in *When Harry Met Sally*.

"You tell them, honey."

"No, you!" she goaded back.

"OK. We met at the Austin Record Convention. It's a huge show, three hundred vendors. Maggie had a booth, and I was shopping."

"Yes, we argued over the price of an album. What was it again?" she asked Matt.

"Miles Davis, *Kind of Blue*."

"Of course. He tried to undercut me. But it didn't work."

"She was very forward. Said I could have it for a little over my price if I bought her dinner!"

They all turned to Maggie and nodded in approval at her

chutzpah. Except Veronica. Veronica came close to her, advancing toward her from every angle, like a moth to a flame. She stared right into her eyes.

"Do I know you?" she asked with a hint of suspicion, adding, "You look so familiar to me."

"I sat behind you on the ferry," Maggie responded, without missing a beat.

Beatrix looked at her watch and shot from her seat.

"Time to start the paella!" she announced.

"Would you like help?" Veronica offered.

Paul nudged his wife.

"Sure," she conceded, "that would be great."

The two walked off the beach together, leaving everyone in the know both worried and hopeful.

Good Day

♩♫♪

Maggie

IT WAS A good day, and though she still hadn't decided to jump into the Silver family pool with both feet, at least she had dipped her toe in without getting pinched by a crab.

Matt accompanied her back to the "Inn" after the beach to charge her phone and pick up some more clothes. Despite her initial ambivalence, she had thrown a few things in her bag suitable for a wedding. Just in case.

When they were a safe distance from the house, he praised her for being so quick on her feet.

"Man, you were good with the comebacks on the beach. 'I sat behind you on the ferry.' If you ever need to testify against a mobster, you'd rock witness protection."

"You weren't so bad yourself—that Austin Record Show bit was perfect. Have you ever been?"

"No, but I'm dying to."

"We can go next year," Maggie laughed.

"Yes, if we're still dating."

Their laughter intensified.

Climbing up the narrow staircase to her room at the Inn,

Maggie felt relieved to know she didn't have to sleep there anymore.

"What is that putrid smell?" Matt asked, affirming that she wasn't being a snob regarding her accommodations.

"I don't want to know—it can't be good."

In the room, Matt did a 360, checking it out. He had never been there, apparently, and from the look on his face, Maggie guessed this would be his first and last visit.

"This may be the smallest hotel room I've ever seen," he noted, before sitting hesitantly on the bed as if it would give him cooties.

Maggie plugged in her phone and waited for it to spring back to life so that she could text Jason. She probably should have called instead of texting but felt weird doing so in a hotel room with a strange guy sitting on her bed. Well, not strange really. She gave him the once-over. It was worse than that. There was a cute guy sitting on her bed.

She wrote a whole paragraph.

> Hi. Hung out with my birth mother on the beach today, incognito. She's not as bad as I previously reported—but I'm still unsure. This is not a very Midwestern family, to say the least. The good news is I got myself invited to the wedding and other festivities, so I should be much surer about things by Sunday! Love you and miss you!

Matt's phone vibrated and he pulled it from his back pocket. Maggie couldn't help but listen to the one-sided conversation—a series of drab "Uh-huhs" and "OKs," with one interesting "Got it. Four o'clock, William Greenberg."

When he hung up, Maggie was standing in front of him, her head tilted like a curious puppy's.

"It was Jake. My mom needs me to pick up the wedding cake in the city tomorrow; apparently there was a big mix-up with delivery, and she's flipping out."

"I've never been to New York City!" Maggie blurted out, then blushed, realizing she wasn't invited.

"Wait, really?"

"Really. I'm just a small-town girl," she sang.

They both laughed, remembering the bartender's reaction to that statement the night before.

"Wanna come with?"

She welcomed a break from lying. It was exhausting.

"Yes!"

"I can give you an abridged tour—we can make a day of it."

"You know what I'm dying to see?"

"How many guesses do I have?"

Maggie lit up—because—a guessing game!

"Five."

"And what do I win if I guess?"

She tilted her head again in thought.

"A first press of Miles Davis, *Kind of Blue*, but you're never gonna guess."

"Well, that was a good hint. I'll cross off the usual suspects. Unless saying 'you're never gonna guess' was a trick."

Matt grimaced; Maggie smiled devilishly.

Matt took his time answering as they rode back to Bay

Harbor. He was very contemplative. He must have really wanted that album.

"Times Square!" he shouted, leaning into the trick.

She squashed it with a dramatic shake.

"Central Park?"

"I would love to see the park, but that's not it."

They reached the house and Matt planted both feet firmly on the ground.

"I hope it's not the 9/11 Memorial."

"Nope. Two more guesses."

"That wasn't a guess, it was a statement."

She leaned her bike against the fence and disembarked.

"Ohhhh, you're one of those."

"One of those what?" Matt questioned.

Maggie put her hand over her mouth and coughed while saying, "Cheater."

"I am not a cheater," he retorted, nudging her on the arm. She found herself pushing into the nudge, adding a few seconds to the encounter before pulling back.

"OK," she said coyly.

"I hate cheating of any kind. I'm serious," he responded with a pout.

"I see that," she laughed. "I'll give you a hint. It is obscure and has something to do with my business."

He paused; now more than serious, his expression was bound and determined.

"You want to check out one of those Japanese-style listening bars."

"Shut the front door!" she gasped.

"I will, as soon as we are inside!"

Maggie pulled open the door to Matt's house and Matt

strolled in, scatting the first notes of "So What" from *Kind of Blue.*

"I can't believe you guessed that!" she marveled as Matt headed to the fridge, grabbing a bag of baby carrots and hummus, and placing them on the counter.

"It was easy. I thought about what I would want to see if I owned a record store—plus I did a piece about them a couple of issues back," he boasted. "So they're top of mind."

"That was you? I tore it out and fastened it to the center of my vision board. I want to open a listening bar in my store. I can't believe you wrote that. How crazy!"

"I'll call my favorite, the Tokyo Listening Room, and get us a reservation for lunch. It's *bashert!*" he declared, dipping a carrot in the hummus, and taking a bite, before nudging the bag in her direction. She took one and dipped.

"You know I'm part Jewish now?"

He laughed. "You weren't before, I guess?"

"Nope. My parents were basically atheists. Atheists who loved Christmas."

"Mine are Jews who love Christmas," he chuckled.

"What's your favorite thing about it?"

"I think the music. I love Christmas songs."

Maggie laughed. "Not Christmas, being Jewish."

He took a minute to chomp his carrot and contemplate his answer.

"Oh. There are a lot of things. The culture, the food, the traditions. The way there are so few of us, yet when I find another Jewish person, I feel instantly connected. First shower or second?" he asked, changing the subject.

"First, if you don't care."

"Have you ever taken an outdoor shower?"

"I have not!" she replied, not bothering to temper her excitement.

"Aaaah. You're going to love it."

They brought her bag upstairs and Matt handed her a towel. She looked at it and blushed thinking about her forthcoming nakedness and how short a time she had known this man. He must have recognized her apprehension because he reached behind the door and handed her his big gray terry bathrobe. Relief flooded her face, and she took the stairs two at a time for her inaugural outdoor shower.

Rock Lobster

♩♫♪

Matt

MATT LAY ON the bottom bunk, googling queen-size beds. It was an excellent distraction from the unfortunate attraction he was developing for his fake girlfriend, his engaged fake girlfriend who lived in Ohio and who was, for all intents and purposes, a total stranger. Looking at her like she hung the moon was great for the believability quotient of their ruse, but not so great for his heart. It wasn't just that she owned a record store, which to him was the closest one could get to heaven on earth, or that it felt like there weren't enough hours in the day to talk with her. And it wasn't the breathtaking contrast between her light eyes and her olive skin, or the way his room suddenly smelled like a rainy spring morning. It was an inexplicable feeling of familiarity, as if he had known her for a long time, even though they had just met.

Plus, it was obviously absurd that he had never thought to replace the bunk beds. He knew why.

Without ever discussing it, he and his mom had gone to great lengths (or the opposite, really) to leave everything in the house as it had always been. It was comforting to them both, after the divorce, to limit change. Now, with his mom marrying Jake, it seemed all bets were off. Jake's house—a 1950s old colonial with multiple fireplaces and good insulation—was much better suited for year-round living. Matt could take his mom's room and turn this one into a gym if he wanted to. His fantasy was cut short by reality. Maggie walking through his bedroom door, her silky olive skin glistening under his oversized bathrobe, was even sexier than it had been in his imagination.

"I'm up," he announced, banging his head on the top bunk. He ignored the sting, grabbed shorts and a decent shirt for dinner, and escaped to the shower.

On his return, he stood outside his closed bedroom door, contemplating whether to knock, when his mother walked by.

"What are you doing?"

"Oh, not sure Maggie's dressed."

"So?" She looked at him with the same suspicious expression she'd get when he came home drunk or high in high school, doing his best to act straight and hold a conversation. Now, he countered with a dubious shrug and entered, praying Maggie was fully clothed. She was lying on the bottom bunk, dressed in a beachy white sundress with her hair tied behind her in a loose braid.

"Sorry, I didn't feel like climbing up."

"No problem."

"The sun really wiped me out today. I can barely keep my eyes open," she added with a sweet pout.

"We have time for a quick nap."

"Do we? That would be amazing."

"We do. I'm tired too," he said, ascending the ladder to the top bunk. As ridiculous as they were, the bunk beds came in very handy when sharing a room with a beautiful, engaged stranger of the opposite sex.

He lay on his stomach staring out the window toward the house across the street, as he had countless times before. The view was prettier now that the olive trees Ben had planted had grown full and tall.

Maggie was still below, and he wondered if she had already drifted off.

"Hi," she whispered, to check if he was awake, he imagined.

"Hi," he responded with a small laugh.

"Paul's nice, don't you think?" she stated randomly.

"Yeah, seems like a good guy."

"I agree. Too bad they didn't meet earlier; they would have made cute kids."

"Very."

She paused, like she was done chatting. She wasn't.

"Do you want kids?"

"I guess. Yes. I want kids. This house will be all mine soon, and is too big for just me," he laughed. "You?"

"Yes. Always. Someone to look like me—you know what I mean?"

"I imagine that's hard."

"It wasn't that hard for me. More like just a gnawing."

"Do you think you'll have kids soon, you and Jason?"

"I don't know. We've never talked about it."

"You never talked about it?"

"No. We only just got engaged, and it's not very official. More like engaged to be engaged," she admitted. "I don't even have a proper ring yet. Wanna hear something funny?" she pivoted.

"Sure," he laughed.

"If I was your real girlfriend, I would feel a little envious of Dylan. She's so gorgeous and free, the complete opposite of me."

He couldn't help but protest.

"You're just as beautiful as Dylan, just two different types."

It was true that Dylan's beach blanket bingo vibe was a far cry from Maggie's vintage store chic.

"Which is your type?" Maggie asked.

"I don't really have a type. You?"

"Hmm. Well, all the guys I've dated had one thing in common: they were all jealous of Jason!" she laughed, adding, "Feeling jealous about Dylan is kind of like a taste of my own medicine really."

"I get that. Who can compete with that kind of history?"

"No one, really. Plus, I was never willing to give Jason up, even just a little."

"I get that too, though I would think if I really fell for someone, they would have to love and accept Dylan because she's a part of me. Especially now that she and I have a life-time guarantee of sorts—you know, with our parents getting married." He yawned, muffling the last part of the sentence.

Matt looked at the clock. "We still have time. You know you only need twenty minutes for a solid disco nap."

There was no response. He took a peek; she was out cold. He set the alarm on his watch, but never fell asleep. Dylan texted about pre-gaming, and he slipped out quietly to partake.

In the kitchen, Matt and Dylan downed their second shot of tequila, sucked a lime, and then licked salt off their forearms before dissolving into giggles. There was truly no one in his entire life that he felt more at home with than Dylan. He contemplated telling her the truth about Maggie, one less person to be lying to. As if choreographed, Maggie came down the stairs, looking quite fetching, just as Dylan's boyfriend, Steve, came through the back door looking quite red.

Dylan reacted.

"Dude, you're really burnt—you look like a lobster!"

"You should see my back."

"I'll get you two Advil and rub some aloe on it."

"Would it be awful if I stayed home tonight? I won't be much fun like this."

"It's fine. I'll run you back a bowl of paella."

Steve headed back out to the guest house while Dylan slipped by Maggie on her way upstairs to fetch the aloe.

"You look pretty," Matt said as Maggie entered the kitchen, for no one's ears but her own.

"Thanks." She looked over her shoulder to see that Dylan was out of earshot. "Funny that a marine biologist is dating someone that burns so easily."

"That is funny," Matt agreed.

Pulling Mussels (from the Shell)

♩ ♫ ♪

Beatrix

THERE WAS NO denying that preparing paella with her sister tugged at Bea's heartstrings. First, she missed her mother terribly, and her sister was the spitting image of her. Second, the act of chopping and peeling and scrubbing clam and mussel shells with Veronica was steeped in memories—even if Veronica did always bail by the time they got to the langoustines. It would not be a problem this time. Bea had ordered them cleaned and beheaded.

Preparing paella, especially for a big crowd, was a true act of kindness that always brought Bea joy. She loved to cook for people, loved inviting her and Paul's colleagues in Gambier over for fondue night or taco night or a big barbecue. Paella, though, was next level. Paella was reserved for Fire Island.

Bea climbed on a chair to retrieve her mother's cookbook from the top shelf of the pantry next to forgotten appliances. It was an old black-and-white composition notebook, the marbled design scribbled in with yellow and orange highlighters, a Silver sister original, no doubt: they were both big

doodlers. The notebook was stuffed with recipes. Some were
ripped from magazines and the *New York Times* Cooking Section, while others were written out in their mother's signature
long hand, with names of Fire Island legends, such as Gicky
Irwin's Scones, Florence Hammer's Fried Chicken, and Joy
Perkal's Five-Alarm Chili.

The yellowing pages of both clippings and recipes handwritten in her mother's telltale loopy script caused tears to
sting Bea's eyes. This was the thing about making up with her
sister. There was no one else on earth who would flip through
those pages with as much emotion as she did. Her mother
was gone. Shep, though he would certainly try, couldn't live
forever. Veronica was the only one left who really knew the
greatness that they came from.

V and Bea's parents were characters, in the most complimentary sense of the word. Gorgeous redheaded Caroline
with her British humor and tremendous style, handsome
Shep with his Yiddish humor and lack thereof. And though
each of the sisters had fine qualities of her own—Veronica's
mostly ornamental, Bea's mostly cerebral—neither rose to
the grandeur and spectacle that were Shephard and Caroline
Silver in their heyday.

When Beatrix and Veronica were growing up, their parents were Bay Harbor royalty. Shep and Caroline's parties,
whether intimate dinners or poolside nights filled with drinking and dancing, were the most sought-after invitation in
town. And not just this town; their parties at their brown-
stone in Greenwich Village were equally epic.

Beatrix hated that her estrangement from her sister had
reduced their parents' massive charisma to a footnote in the
Silver story. A mark of good parenting is knowing that your

children care for each other and will do so after you are gone. Bea, being older by four years, could close her eyes even now and picture teaching Veronica how to put on her winter coat by placing it upside down on the floor and flipping it over her head. She'd shown her how to tie her shoes with bunny ears, and even how to ride a two-wheeler after Shep threw in the towel (and threw out his back). For all the family values they'd instilled in them when the girls were growing up, Shep and Caroline knew that the lifeguard debacle was the beginning of the end.

Beatrix observed that the page containing the paella recipe had a distinct yellow hue from the saffron. She began by listing the ingredients for Veronica to check off, just as their mother would have done.

"A quarter cup olive oil,
one onion, diced,
four cloves garlic, minced,
one cup mushrooms, roughly chopped,
one cup zucchini, diced."

"What's the difference between minced, diced, and chopped?" V asked her wordsmith sister.

"I think minced is the smallest, then diced, then chopped."

V nodded and continued setting aside the items in the recipe.

"Half a cup carrots, diced,
half a cup bell peppers, diced,
one bay leaf,
one teaspoon paprika,

one pinch saffron,
a quarter cup white wine."

"To Mom," Bea said, before taking a swig.
They both chuckled.

"Two cups short grain rice,
five cups lobster stock,
one pound cockles."

"Oh my God, remember how hard we used to laugh when
Mom said, 'Hand me the cockles!' Did you even buy cock-
les?" Veronica inquired.
"Nah. I just got littlenecks."

"One pound mussels,
one pound squid,
one pound shrimp or langoustines, peeled and
    deveined."

"I'll leave the seafood in the fridge till we're done chopping, but I got all of it," Bea assured.

"A half cup peas,
a quarter cup fresh parsley, roughly chopped,
salt and pepper, to taste,
lemons, for serving."

"And that's it!"
"You know we have to quadruple all of this," Bea informed V.

"I did not."

"Let's get chopping."

"Can I put on the stereo?"

"It's not my house."

"It's not mine either."

They both laughed again. The small house across the street where they'd grown up sharing a bedroom would always be their house—even though it was now occupied by another family.

Veronica set all the ingredients in need of chopping on the kitchen table with two cutting boards and a big silver bowl in the middle. The two women began chopping and mincing and dicing—and with each motion of the knife, more conversation slipped in.

Bea told V all about Paul and their life in Ohio. Veronica seemed mesmerized by her tales of the academic life, the energy on campus, and the boast-worthy success of her former students—one had been shortlisted for the Booker Prize, another was editing the *Kenyon Review,* and a third had published a debut novel that made the list. Even Veronica knew that meant the *New York Times* Best Seller list.

V told Bea all about her life in LA, the pressure to keep up her looks, the loneliness of her ten-thousand-square-foot home with a pool and a tennis court, and how the highlight of her day, after completing Wordle, was picking flowers from her garden and arranging them in vases all over the house.

Beatrix expected to be annoyed by her sister complaining with two loaves of bread in her hands, but she felt for her. Her days sounded empty compared to her own, a fact she never would have imagined. And with Veronica's kids grown and flown, she seemed to have little of interest on the horizon. She knew it was awful, but Veronica's unhappiness made it harder to hate her. She certainly never wished bad things for her sister, but it did cut at the anger a bit.

Veronica asked Bea a million questions about the kids they grew up with, where they lived now, what they did, their marital status. When Bea visited Fire Island, she made sure to catch up with everyone she could, while Veronica did the opposite.

"Too fair for the beach, and too sober for the bars," as she described herself, Veronica mostly hung by the pool and read under an umbrella.

"When did sober happen?" Beatrix inquired.

"I got my seven-year chip last week. After an unfortunate incident at a pool party, Larry said it was him or the gin. I sometimes wonder if I made the right choice."

Bea laughed. "You did. I'm proud of you. You never could hold your liquor."

"Back then was far worse—back then I couldn't hold my quaaludes and my liquor."

Bea had an uneasy feeling that the conversation was taking a dangerous turn, and right before it was time to cut the onions no less. She changed the subject.

"Remember that Labor Day party when that neighbor in the white dress jumped into the pool?"

"Yup, and she did a handstand."

"Yes, and she wasn't wearing any underwear!"

"Oh my God, how old were we?"

"You were like six and I was ten."

"Do you remember she had a giant vagina?" Veronica asked, making the biggest V shape she could with her hands.

Their laughter filled the room. Veronica continued, "I'm sorry to say, I think it's my earliest memory. I can still picture it. It was covered in so much black hair; it looked like Uncle Lenny's Jew-fro! I swear that scarred me for life."

"Me too. Remember that other party, when Dad threw that guy in the pool, and he got so mad?"

"'Dogs get mad, people get angry,'" Veronica intoned in her best British accent. They both laughed at the perfect imitation of their mother.

Bea pulled out a large skillet and sautéed the onion and garlic in olive oil on medium heat. They added the mushrooms, zucchini, carrots, bell pepper, bay leaf, paprika, and saffron and cooked them for five minutes before adding the wine and cooking them for five minutes more.

Veronica read the rest of the instructions slowly, while Bea performed them.

"Add rice to the skillet and cook for two minutes. Pour over broth and shake pan to make sure the rice is in an even layer."

Next came the most important directive, according to their mom. Veronica broke out the accent again to do it justice.

"At this point, you will no longer stir the paella!"

When the rice was cooked, they added the seafood, topped the dish with peas, and cooked it for another five minutes or so.

And that was it! The house smelled delicious, like a savory memory.

When it was finally time to go upstairs to get ready, Bea admitted, "This was really nice, Veronica. Brace yourself: I'm going to say something sweet." She took V's hands in hers and declared, "I think it's time we put the past behind us, and not just for Daddy's sake. I'm glad you came this weekend. I'm even going to ask Renee to officially invite you to the wedding."

As per usual, just when she let her in, Bea was quick to regret it. The floodgates opened and Veronica wept.

"I'm sorry," she managed, snot now mixing with the tears running down her face. Bea couldn't bring herself to comfort her. She knew one hug would do wonders for her sobbing sister, but Veronica playing the victim card was number one on the list of traits that Bea detested in her sister. She couldn't give in to it.

"I've waited so long for you to forgive me," Veronica continued. "You have no idea how I have dreamed of this moment."

Beatrix let loose an eye roll—not one of her bigger ones, but it did not escape her sister's notice.

"Go ahead, Bea, roll your eyes, but no one loves you and looks up to you like I do. No one."

Her words gave Bea pause. Veronica didn't give her a chance to respond, however, and continued in her steamroller style.

"Do you know what it was like for you not to come to my wedding?" she sobbed.

"What are you talking about? You eloped."

"I eloped because Mom and Dad were shattered by the thought of you not being there. And I knew I would spend my whole wedding day heartbroken."

"I was still feeling very raw."

"It was years after it happened."

"Well, I'm sorry."

Bea could have admitted she'd been jealous, but hoped her apology was enough to put an end to the pity fest. It wasn't. Apparently Veronica had a list.

"Every year, on my birthday, I spend half the day checking my emails to see if you sent me one. The constant chatter in my brain: Is she purposefully trying to hurt me? Does she even remember that it's my birthday?"

"Of course I remember your birthday."

"Then why don't you ever reach out to me? It's been thirty years since you've wished me a happy birthday."

"You know what you don't seem to get? It's not just because you screwed the one guy out here who was ever into me, which had cataclysmic repercussions that fueled a lifetime of rumination and regret. It's because you chose the attention—your insurmountable need for attention—over me, your sister, your loyal devoted sister."

"And I've paid the price a hundred times since. You've punished me over and over with your caustic words and total abandonment."

"Stop acting like the victim, Veronica! I am the victim!"

Paul, who'd returned from the beach an hour earlier to find the two sisters cooking to the soundtrack from *Pippin*, came running down the stairs, intent on defusing the situation. Shep entered from the back deck, and instead of remembering that he was the reason for their ceasefire, Veronica doubled down, guns blazing.

"You know what, Daddy?" she said in a biting tone.

He didn't respond; he just backed up against the wall, clearly bracing himself for what was next.

"You always favored Bea. Maybe that's why I looked everywhere else for male approval! There, I finally said it!"

"Of course, nothing is ever your fault," Bea chided her.

Veronica shot her a death stare and stormed out.

"Just let her go. She'll come back when she cools off. She always does," Shep advised.

Bea kissed her father on the cheek on her way upstairs.

"You were a good dad, to both of us. I'm going to take a quick shower and get dressed. I smell like cockles," she said, hoping for a laugh. She didn't get one.

The Joker

♩♫♪

Maggie

YOU COULD HAVE closed your eyes and followed your nose from the Tucker house to the Silver house—that's how potent the delicious aroma of paella was. Maggie, Matt, and Dylan walked over with Renee and Jake. The betrothed couple entered first, to a rousing standing ovation and a boisterous rendition of "Here Comes the Bride." Many in the chorus had been on the beach that day, so luckily for Maggie, introductions were mostly behind her.

"Ping-Pong?" Dylan asked Matt with a competitive grin.

"Do you mind?" he asked Maggie.

"Not at all," she said with a smile.

Maggie weaved her way through the crowd, taking in everything and everyone around her. The house itself surprised her. It was decorated in a minimalist fashion with an aesthetic that was beachy but chic. The walls were dotted with eclectic artwork, from oversized photographs of far-off beaches to European travel posters to a huge oil painting that Maggie later learned was done by a famous artist who had lived nearby. The hardwood floors were softened with sisal

rugs in muted colors. Guests were gathered around a pale
gray mid-century-style sectional in the living room, socializ-
ing, sipping cocktails, and munching on Manchego cheese,
Spanish nuts, and olives served on a massive coffee table with
a glass top and a driftwood base.

Shep was the first to approach Maggie. She had seen him
only briefly while he was faking death, so she was happy to have
the chance to speak with him. To speak with her grandfather.

Heavy stuff.

She felt her eyes begin to water when he smiled at her and
offered her a glass of sangria. She squeezed them tight and
took it happily.

"You must be Matt's girl? Shep Silver, nice to meet you."

He reached out for a hug, like a bro. She sank into her
grandfather's arms, fighting the urge to weep. He smelled like
both Tide and the tide. She memorized the scent.

"He's a keeper, that Matty. As good as they come," Shep
said.

"I couldn't agree more," she said, meaning every word. In
the short time she had spent with him, she was amazed at
how good Matt really was. He seemed to emanate decency,
which was why she had instantly trusted him. "He says the
same about you."

"I'm more like as bad as they come, but I've loved that boy
since he was a baby."

"That's sweet. He must have been a cute baby."

"The cutest. Wanna see?" He motioned to the stairs.

"Yes!" She'd been hoping to get the full tour, but her Mid-
western manners had prevented her from asking.

She followed Shep up to a long hallway lined with white-
framed photos.

"This started out as a family wall," Shep explained, "but after nearly sixty years on this crazy island, the definition of family has blurred like a line in the sand." He moved across the pictures. "Here's the one I wanted to show you: my wife, Caroline, pushing Matty down the block in his pram."

Maggie looked closely at her beautiful grandmother before taking in Matt's chubby cheeks and gummy grin. It was just the kind of photo a girlfriend would go gaga over, picturing what her own baby would look like if the two were ever to be fruitful and multiply.

"He really was adorable," she gushed. "And your wife, wow, so beautiful!" Caroline was barefoot in the photograph, dressed in an A-line sundress covered in big bright flowers. Her auburn hair was effortlessly tied in a knot, and her sunglasses were white and glamorous. Maggie could see the strong resemblance between Caroline and Veronica, and she wondered if looks were where the similarity ended.

"Inside and out," Shep mused, and she had her answer. Although clearly those two sisters brought out the worst in each other.

"And over here, this is the team picture of Matt's first homeowners' softball game." Shep searched the line of men, stopping at a lanky teenager with a big goofy smile on his face. Maggie looked closely.

"He was cute then too," she remarked, a big goofy smile lighting her own face as well. She couldn't help herself.

There was one thing about being adopted that she had never much thought about until she received the 23andMe report—ancestors. Neither of her parents had many people left in the family department. She had a faint memory of her dad's mother, who passed when Maggie was around five—the only one of the four grandparents who was alive when she was born. She'd met a few distant cousins here and there, but they were older. When she and Jason married, she would have zero family of her own present. As she stood there now, in the presence of her grandfather, that fact, which had never bothered her before, suddenly stung.

Shep continued his narration as he went down the line.

"Bea and V in the Fourth of July wagon parade, me and Caroline at a seventies disco party."

Maggie met each image with a smile.

"This one's a camp show, *Kiss Me Kate*, I believe. They both loved being in camp shows. They would sing those songs all summer long. Caroline used to refer to those summers by the name of the show—The *Oklahoma* summer, the *Pippin* summer, the *Fiddler* summer. Those years—the Broadway years when the girls were young—they were the best of our lives."

"What's this one?" Maggie asked, pointing to a photo of what looked like a hippie dinner party.

"That one comes with some story. Summer of 1969. The summer I met Caroline. She came to the beach with her friend Florynce Kennedy. Ever heard of her?"

"I have not."

"She was an amazing gal—a radical Black feminist—she once led a mass urination protesting the lack of ladies' rooms at Harvard. Not her greatest accomplishment, but my personal favorite."

Maggie laughed. She had known him for all of five minutes and she had already fallen in love. "How did you meet Caroline?" she asked.

"We were in a share house together, filled with civil rights activists. I didn't really fit in at the start of it, but by the end I became assistant counsel for the Black Panthers."

"The Black Panthers? Oh my God!"

"What I wouldn't do to impress Caroline!"

"That's them"—he pointed to the photograph—"in the berets and button-down shirts. We had decided to take the Panthers to a restaurant in a town on the island that didn't permit Blacks or Jews. It caused quite a ruckus. We ended up coming back with more friends the next day, demonstration-style. We jokingly demanded they serve us herring and ham hocks and yelled things like 'Guess who's coming to dinner?' The sixties. That was some time in this country. Some time."

Maggie was blown away that this man was her grandfather. And more than a little excited to be the beneficiary of his miraculous genes.

They moved farther down the wall to more family snaps. A gorgeous shot of the four of them on the ferry. A big group of kids with Bea and V in the center on the swimming dock on the bay, and some older pictures of their forbears, she assumed, more sepia-toned than black-and-white.

It was the first time Maggie had looked at old photographs and been able to think about where she came from. She studied them to see if there was something of herself in the smiles she saw on the wall, or in their physiques or expressions. She stopped in front of one photograph that showed a young woman around her age wearing one of those old-fashioned one-piece bathing suits that look like modern-day workout gear. The woman had her same dark curls, her same broad smile. Maggie leaned in.

"That's my mamma," Shep said, with a mixture of longing and pride.

"Is that on Fire Island?"

"No. Coney Island, by way of Yemen. I was the first to come to Fire Island. First to go to college and law school too. I adored my mother. My Beatrix takes after her."

As if on cue, Beatrix flew past them down the hall, giving off a frazzled energy.

"Oh my God, Dad. Why are you torturing this poor girl?" Bea looked toward the room below. "Where's Matt?"

"Outside playing Ping-Pong with Dylan and some of the others."

Bea was very distracted.

"It's time to serve dinner," she told them.

"Veronica's not back yet?" Shep asked.

"Please, Daddy. Let's not."

"I can help," Maggie volunteered, twisting a brown curl around her finger nervously.

"I'm fine, honey, don't worry."

"That's a good idea," Shep whispered in Maggie's ear. "If you don't mind."

"Not at all." Maggie smiled. "Thanks for showing me all of this."

"Thanks for pretending you were interested."

If he only knew.

On the way to the kitchen, Bea peeked out back, where, not surprisingly, the game had morphed from Ping-Pong to beer pong.

"You're sure you want to help? It looks like you're missing some fun out there."

They peered outside to see Dylan and Matt hugging in victory.

"I'm sure," Maggie responded, her cheeks burning. She touched her hand to one and then the other.

"Dylan and Matt are just old friends, you know," Bea said, quickly catching on and looking at Maggie with empathy.

"Oh yes, I know. That doesn't bother me," she replied, though she wasn't so sure. Dylan seemed so exotic to Maggie. Blond, sun-kissed, and able to leap giant waves in a single bound. She was probably happiest with sand between her toes, while Maggie would yell "First shower!" while still packing up her stuff on the beach.

Bea put her hand on Maggie's shoulder, directing her toward the kitchen. Maggie fought the urge to ask her for a hug. After experiencing the hug from her grandfather, she was curious what her birth mother's embrace would feel like.

Was she a hugger now?

"It's hard to be the new one around here," Bea offered. "From the little I've seen of you two, you're a perfect match, like two halves of the same person."

If lying to your mother was a rite of passage, Maggie realized that she'd accrued a lifetime's worth in one long weekend. She felt bad about it.

"Thanks," Maggie said, appreciating the compliment.

"Thank you. I could use the help since my sister disappeared. Surprise, surprise. Do you have siblings?" Bea added.

"Nope, only child."

"Lucky you."

"I'm not so sure about that. Both my parents are gone, so, you know."

She wasn't sure why she was telling Bea this. The whole conversation was so . . . meta.

"I'm sorry. My mom is gone too," Bea commiserated, pulling off the fridge a handwritten list of everything she was serving that night.

"She taught me to do this when having a big party. She loved to entertain. I like doing things the way she did, makes me feel like she's still here."

A timer went off.

"Warm rolls," Bea proclaimed, slipping on oven mitts, and pulling the pan from the oven. Maggie grabbed the basket from the table and lined it with a cloth napkin.

"I did the same thing with my mom. Especially at our store. I run the family business now that my parents are gone."

"Right, the record store."

"Maggie May Records." Maggie's face lit up when she said it. And then again when she witnessed her birth mother's enthusiastic reaction.

"Wow, it's named for you, how cool is that? I've always dreamed of owning a bookstore. I imagine the two are very similar."

"Very. Lots of people browsing and sharing recommendations. Our local bookstore and my shop are the most popular attractions on Main Street—other than the Popcorn Shop, which sells candy and ice cream and drops that big New Year's Eve ball we were talking about on the beach."

"Hard to compete with popcorn, candy, and ice cream."

"Exactly."

Beatrix went to work stirring the huge pot of paella. She scooped up the perfect bite with her wooden spoon and blew on it. "Want to taste?" she asked Maggie, who signaled yes by opening wide.

It was delicious in every way. Maggie's eyes teared up a bit, and she scrunched them tight as soon as she felt it. Too late.

"Too spicy?" Beatrix asked at the sight of Maggie's watery eyes.

"It's perfect," Maggie replied.

She thought about this crew she had landed among. Individually they were great, but there was no denying that together they were complicated. Even though her birth mother had just fed her paella off a wooden spoon, she still was not sure what to do.

"Great. Let's put the salad and the rolls on the table. Then we will muscle up and bring out the main course. You look strong enough!"

Maggie flexed her biceps, and they laughed.

Soon the hungry guests appeared. Matt took a minute to check in on Maggie, covering her eyes from behind and saying, "Guess who?" in a funny voice—maybe Elvis. She put her hands over his, and it made her heart jump. The feeling surprised her, but she quickly pushed away any concern. She was crazy vulnerable right now and this stranger had quickly become her person. Of course, she was feeling all kinds of emotions.

"Let's eat outside," he said when she spun around to face him. "You can meet some of my old friends."

~~~

MATT'S FRIENDS WERE great, laughing and reminiscing and teasing one another in between bites of the scrumptious paella. Her mom's scrumptious paella. Maggie began fantasizing about visiting Bea in Gambier, being introduced at some professors' mingle. "This is my daughter, Maggie."

She smiled at the thought for a second or two before her real mother's image ran through her head. Maggie pictured her face hurt by the betrayal. But was it really a betrayal? She debated the possibilities in her head. There was no doubt that her mother would want her to have a family of her own. Though marrying into Jason's would have the same result.

"You OK?" Matt whispered in her ear.

She nodded, shrugged it off, and smiled at the group.

She felt Dylan's eyes on her, checking her out on more than one occasion. She could picture Matt and Dylan as a couple, were it not for the circumstances. Though both New Yorkers, they each had a California vibe to them—Dylan with her cropped blond hair and lithe build, and Matt with his laid-back style and Ryan Gosling crew cut. Matt looked like a better match for her than Sunburn Steve back at the guest house.

"What do you do?" a guy in a Wesleyan T-shirt to Matt's left asked.

"I own a record store."

All eyes turned to her in complete amazement. The reason soon came tumbling out of their mouths.

"Oh my God, Matt, you hit the lottery!"

"Matty always dreamed of owning a record store."

"Are you just using me, Matthew Tucker, to fulfill some childhood fantasy?" she teased, messing with Matt's hair.

"You got me." He smiled back, messing with hers. The conversation turned away from them, and Maggie half whispered to Matt, "It's so cute how some people call you Matty."

"*Well, some people call me Maurice,*" he joked.

"That's funny, because *some call me the gangster of love*," Maggie countered, literally without missing a beat.

They cracked up over their consecutive references to "The Joker" and Steve Miller's lyrics, laughing too hard and too privately. When they were through, five sets of eyes were staring at them.

Dylan had no problem voicing her objection.

"Hello, we're here too! You guys see each other all the time."

Maggie wasn't sure whether Dylan was a little jealous or just wanted a share in the fun. She and Matt both gazed downward, their cheeks three shades of red, before peeking up at each other and laughing again.

The five pairs of eyes looked back at them. It was clear they agreed on something: Matt and Maggie made a very cute couple.

After Midnight

♩♫♪

Beatrix

IT WAS AROUND midnight when Bea and Paul finished straightening up and crawled into bed. Bea was happy. It had been a great party and she was overjoyed to have hosted it for Renee and Jake. Bea took her responsibilities as matron of honor extremely seriously.

She slid into her favorite spot, in the crook of Paul's arm, and waited for her eyes to get heavy. She was about halfway there when the house phone rang. Flipping over, she lay on her back and stared at the ceiling. She knew the call would involve Veronica, who hadn't come back to the house since their unfortunate exchange.

Paul, of course, was already lightly snoring.

Reluctantly, she picked up the receiver, not wanting to wake him or her dad, who fortunately always removed his hearing aids before going to sleep.

"Hello," she grimaced, her annoyance evident in her tone.

"Bea?" the strangely recognizable voice replied. "It's Chase Logan, you know—the lifeguard."

"Yes, I know who you are, Chase."

"Your sister is here, and I think someone should come get her."

"Where is here?"

"The Salty Pelican."

Bea hung up and rolled back over. She had put her days of saving Veronica way behind her. Forcing her eyes closed, she attempted to override the call with happy thoughts: how delicious the paella had turned out, how good it was to see Renee so happy, how sweet Matt's new girlfriend was for helping her—and just sweet in general.

Five minutes later, she was on her bike pedaling to Ocean Beach.

Bea hadn't been to the Salty Pelican in a few summers and did not know that Chase now tended bar there. She entered the familiar establishment, filled with memories from her youth, in search of her sister. She looked under the bathroom stalls and thankfully didn't find Veronica. If she was already leaning over the toilet bowl, getting her home would be a two-person job, and she wasn't about to ask Chase for help. It was then that she remembered that Veronica was sober.

Fuck, she thought, *seven years*.

She tried not to feel guilty if she had played a part in pushing her off the wagon.

With no other choice, she approached Chase behind the bar. It was nearly impossible to align the paunchy middle-aged man with the gorgeous young lifeguard she had known. Eager to avoid speaking to him, she held her hands up like the "I don't know" emoji that she often sent Paul when he inquired about dinner.

"You just missed her. She made a scene and left with Dave Acres."

"Handsome Dave?" she asked.

"Yeah, but he's not so handsome anymore."

"Is he still on Wilmot?"

"Three from the beach."

This place was like a freaking time capsule, she thought, locked in 1989.

"Thanks," she managed.

"No, thank you," he retorted in a curiously biting tone.

"Do you have something to say, Chase?"

"Only that it would have been nice to know from you that we had a baby, instead of from a book years later."

She paused for a second, feeling confused as to why he was bringing this up out of the blue. She knew she had run into him a few times over the years. Was it possible she hadn't seen him since *On Fire Island* was published? It was so long ago now. He must be a slow reader, she thought amusingly.

A million responses to his question flooded her brain. She went with the most succinct.

"We didn't have a baby. *I* had a baby, Chase."

With that, she left and headed for Wilmot Road, having not the slightest clue what she would do when she got there. She was surprised at the thought that Veronica would risk her marriage and family for a romp with not-so-handsome-anymore Dave. She'd never thought he was handsome to begin with. Nevertheless, Veronica had apparently been drinking, and Veronica and alcohol didn't make for logic.

The house was dark. Bea parked her bike, went right up to the front door, and rapped her knuckles on it loudly. A light switched on in a window upstairs. Soon, handsome Dave's wife stood in front of her, barefoot and angry.

Bea did not know there was a wife. She'd step lightly.

"Do you know what time it is?" the woman asked, and not because she didn't own a clock.

"Um, yes, sorry. I'm looking for my sister."

"Is she a pathetic middle-aged drunk with bleached-out red hair?"

"That's a little harsh," Bea responded, genuinely defensive.

"Yeah, well, it's one a.m. and my husband had to walk her home to Bay Harbor."

"Oh. That's great. Thank him for me. And sorry for waking you."

The door was already shut by the time she got in that last part.

Bea pedaled back to Bay Harbor, exhaling her resentment toward Veronica, and inhaling the anticipation of climbing back under the light summer quilt next to Paul. She threw her bike in the shed, kicked off her Birkenstocks, and wearily stomped down the hall to check on her sister. She cracked the door open gingerly. The last thing she wanted to do was to wake her, certain that any conversation between them right now would be even uglier than before. She peered into V's bedroom, only to find her bed untouched. *What the hell?* Concern for her sister, which lay deep down under layers of indignation, suddenly grabbed her by the throat.

Holding her breath, she searched the house, expecting to find Veronica passed out somewhere else. Yet she was nowhere to be found. It was then that real panic set in.

Bea grabbed a flashlight and ran down to the beach. It was an old habit of Veronica's to make it home as far as their block, but not to complete the journey, passing out on the cold night sand. It was amazing that she could still keep up these kinds of antics. Having just binged all six seasons of *The Crown*, Beatrix's mind flashed wryly on the fact that she and her sister were like duty-bound Elizabeth and uninhibited Margaret.

Heavy is the head that wears the crown.

Bea stood at the top of the stairs and shined the flashlight in every direction. The beach was empty. She made her way to the bottom step and sat down. Exhausted, she wanted nothing more than to go back to sleep.

"Calm down," she said out loud, chiding herself for even taking the bait. Her sister was a grown woman who could take care of herself.

Then, something sticking out of the sand caught her eye. She aimed her flashlight on a pair of bright pink pool slides with the Balenciaga logo emblazoned across them. She couldn't fathom them belonging to anyone on their block other than Veronica. She slipped them onto her feet. They fit perfectly. She and Veronica were the same size; she'd made a habit of stealing her shoes long before she stole her boyfriend. Bea grabbed the Balenciagas and sprinted toward the ocean. With each step, she ricocheted between feeling annoyed, worried, and panicked, ending with one beyond-distressing thought.

I killed my sister.

SOS

♩♫♪

Matt

MATT LAY ON the bottom bunk trying again to distract himself from thinking about Maggie. Maggie, who he had just met and who was marrying her best friend. Maggie, who lived five hundred miles away. Maggie, who he felt instantly connected to, like something out of a movie. Maggie, who was gingerly tossing and turning on the bed above him. He squeezed his eyes tight, trying to push her from his mind. Within seconds she made that impossible, leaning her torso over and dangling off the bed like a teenager. It made him laugh. This girl was freaking adorable.

"You up?" she asked.

"Nope."

"Ha ha. What are you thinking about?"

"Nothing," he lied.

She pulled herself back up, and Matt could feel her resume her tossing and turning. No more than a minute later, her head was dangling in front of him again. He laughed some more and asked:

"What are *you* thinking about, Maggie?"

"Funny you should ask. I'm thinking that maybe they're not such a crazy family after all. Maybe that scene on the roof was just a one-off thing? I mean, have you ever witnessed my birth mother swearing from a rooftop before?"

"I can't say that I have."

"I had such a nice time with her tonight. She fed me from a spoon, and I almost told her right then and there."

"She fed you from a spoon? Did she do it choo-choo train style or like an airplane?"

"Don't be silly. Oooh. All the blood is rushing to my head." She pulled herself back up but kept talking.

"I feel awful about lying to her. I hate the thought of doing this all over again tomorrow."

"We won't be here tomorrow, remember?" said Matt, reminding her of the lightning-fast tour of New York they had planned. "Let's see how we both feel after a day away."

"I think I've made up my mind. If it's OK with you, I'm gonna stay back tomorrow and tell her. I'd rather it not take away from the wedding and I'm feeling confident that the big drama was a one-off thing."

While saying it, she glanced out the window.

"Look outside!" she said, clearly alarmed.

In the light of the moon, they spotted Beatrix darting down the street, zigzagging between people's yards like a lunatic.

"What the . . . ?"

"On second thought, taking some time off tomorrow to reflect on it all might be smart," she said uncertainly.

Before they had time to figure out what Bea was up to, a long blasting alarm sounded outside. The noise seemed to fill the whole island.

"What's that?" asked Maggie, her body now rigid with apprehension.

"It's not good," Matt replied. "One long alarm usually means someone's in trouble."

He got out of bed and opened his door to see Jake running down the hall, hastily pulling on his jacket.

"What's going on?"

"Possible ocean drowning."

"Do you need help?"

"More eyes can't hurt."

Maggie slid off the top bunk and followed Matt and Jake downstairs. Dylan emerged from her room and came into the kitchen, wiping the sleep from her eyes.

"What's going on?" she asked.

"Possible ocean drowning," Matt reported. He only recalled one other instance like this in the middle of the night, and it didn't end well.

"Do you think it's Veronica?" Maggie asked cautiously.

All their faces turned to her in fear.

They knew she wasn't at the dinner party, and that Bea hadn't been sure where she was.

"We just saw Bea running up and down the street in a panic," Matt informed the others.

"Oh my God," Renee said, appearing in the kitchen just in time to hear Matt's words.

"Everyone calm down," Jake insisted before passing out flashlights. "Dylan, Matt, and Maggie, come with me. Renee, please go over to Shep's and see what's going on there. Bring your phones so we can connect."

"Should I wake Steve?" Dylan asked the group.

Their answer, a resounding "No."

Maggie and Matt ran back upstairs.

"Do you really think she could have drowned?"

"I highly doubt it. She's probably asleep on the beach somewhere."

"Would it be wrong to note that you definitely have the more popular wedding date?"

Matt threw her a sweatshirt and pulled one over his head.

"Just put this on," he laughed, secretly satisfied that she spoke the truth.

Instinctively, Maggie reached for her phone. "Oh no! I left my phone charging at the hotel. Where is my brain?"

"We'll get it later. Come on."

Outside they slammed right into Bea, who collapsed in tears in Renee's arms.

"I killed her. She drowned herself."

"Take her home. She's hysterical," Jake instructed Renee. Maggie instinctively reached out to Bea and hugged her, and Bea sobbed on her shoulder. Jake switched things up. "Maggie, go with Renee and Bea. Dylan, you go with Matt."

Within minutes, a chopper from the Marine Bureau was overhead, its enormous floodlight searching the vast ocean. Jake headed west and sent Matt and Dylan east. It was cool and dark. They linked arms and searched the shore with their flashlights.

After an hour of looking, they retraced their steps and rested in front of the dunes near their home block. The helicopter was still following the shoreline, while in the distance two police boats were scouring the ocean.

"It's OK to rest," Dylan said, "but we should try to stay awake."

Matt had no idea how they would stay awake. The adrenaline

that had fueled the first hour of their search had now faded. It felt like coming down after a sugar high.

A few minutes in, Dylan spoke.

"Hazmat?" she asked, in homage to her childhood nickname for him.

"Yes, Dyl pickle," he responded in kind.

"Remember the summer we tried to stay awake on the beach to see the Red Moon?"

"Yes, we didn't make it—we were, like, twelve."

"We played that Oreo hand game over and over till our palms were chafed to stay awake."

"I remember."

"The game or playing it?"

"Both."

"Me too."

After a minute more, Dylan asked, "Would it be wrong to play it now, under these circumstances?"

"Not if it helps us stay awake."

Dylan crossed her legs and turned to face him. He did the same. And they began, as if that Red Moon were yesterday.

"Do you know exactly how to eat an Oreo? Well, to do it, you unscrew it, very fast, 'cause the kid who eats the middle of an Oreo first can save the chocolate cookie outside for last!"

They messed up a little with the hand motions, causing Dylan to insist they do it again. After four times they got it down perfectly, and even under the awful circumstances, they both crashed down into the sand laughing.

"We did make it to see the lunar eclipse—remember that?" Matt asked, after calming down.

"That was awesome," Dylan replied, both of them now lying flat on their backs, staring at the moon.

The somberness of the situation sank back in.

"Do you think we should stay, or go back to the house?" Matt asked.

"I think we should stay here at ground zero. You know my dad is very into respecting orders."

He remembered how Dylan had to say, "May I be excused?" before leaving the dinner table as a kid.

"I hate lying here thinking the worst," Matt said sadly.

"I'll distract you. So, Maggie's nice," she said. "Are you two serious?"

"I just met her at the Salty Pelican two nights ago."

He let out an audible sigh of relief. Matt had never been much of a liar.

"Shut up! OMG! You two have such chemistry, I was jealous!"

"There's nothing to be jealous about. Also, she's engaged!"

"Engaged?"

"Yes, to her childhood best friend, in Ohio. Could have been us," he laughed.

"No offense, but I'm glad it worked out this way," she said, rolling on her side to face him.

"Remember," she added, "before we dreamt about getting in each other's pants, we dreamt about being brother and sister."

She reminded him about the time the two of them, aged seven or eight, went running around the ball field in early spring, blowing on wishing weeds and shouting to the heavens,

"We wish we were brother and sister!" Dylan laughed at the memory.

"On Saturday we will be," Matt said.

"I know, I'm so glad we're on the same page. I was worried we wouldn't be. That's kind of why I brought Steve." She buried her face in her hands. When she removed them, her cheeks were bright red.

"Are you telling me that Steve is a fake boyfriend too?"

"Not exactly. We have been dating on and off for a few months. But I only brought him to the wedding as a buffer."

"Oh my God, we should really talk more," Matt laughed.

"We should." She reached out her pinky and he looped his around hers as they had dozens of times before. The moment felt deep, until Dylan broke the mood.

"I really need to pee."

"Run back to the house."

"'Kay, I'll be right back."

Sometime during her absence, he fell asleep.

Riptide

♩♪♪

Maggie

MAGGIE SAT FROZEN on the couch, scared to move even a muscle for fear that she would wake Beatrix. She had comforted her crying birth mother as best she could, stroking her hair until she eventually drifted off. Now her mind bounced around in that way one's mind does at 3 a.m., on an indirect route from the insanity of rocking her birth mother to sleep all the way to what she did and didn't say to Kimberly Kahn when Kimberly falsely accused her of copying in the seventh grade.

She knew she had promised to think deep thoughts regarding her future on this outrageous trip, to journey inward as well as east to the Long Island shoreline. But it had been too much of a roller coaster ride thus far to allow much time for introspection. Maggie did not like roller coasters. Maggie was happiest on a carousel.

Next, her mind ran to college and her senior year when she had wandered into the student health center and asked to make an appointment with a therapist. After a few sessions, she and the old male shrink she was assigned to, whom she doubted could crack her code, got to the bottom of the weird sense of impermanence she had felt since her parents had told her she was adopted. At least that was how the old (and possibly genius) shrink had labeled the thin layer of anxiety that cloaked her like the fine mist of patchouli her mother would spritz over her head every morning.

"Your parents should have explained that you were adopted before you ever thought differently," he had said.

Probably true, but attributing anything negative to her parents now that they had passed only added to her feeling of instability. The idea that Jason wanted to make permanent what had become the longest and most loyal relationship of her life felt like the best way to restore balance.

She questioned why she had hesitated. Of course she should marry Jason. She would tell him the minute she stepped off the plane.

And that's where she was on her "journey" when Dylan walked into her grandfather's house holding two cups of coffee.

Maggie put one finger to her lips before motioning to Bea asleep next to her on the couch. Dylan smiled.

"Here," she whispered, handing her a mug.

She took a sip and smiled back at Dylan.

"Want to bring this one down to Matt, and I'll stay here with Bea?" Dylan suggested.

Maggie's legs were starting to cramp, and though she didn't want to risk waking Bea, she wasn't sure how much longer she could last in her current position. She took Dylan up on the offer and carefully eased herself off the couch and out the door.

~~~~~

MAGGIE WAS THINKING of all that had gone on since she arrived as she walked down the beach in the moonlight with the two coffee cups, looking for Matt. When she eventually spotted him in the distance, her heart shook in her chest. The sensation was unusual for her. "You're just tired," she said to herself out loud.

"Coffee," Maggie whispered, gently nudging Matt awake in the sand.

He shot up. She laughed and apologized for startling him.

Brushing his hand through his hair and wiping speckles of sand off his cheeks, he got himself together.

Maggie sat down and handed him his cup.

"Any news?" Matt asked.

"None. Renee left to find Jake, and Dylan suggested I switch with her."

Matt smirked and shook his head. "Of course she did. She thinks we make a cute couple."

"So, I guess we are fooling everyone."

"I told her the truth about us. Don't worry, she's a vault," he added. "How's Bea?"

"She fell asleep, probably to save herself from thinking. I slept for, like, a month after my mother died—just as a respite from reality—not that anyone's dead."

"Let's not go there. I'm so sorry for your loss—your losses. I can't even imagine."

"I try and imagine that they are together somewhere. They were the best, both of them." She smiled. "I guess it's why I never looked for my birth parents. I felt so blessed to have the ones I did."

"And now? This seems like a big effort; I mean, you could have waited till Bea was back in Ohio, no?"

"Once I found out who she was, and then learned that she was going abroad for the year, I didn't want to wait."

"But you could have called her or emailed—even FaceTimed—just saying."

She felt foolish. She knew that her coming here was more of a stall tactic to delay responding to Jason's proposal than she cared to admit.

She toyed with telling Matt the truth, saying how badly she wanted a family and explaining that when Jason proposed, her mind had gone right to that—to Jason's family— and it gave her pause. Realizing that somewhere out there was a family of her own who could possibly fill that void and give her more clarity in making the biggest decision of her life, she'd had to act.

Instead, she just shrugged and took another sip of coffee. Stalling again, she took in her surroundings.

"The moon is so bright," she remarked. "It almost looks like it's inviting us into the ocean." She motioned to a narrow path between the waves where the water seemed motionless.

"That's a riptide. They're very misleading, and dangerous," he said.

Her mind went right to Veronica wandering in and drowning. She wished she hadn't pointed it out. Ugh, she had gone there again.

"Sorry," she added.

"It's OK. I've been staring at it all night," he said, slowly rotating his head in a circular motion before stretching it from one side to the other.

Maggie instinctually reached over and massaged his neck with one hand.

He leaned in and smiled. "Thank you, that feels so good."

She put down her cup and wiggled behind him to use both hands. He pushed back into her, his muscles pining for the pressure of her touch. His arms felt strong, muscular. She pushed from her head the image of him wrapping them around her. The thin space between his back and her torso suddenly felt charged—almost electric. The moonlight caught her mood ring. It was lavender—the color of her eyes. She didn't need to look it up—she knew it meant excited.

Before, when she was feeling things that she shouldn't about Matt, she chalked it up to their playacting, but now that they were alone, it unnerved her. This guy stirred things in her that she'd never quite felt before. Things she'd read about, or heard about, but never really believed to be true. She stopped, rubbed her hand as if it were cramping, and slid back next to him.

A line from the song "Riptide" ran through her head.

She's been living on the highest shelf.

Is that what she had been doing? Living up high, where nothing could break her?

From nowhere (or everywhere) she began to cry.

"What is it?" Matt asked with a pained expression.

"Nothing. I'm OK. Just so tired."

"It's a lot," he said, patting his leg, offering for her to rest her head on it.

There was no doubt that their fake coupling had blurred all sorts of lines. She put her coffee cup down in the sand and silently accepted his invitation. He rested his hand gently on her back, rubbing it as one would a baby, or a puppy. A Zen-like feeling inexplicably flooded her body, which, given the awful circumstances and the fact that she didn't typically crave physical comfort, felt miraculous. Her lids grew heavy and she closed her eyes.

She woke an hour later, prone, in Matt's arms. *He* was now sound asleep again. She marveled at how well she fit on his chest, her head tucked perfectly into his neck, their bodies rising and falling and rising and falling in sync, seemingly orchestrated by the tide. She imagined what it would feel like to kiss him. She wished she could kiss him. Just once. Just to know.

She felt completely at ease until the guilt of her thoughts squashed that emotion. Then she felt completely ill at ease.

Again, the lyrics to "Riptide" ran through her head.

She had been living on the highest shelf.

The sun began to rise, adding the dreadful feeling to her woes that finding Veronica Silver was a lost cause.

She wiggled out from under Matt's arms, slipped away, and headed back to her grandfather's house.

The House That Built Me

♩♫♪

Maisie and Juno

MAISIE AND JUNO tiptoed into their parents' bedroom early on Friday morning. Juno was six and Maisie was five. Irish twins, Shep called them, though they were too young to understand why. Their dog, Sally, named for the book *Sally Goes to the Beach*, was sleeping in the bed, wedged between Ben and Addison. It was a big bone of contention in the Morse family: Why was their old dog allowed to sleep in their parents' bed and they were not?

"She was here first," their dad would insist.

They still tried, as they did now, slipping between them quietly. Only Sally noticed, lifting her head to look at them and acknowledging the interruption with a long, wet lick of her tongue on each of their cheeks. They were both careful not to giggle, even though it tickled.

The girls succeeded in crawling under the covers unnoticed. Such success had little to do with their baby ninja skills and more to do with the level of their parents' indulgence the night before. The first night of festivities in honor of the marriage of Captain Jake to their across-the-street neighbor,

Renee, was soaked in sangria and grappa, and both Addison and Ben partook as if two sun-kissed little faces would not be peering down at them wanting breakfast a few hours later. They were both effectively still tipsy.

The girls lay still for a bit, relishing in the fact that they were sleeping in Mommy and Daddy's bed. They smiled at each other over the rise and fall of Sally's chest between them, creating a game of doggie peekaboo with each breath. Maisie giggled when her sister came back into sight. Juno reprimanded her with a finger to her lips. She looked crushed. Juno felt bad for crushing her. She already recognized how much her approval meant to her little sister. Feeling guilty for hurting her feelings and bored from staying so still, she mouthed the call to action that Maisie was likely hoping for.

"JUMP!"

And they did.

Addison and Ben grabbed the sides of their king-size bed as if it were balanced on the San Andreas Fault—trying their best to keep down the paella and alcohol that the sudden jerky movements were stirring. Ben had no patience for it. He yelled:

"Girls, for the love of God, stop jumping!"

They listened, but ended with the biggest flop their two little bodies could create, giggling hysterically. They lay flat on the bed afterward, arms to their sides like tiny wooden soldiers, hoping for tickles, no doubt.

"What time is it?" Addison managed.

Ben reached for his cell on the nightstand and finally found it between the book he was currently reading, used tissues, an empty pack of Tylenol, and the case for his earplugs. The phone was dead.

"Ugh. I never charged it."

Addison sat up, pushed herself back to the headboard, and pulled out hers.

"Eight oh-seven. Not bad."

"Not bad at all," Ben agreed. "We got a solid seven hours."

"Really? You didn't hear all the noise last night?"

"Not a thing," Ben stated. "What happened?"

"No idea, but something big was going on. Hangover pancakes?" Addison offered.

"Yes, please," he replied gratefully.

The girls sat up, crossed their legs, and smiled proudly that they had apparently slept in, as their parents begged them to do most evenings when they kissed them good night.

"Make extra pancakes for our friend, please, Mommy?" Maisie requested.

"Who? Imogene?"

"No, Mommy. Imogene is just pretend. She doesn't eat pancakes. They're for the lady with the red hair who slept in Juno's bed last night!"

The Search Is Over

♪♫♪

Maggie

THE MORNING SUN streamed through the living room window of her grandfather's house as Maggie opened one eye and then the other. She had returned from the beach and taken back her position on the couch next to Bea, who, though now awake, was staring straight ahead in a trance. As far as she knew, Paul and Shep were still at the police station in town, filling out paperwork and questioning everyone who had seen Veronica the night before. And the rest were out searching.

Maggie couldn't help thinking about what she was holding back from poor Bea and the Greek tragedy that would unfold if she were to reveal herself on the same morning that her sister died. It was too much; it was all too much. She silently begged her parents to help her, as she did when things were bad, replacing *Please, God* with *Please, Mom and Dad.* This time she threw in, *If you bring her back alive, I will never ask you for anything again.*

It was then that the neighbor, Ben, strolled into the house. "If you're looking for Veronica, she's asleep in my kids' room. Must have had one too many and forgot where she lived."

He said it real casual, as if it were a joke he had rehearsed on the way over. Bea's reaction, guttural sobs of relief, were the polar opposite of the light chuckle he'd probably been expecting. Maggie quickly jumped in.

"We thought she'd drowned. Her shoes were found on the beach. There's been a manhunt all night."

At least she thought it was called a manhunt. She wasn't sure if manhunt was reserved for escaped convicts; she didn't know what the term was for last night's valiant effort—maybe a search and rescue?

"Oh my God. I had no idea!" The color drained from his face, and he directed them to "Come with me."

Bea gripped Maggie's hand tightly and pulled her along as they raced to her old house. Part of her now felt a connection to Bea that bound them together, while another part of her thought to run in the opposite direction.

Inside the neighbor's house that had once been Shep and Caroline's, Ben's wife, Addison, pointed to the bedroom where the Silver sisters had slept as children. There they found Veronica curled up under a *Little Mermaid* comforter, sound asleep.

Two young girls were sitting up in the other bed, watching her. Maggie imagined one sister waking the other in the night to reveal her discovery, the two of them tucking Veronica in with the comforter and snuggling up together in the other bed, lids heavy, but imaginations running wild over the identity of their surprise guest. From the images on their bedding, Maggie was sure they were hoping for a mermaid or a princess or some other Disney iteration of a damsel in distress, not a drunk Beverly Hills housewife desperately clinging to her youth.

Bea pulled her phone from her pocket and called Paul.

"I found her. Tell my dad she's fine. She was at the old house."

Veronica rolled over, opened her eyes, and looked curiously at the scene in front of her.

"Come here, girls," Addison instructed her two little ones, leading them out of their room to give the older sisters, who once shared it, their privacy. Maggie tried to follow Addison out, but Bea refused to release her hand.

"I thought you were dead," Bea cried, finally letting go of Maggie and climbing into the little bed next to her sister, holding her shocked face in her hands.

"I am," she cried.

"No, you're not," her sister assured her.

"I dissed the lifeguard."

"Good job. Me too."

"And I drank."

"I'll help you find a meeting."

Veronica motioned to the space between them.

"This ridiculous mountain between us. I'm so tired of climbing it, only to fall back down again. Could this be over now, please?"

Bea looked at her sister, so thankful that she was right there in front of her in one piece. She thought back to the time in their lives when they were a single unit, an unbreakable force in so many ways. Life was better like that, safer, kinder, more fun. Sitting in their old bedroom, it hit her hard: the years had flown by, and Veronica was the only person who had seen them all with her—well, almost all. She suddenly longed for the moments they'd missed.

"Yes." Bea hugged her and Veronica melted into her sister's arms. Bea melted right back.

"C'mon. Let's go," she whispered.

"But—"

"We can't stay here," Bea interrupted her, reading her sister's mind.

Veronica nodded in reluctant understanding and sat up.

"Can we do one thing, please, before we go?" she asked, nodding her head toward the closet.

"Wow, I never even knew you read it."

Bea reached into a bucket of markers on the girls' dresser and pulled out a dark purple one that, when opened, filled the room with the scent of grape jelly. She slid open the closet door and gingerly stepped in between pairs of tiny flip-flops, sneakers, and rain boots, bending her head back to see if the hateful words she had scrawled underneath the shelf in Sharpie thirty years before were still there.

She scribbled over the decades-old graffiti as best she could.

"Let's go home," she said, taking Veronica's hand.

"This house is our home," Veronica replied.

"Then let's go make that one our home."

Maggie was left awkwardly alone in the room, clutching a stuffed orangutan that she hadn't even remembered picking up.

Talk about baptism by fire. She was happy to have been left behind.

She stuck her head in the closet and tried to decipher the

words still visible through the scratch-and-sniff marker Bea had used to cross it out.

You are dead to me V!

It was a declaration that Bea had mostly adhered to for thirty years. A lifetime. Maggie's lifetime.

If she wanted to be a part of this family, she would have to remove "drama-free" from her list of criteria. She needed space to think. Tired as she was, she would take Matt up on that day in the city.

TRACK 30

All

♩♫♪

Matt

WHILE EVERYONE ELSE tried to catch up on their sleep, Matt and Maggie walked to the 10 a.m. boat—or more correctly, Matt walked, and Maggie dragged herself a few feet behind him.

"How many hours do you think we slept?" she called out.

Matt laughed as she caught up.

"I left extra time to pick up breakfast and coffee at the market for that reason. And the answer is, maybe three hours."

"Even when I did sleep, it felt like I had one eye open," she whined.

"Well, as your grandfather would say, there's plenty of time to sleep when you're dead."

Maggie smiled, and Matt interpreted it correctly.

"Yeah. If nothing else, I am so glad you got to meet Shep. Somehow, the old man is the least messed up of all of them. What a train wreck you walked into."

"Yes, but family is hard, and maybe they've turned a corner."

"Aaaah. I was curious to see if you would defend them—and you did! I think you're in too deep to back out now."

"I don't know. I was so content in my life before this all happened. I still don't see why I would upset that."

"Yes, because when you were young, dreaming of the life you would have one day, you closed your eyes, crossed your fingers, and said I hope I'm content when I grow up."

"I'll have you know I did dream up my life when I was little, and aside from the obvious, and the fact that I'm not married to Justin Bieber, it is as I wanted it to be."

They turned the corner, the ferry dock and market in sight.

"OK, then, maybe I should drop you at the airport on the way to the city, and you can head home."

"Ugh, home!"

"What about it?"

"I need to call Jason!" The revelation caused her to dramatically plant her hand on her forehead.

"Now what?"

"My phone. I forgot about my phone again. I don't know what's come over me."

"We don't have time to get it and make the boat. Here. Use mine and I'll get us breakfast."

A few minutes later, she was back next to him at the deli counter.

"It went straight to voicemail. I left a crazy-long message," she said, returning his cell with a sad expression.

"You'll try him later."

"Wakey wakey, eggs and bacey?" the guy behind the counter asked.

"Yeah—two BEC SPKs, please," Matt specified.

"What's that?" Maggie questioned.

"She's not from here," Matt told the guy, then explained to her, "Bacon, egg, cheese, salt, pepper, ketchup."

"Ketchup?"

"Trust me."

They ate their sandwiches on the ferry, seated up top on the most coveted bench: a single row facing the others, behind the captain's deck, which doubled as a block from the sun and wind. Today there was no competition. It was just them. Friday ferry traffic, which packed the boats from port to starboard, was mostly reserved for coming, not going.

Matt watched Maggie take the inaugural bite of her Long Island Bacon Egg and Cheese, her closed-mouth smile signaling total satisfaction. He couldn't wait to introduce her to more delicious things in the city, and hoped she would be equally enamored. The wind took her hair, leaving a few strands adrift on her lip, where a remnant of yolk sat, imitating glue. Matt gently pushed the strands aside with his finger, suddenly aware that he was using any excuse to touch her.

Long-distance, engaged, and extremely comfortable with lying.

He repeated the roadblocks in his head before committing to keeping his hands to himself.

"Wow, what a good combo," she gushed.

"Told you!" he said, patting her knee.

He hadn't made it thirty seconds.

"Speaking of good combos," she said, "I never asked you how you feel about your mom marrying Jake."

"I'm cool with it. I mean, it was hard to wrap my head around it at first. If anyone was marrying a Finley, I would have bet on me marrying Dylan. But now, when I see my mom so happy, I'm happy too."

"They seem perfect for each other, from the little I saw."

"They are. But when you see how different the city is than Fire Island, you'll know why I was worried at the start."

The 59th Street Bridge Song

♩♫♪

Matt

BY THE TIME Matt pulled his car out of the ferry terminal parking lot, Maggie was already fading.

"You can close your eyes," Matt suggested.

"*No sleep till Brooklyn!*" she yelled, channeling the Beastie Boys song.

Matt laughed, and they sang a few verses as she sat up straight, intent on taking it all in.

She was asleep by the first traffic light.

When Matt looked at Maggie's sleeping face, he saw a beautiful combination of two people who were nothing alike. Her mouth and her coloring were like Bea's. They shared the same olive-toned skin, and her wavy chocolate-brown hair was a looser version of Bea's curls. But her long legs, sharp nose, and unreal eyes came right from Chase Logan's DNA.

The car behind him honked its horn impatiently. Matt blushed, realizing the possibly creepy reason for his delay, and drove off.

During the hour-long drive to Manhattan, he organized their day in his mind. The bakery where Renee and Jake's

wedding cake was waiting for pickup was located on the Upper East Side, while the Japanese listening room he wanted to
show her was way downtown. It was one of the coolest new
concepts in music he'd seen in years. THE NEXT KARAOKE was
the headline he'd given his article on the subject. He was
psyched for Maggie to experience it firsthand, stoked for her
to bring the concept to her space in Ohio.

He hoped that he and Maggie would keep in touch. He
hadn't made a new friend whom he had felt such an immediate connection with in a long time. It seemed as if he had
known her for much longer than a few days. And nights. For
strangers, they had certainly spent a lot of time together.

Matt broke his no-touching rule again, gently nudging her
when the skyline appeared in the distance. She barely took in
the sight of the city, though not for lack of trying. It was adorable how she propped herself up, holding on to the door with
one hand and the middle console with the other before resting her head back on the window and shutting her eyes again.
She would have to look backward on the way home.

He purposefully chose the 59th Street Bridge to enter
Manhattan, cueing up his Spotify to the song of the same
name—he loved adding his own soundtrack to life. He had
recently heard Paul Simon tell Stephen Colbert that he
loathed singing the song, specifically the line that said, "Life
I love you, all is groovy." Matt got it—it was quite the corny
line—but to him, that was part of its charm. He wondered if
Maggie would roll her eyes or sing along, lowering the win-
dows and cranking up the stereo to bring her to. The moment she heard the first notes, she perked up and harmonized
with Simon & Garfunkel, leaning out the window to lap up
the Manhattan skyline like an excited puppy.

By the time they got to the other side, they were both loving life and feeling groovy.

"We can park in the garage near my apartment and walk through Washington Square Park to the restaurant. Sound good?" Matt asked.

"Sounds wonderful," Maggie replied. "Do most people have a car in the city?"

"Not really. I use it a lot for work. It's more affordable to park at the airport than to take a cab, and I drive to local shows in Long Island and Asbury Park, plus a lot of college towns—you know, for the indie stuff."

"Love that! I'd love to hear who you're listening to."

"I'll share my latest Spotify playlist with you."

"I'll send you mine too. I carry some great local musicians. I get pitched all the time."

"Same. How do you decide who to buy for the shop?"

"I'm not great at saying no. I have a special section in the store for local indie groups, and I usually sell them on consignment. You?"

"I'm a sucker too. I always think I'm going to discover the next Bruce Springsteen. You know, this guy I know at the beach was the first to write about him in the press."

"No way. You know the guy from *Crawdaddy* magazine? I can't believe it."

"I can't believe you know *Crawdaddy* magazine."

It was rare to be with someone outside of work who considered his trove of useless music trivia interesting.

"Of course I do. I literally grew up in a record store. I used to cover my textbooks with their magazine covers. Not the original ones, the reincarnated version, but still."

"The other kids must have thought you were so cool."

"More like so weird. But I didn't care—I always had Jason."

He swallowed the lump that formed in his throat and reminded himself again that Maggie was not available. Even though it hadn't felt that way last night when he was comforting her on the beach.

Matt circled around the Plaza Hotel, pointing out Central Park to the north and his favorite movie theater, The Paris, to the south, before heading down Fifth Avenue to the sounds of Leonard Bernstein conducting *Rhapsody in Blue*. Maggie's head was flipping right to left as he pointed out the guidebook-worthy sights. He worried she'd get whiplash.

There was Tiffany's on the left.

Rockefeller Center on the right.

St Patrick's.

The New York Public Library.

The Chrysler Building.

The Empire State.

The Flatiron.

They continued all the way downtown until the arch of Washington Square Park appeared in the near distance. Since he'd grown up uptown, the sight of it still thrilled him.

Matt pulled into his garage, where he was greeted like a bro by the usual attendants. It made him laugh as they watched Maggie get out of the car, not in a catcalling kind of way; more for the gossip. They were like a bunch of bored teenagers and would surely ask him what the deal was with the pretty woman later.

"I live in an L-shaped studio apartment right up the street." He pointed north as they climbed the garage ramp, squinting in the bright sunlight at the top. "But I travel so much, I'm hardly there. I could really live anywhere. I have a friend who's been living in Nepal since Covid. She works remotely."

"I think it would be pretty amazing to live right here where you do!" she marveled.

"That's funny, because I think it would be pretty amazing to live over a record store!"

"It is pretty amazing," she admitted. "Plus, not to be a downer, but you know, the spirits of my dead parents are there, so I'm always happiest at home."

He thought to hug her, then thought better of it.

They walked under the arch of Washington Square Park. Well, he walked, she skipped. Her eyes widened, as did the perpetual smile that had lit up her face since crossing the bridge. She was beautiful when she smiled. She was beautiful when she didn't smile too.

She spun around in front of the fountain in the park like Julie Andrews at the start of *The Sound of Music*, taking it all in.

"I can't believe you grew up here," she shouted.

"I didn't really grow up here. I grew up on the Upper East Side. It couldn't be more different."

"I've only ever seen New York in the movies."

"OK, then, I grew up in a Woody Allen movie, and the kids down here grew up in some sort of Martin Scorsese–Ed Burns collaboration."

Maggie laughed. "I totally get it!"

Washington Square Park rarely disappointed. Any visit more or less guaranteed sightings of an unhinged woman feeding squirrels, a kid from the suburbs buying a dime bag, a plethora of dogs, or a protest about whatever was worth protesting at the moment, all of it set to the music of a street performer singing Dylan. In this case one of his lesser-known tunes, "Simple Twist of Fate."

Matt could swear the guy looked at him prophetically as he crooned in a gravelly, nasal tone.

"They sat together in the park . . . she looked at him and he felt a spark. Tingle to his bones."

Why is it when you are falling for someone that every love song feels like it's written for you? If he hadn't gone to that bar, sat on that stool, talked to that girl . . . all simple twists of fate. He wondered if she was feeling it too, or if she was on a totally different page.

She stopped in her tracks and wrapped her hands around his middle in what he could only describe as a love-filled hug. His cheeks turned ten shades of crimson and, upon realizing that, ten shades more.

"What was that for?" he asked after she released him, the journalist in him looking for a straight answer.

"Everything. I don't know what I would have done without you this week."

"It has definitely not been what I expected." He laughed to cover up his hope; maybe she *was* on the same page.

"Me neither," she said, twirling in front of him. "I can't believe I'm in Washington Square Park! Jason would love this!"

His face dropped, along with his ego.

Not even the same chapter. Maybe it would be best if they didn't keep in touch after all.

Maggie followed Matt out of the park and through a non-descript door below a neon sign that read TOKYO LISTENING ROOM. Inside, Matt was greeted like a celebrity by the man-

ager, an upbeat woman named Justine, grateful for the glow-
ing feature he had recently written about them in *Rolling
Stone*. He introduced Maggie and explained her dream to
open a similar space in her record store back home. Justine
was generous and encouraging.

She led them down the narrow stairs from the bar to the
tiny basement restaurant, where she directed them to the last
remaining stools in front of a small open kitchen. The chef
greeted them with a smile as he polished white soup bowls as
if preparing to serve a queen.

It was a full house, meaning the two tables and dozen bar
seats were taken. Justine called for everyone's attention.

"Welcome to the Tokyo Listening Room. My name is Justine, your host, your friend, your Sakesan. On the turntable
today, we welcome DJ Amanda Panda!"

Following a boisterous round of applause, she continued:

"If you care to have a song played, check out our song list,
write down your choice on your chopstick sheet, and turn it
in. If you don't, by all means we're good with that too. Our
playlist is fabulous, we love Beyoncé and all that, but we do
want to play your faves, so write them down. As for booze
down here, our magic water keeps you hydrated and is somewhat good for you. We also have beer and wine and champagne."

"The magic water is sake," Matt whispered to Maggie.

"I figured—I'm going to serve magic water too! The sushi
place next door already has a license for it."

Justine went on to explain that the four-course tasting
menu was set by the chef, before turning things over to him.

"Hello, Tokyo Listening Room, if I can have your attention for one moment, please," the chef bellowed over A Tribe

Called Quest rapping their hit "Buggin' Out." It was quite appropriate because Maggie was most definitely bugging out. Matt could see her brain bouncing in ten different directions. She was wide awake now; that was for sure.

The chef placed a small white bowl in front of Matt and another in front of Maggie, while a waiter left the kitchen with a trayful of the same.

"Thank you for joining us to start off the weekend early," the chef said. "This is a miso clam chowder topped with watercress and sliced thick bacon."

They each took a sip. It was otherworldly.

Matt grabbed a tiny pencil from its holder and handed it to Maggie. "Write down one song from the list on your paper chopstick holder."

Maggie perused the selection of songs, sorted by decades.

"Let's not say what we picked—and then guess when the song comes on?" he suggested.

"Duh." She smiled, psyched for the challenge.

She finally scribbled something down before folding the paper as many times as possible, as if Matt had X-ray vision. He laughed and took the pencil, writing down his choice. He toyed with putting down his usual, "Rock and Roll" by Led Zeppelin, but went with a not-so-subtle hint of his feelings for her—there were so many songs to choose from in that category. He doubted she would guess it was his, but maybe it would resonate with her all the same.

Justine brought over the first flight of sake and poured it to Madonna's first hit, "Holiday." Matt asked for a half pour. Even though it was hours away, he did have to drive back to the beach later.

"This one is fruity and floral, it's called Southern Beauty, and it's from Oshu, Japan."

"Ahh, like Shotime," Matt interjected, touting the famed young Japanese baseball player who had signed with the Dodgers. He turned, intending to explain his comment to Maggie, who retorted with, "I bet you hoped he'd be a Yankee."

He looked at her in awe. There was no way this girl could know about both music *and* baseball.

She smiled her beautiful smile at him. "This is amazing," she said.

You are amazing, he thought.

Salt-N-Pepa started singing "Whatta Man."

"You shouldn't have," Matt joked.

"As if," Maggie laughed.

The chef served the next course, hamachi sashimi over arugula salad sprinkled with jalapeño, toasted shallots, and crushed black and white sesame seeds. It was paired with a mash-up from DJ Godfather and a delicious dry sake made locally in Sunset Park, Brooklyn.

"I wish I could show you around Brooklyn," Matt commented.

"Next time," Maggie said, clearly meaning it. Her words made his heart swell until it hurt, like an ache.

That's it. He would not fall for this unavailable woman. He toyed with asking for his song choice back. Maybe she would pick a bad song and he'd be turned off. He once broke up with a girl because she picked Toto's "Africa" for karaoke.

As if on cue, Maggie's song came on.

He knew it in an instant by its perfection and obscurity.

If she had picked "New York State of Mind," or something equally on the nose, he would have been disappointed. "New York City" from John and Yoko's 1972 studio album with the Plastic Ono Band blasted from the speakers, and Maggie casually bopped along to the beat, trying to play it cool. As the bridge faded and the last stanza played, she broke.

"This is my song!"

"What! No way, this is my song," he lied.

"Stop! You have got to be kidding me!"

"I am, I am kidding, I knew it was your song from the first note. Great choice."

The third course came, nori lentils with Swiss chard and shiitake mushrooms followed by dessert—a sweet potato cheesecake topped with caramel, fresh raspberries, and one spectacular sweet potato chip. It was nothing short of sublime, as was the song pairing, Matt's choice, The Proclaimers singing "I'm Gonna Be (500 Miles)" in honor of the distance that would soon be between them.

Yes, he had calculated it.

"Is this you?" Maggie managed in between decadent bites.

"It's my go-to," he fibbed again, taking a slow bite of the heavenly cheesecake.

"I love it," she said, taking her own slow bite.

"The dessert or the song?"

"Both!"

TRACK 32

The Shoop Shoop Song

♩♫♪

Maggie

ON THE WAY to the car, they stopped at a window cut into the side of an Italian restaurant. Matt knocked three times on the glass. It slid open, reminding Maggie of the scene in *The Wizard of Oz* when Dorothy and her posse reach the Emerald City.

"We're here to see the wizard!" Maggie joked. "I need to get home, and he needs a shot of espresso."

Matt cracked up. The barista not so much.

"*Due caffè espresso*," Matt ordered, with an Italian accent that felt more respectful than pretentious. The window slammed shut with zero acknowledgment.

New York City, with its cranky, kooky residents and surprises at every turn, was exceeding Maggie's expectations.

Matt was exceeding her expectations at every turn as well. Being alone with him in the city, away from all the messiness on Fire Island, felt completely right. She had never felt so instantly connected to someone. Like two halves of the same person was how her birth mother described them.

It was different, being with Matt, than it was with Jason.

She knew she shouldn't compare the two. What good would that do her? And if she did (like really did on a piece of paper with pros and cons), she knew Jason's list of pros would run circles around Matt's. But when she woke up in Matt's arms on the beach that morning, it had stirred her in ways she'd never quite felt before. *Could lust outweigh a lifetime of pros?*

The line from "Riptide" played in her head yet again.

So what if she had been living on the highest shelf? There are worse things in life than playing it safe.

The barista placed two steaming shots of espresso on the small wooden ledge that protruded from the windowsill, served in bone china cups with lemon rinds adorning their saucers like miniature crescent moons. Matt downed his, Maggie sipped hers. The humorless barista stood there, waiting for their cups, she assumed. She fell to the pressure and downed the rest. It tasted bitter, and she felt the bolt of caffeine nearly instantly. Not that she needed it. She was high on the excitement of being in Manhattan, with Matt. He was looking down at her, patiently waiting for her to finish. His eyes seemed to be smiling. Her mind ran to kissing him again, but she quickly pushed the delicious thought away.

Concentrate on your new venture, she admonished herself.

She didn't shut up on the car ride uptown. Matt didn't even turn on the radio. He just listened to her big plans, smiling and nodding his head in approval. She was on fire, starting one sentence before finishing the last, a rambling jumble of everything she loved about the listening bar and everything she hoped for her own.

If someone had taken notes and organized them in a business proposal, it would have been quite sensible. Initially, she planned to open only on weekends. She would serve in shifts, a seven o'clock and a nine o'clock seating. The nine might be a little late for Chagrin Falls, but the sushi chef she was partnering with promised that his place was hopping till midnight on Friday and Saturday nights. She would switch on mood lighting after closing the store and add candles, Japanese cherry blossoms, and one long line of maneki-neko: porcelain paw-waving cats considered to bring good fortune. Her favorite employee, Phoebe Buffay, who was watching the shop now (she had officially changed her name from that of another *Friends* castmate, Monica, when she turned eighteen), was a musical theater geek and would be the perfect hostess. Maggie would spin the records and her partner, the chef from the sushi place next door, would work the menu. Soon her little nine-to-five (really ten-to-six) shop would be rocking through the midnight hour.

"This could really work," she squealed, as Matt happily agreed.

They pulled off the FDR Drive at East 61st Street and headed west to Park Avenue. When they turned, so did the city. Maggie stopped babbling and looked out the window.

"Aaah, the Upper East Side, I presume."

"Yup, my childhood hood."

"Do we have time for a little drive-by tour before we get the cake?"

"Sure, what do you want to see? The shops on Madison Avenue, the Museum Mile?"

"No, no. I want to see *your* Upper East Side. Where you went to school, hung out, that kind of thing."

Matt sat up straight and leaned into the wheel, clearly pumped for a trip down memory lane—or up Park Avenue, as the case may be.

He paused at the corner of East 82nd and Park and pointed up to his childhood apartment. The uniformed doorman came out, thinking they were stopping to drop someone or something off. Recognizing him, Matt jumped from the car.

"Anthony!"

"Matty!" They went in for an exaggerated shake. "How's mom?" the doorman asked.

"Getting married tomorrow, if you can believe it. This is my friend Maggie." He motioned to the passenger seat, and Maggie rolled down the window to wave hello.

"I'm giving her a little tour of the old neighborhood."

"Oh. See that planter?" Anthony pointed to the corner. "That's where Matty puked the first time he drank too much."

They laughed, and the two leaned in for a quick embrace goodbye. Matt got back in the car, turned on East 89th Street, and pulled up in front of the Dalton School. Even Maggie had heard of it.

"Oh my God. I went to college with a girl who went here. Becca Green, do you know her?"

"Look at you playing Jewish geography! I'm gonna buy you a babka at the bakery. Have you tasted babka yet, you newish Jewess?"

"Nope," she laughed.

"Ah. You have so much to learn—in baked goods alone. Becca Green was two years ahead of me. I had a big crush on her."

"Yeah, well, she was gorgeous, and so sophisticated, who wouldn't?"

"A lot of the girls were that sophisticated."

"Like in *Gossip Girl*?"

"There were a handful in each grade that were over-the-top Serena and Blair level. A few girls from each private school traveled in a pack, armed with their parents' Amex cards, going to all the hottest places. My group was more erudite. We all thought we were brilliant. Until we got to college and found out we were just overeducated."

"I can't even imagine growing up here."

"I went to college in California, you know, to get away from all of it. In the end, I couldn't get back fast enough. Though lately I'm such a nomad because of work, it seems ridiculous that I live in the most expensive neighborhood in the most expensive city when I could live anywhere."

They turned on Madison Avenue and Matt pointed to a restaurant called Three Guys.

"You see that place? We ate there so much that my mother called it the west wing. We had an account. Whenever my parents worked late, I would sit at the counter under a fresco of Mykonos with a book and a burger and fries. The book was a prop, really. I would chat with the old Greek waiters and the chef the whole time. They were awesome."

"My parents were always home for dinner," Maggie countered, "but we did live above the store till I was ten, so you know, no big commute."

He turned again down a side street and stopped in front of the famous steps at the Metropolitan Museum of Art. The place was huge—like four blocks long. She waited for him to get all erudite on her. Instead, he pointed. "You see that bench?"

She nodded.

"That's where Sophie Michaelson let me feel her up for the first time. 'Let me' may be an exaggeration. She took my hands and placed them on her boobs. I was twelve. I just sat there twisting them like they were the hot and cold knobs on a shower faucet."

He laughed at himself, and Maggie laughed with him.

He looked at his phone.

"We gotta get to the bakery," he warned. "There's going to be mad traffic on the way back out to the beach."

They circled around the block and Matt let out an alarming, high-pitched "Oh my God!"

"What?" Maggie shrieked, circling her head around expecting to see a mugger or a movie star.

"There's a spot right out front! You can come in!" Matt exclaimed as they pulled up in front of the famous Madison Avenue bakery, William Greenberg, just as an idling taxi pulled out.

She'd never heard such excitement over a parking spot but followed his lead.

The shop was crowded with customers, real-life Upper East Siders, picking out their challah and desserts for Shabbat dinner, she imagined. In high school, Maggie was a frequent guest at a Jewish friend's house on Friday nights. The girl was allowed to go out afterward, but sitting down with her family every Friday night to break challah bread was mandatory. Maggie loved everything about it. The girl and her mother would light the candles and the father would place his hand on the head of each of his children, bestowing blessings on them for the week. Maggie had already decided that she would incorporate some iteration of that into her own family one day, now that she had discovered her roots.

Her mouth dropped open at the display of cookies and cakes in front of her.

"What would you like?" Matt asked.

"One of everything!" Maggie replied, while taking in the other ladies in line. An older woman in a tailored cotton shirtdress with beauty parlor hair, a young mom sporting a high ponytail in head-to-toe Lululemon with two little legging-clad mini-mes at her side. She had never seen anyone look that chic in workout clothes. Matt told the lady behind the counter that they were there to pick up the wedding cake and she disappeared into the back. One of the little girls tugged on Maggie's skirt.

"Are you getting married?"

Not wanting to douse the hopeful twinkle in her eyes, she nodded yes with a big smile. Matt laughed and whispered, "From fake dating to fake marrying in three days."

"They're getting married," the girl told her sister.

"Kiss, kiss!" the sister got in their faces and pleaded.

Maggie and Matt smiled at them and turned to face the counter. Matt asked the other attendant:

"We'll also have a chocolate babka, four rugelach, two black-and-whites and two schnecken, please." Maggie had never even heard of the last one. She was excited.

The skirt-tugging sister joined the uproarious one, taking their shouts up a notch, now a duet.

"True love's kiss! True love's kiss!"

Matt turned to the mother and smiled. "Do they have an off button?"

"Not that I've found, sorry," she said, though not sorry enough to tell them to stop.

"True love's kiss! True love's kiss!"

They were loud and relentless. Now the customers at the back of the line were giving Matt and Maggie come-on-already looks, as if they alone held the key to their serenity.

"I'm sorry," the mother addressed the group, "too many Disney movies."

"Just kiss her already, I'm getting a headache," a cranky old man at the rear pleaded.

Maggie knew Matt wouldn't do it and felt that taking the lead would be a good feminist lesson for these two. Plus, maybe kissing him, just this once, would put an end to the curiosity that had been plaguing her, if she was being honest, since he gave her a ride home that first night on the back of his bike. It would be better (for her and for Jason) than wondering about it for the rest of her life, she rationalized. She could kiss him, explain to Jason what happened, and put it behind her.

Maggie stood on her tippy-toes and planted a sweet smooch on Matt's lips before looking down at the cheering squad, expecting satisfaction and silence.

The girls' faces dropped from gleeful anticipation to utter disappointment. The older one vocalized her dissatisfaction.

"That's it?"

Everyone laughed, except the two little girls, who looked as if their entire vision of true love had fizzled before their eyes. She couldn't have that. Her competitive side (really her only side) kicked in.

She met his eyes before his lips and saw that they were filled with apprehension and longing, as, she was sure, were hers. It was too much, so she closed them. When her mouth touched his, time seemed to stand still and everything else faded away. The girls, the older lady, the old man, the smell of fresh-baked cookies and babka, gone, replaced by passion, wonderment, and truth. It was the truth that concerned her when they finally broke away. Her lips had never felt more at home, though it was no home she'd ever known. How was that possible? Her alarming observation was quickly doused by the old man's snarky commentary:

"She said Disney, not *Debbie Does Dallas!*"

Even the woman behind the counter laughed as she passed over the first boxed layer of the wedding cake. Matt, red-faced and smiling ridiculously, grabbed it with two hands, nodding for Maggie to get the door. He went back and forth with the three boxes that they would lay on top of each other at the wedding to form the traditional vanilla frosted tower. The bag of treats sat on top of the last box, and Maggie couldn't decide which to try first. She climbed into the back seat of the car, insisting she should keep the boxes safe. But really, it was her virtue that she wanted to keep safe. She was worried that her commitment to Jason wouldn't survive a two-hour ride sitting next to Matt.

"It's a good thing you're back there guarding the cake. This could have been quite the disaster," Matt said.

In more ways than one, Maggie thought.

"Happy to be of use," she replied, instead, in a shaky voice that she didn't recognize. It had been some kiss. Their first and their last, she swore to herself, as the lustful memory of it was overshadowed by guilt. She repeated her prior rationalization.

I did it and now I won't have to spend my whole life (with Jason) thinking about what it would feel like to kiss Matt. I climbed off the top shelf and now I can return to it—safe and sound.

Matt grabbed a black-and-white cookie from the bag and passed the rest back.

"A little nosh," he said, in his best old Jewish man accent, adding, "I like to eat the vanilla half first, and then the chocolate, but you do you."

And she did, starting right down the middle.

Matt had been right about the traffic. The ride that had taken an hour on the way in looked like it would be twice as long on the way back. They filled the time with a back-and-forth game of music trivia. They were safely back in the friend zone.

"Best album?" Matt asked.

"Favorite or best?"

"Best."

"Prince. *Purple Rain*."

"Not even in my top five."

"Pull over, I'm getting out!"

"But the cake!"

"True. OK, give me your top five."

"*Nevermind*."

"Ha ha. You can't trick me. I own a record store."

"OK. Nirvana's *Nevermind*, *Abbey Road*, duh, Radiohead's *In Rainbows*, *Zeppelin IV*, and—don't laugh—Fleetwood Mac, *Rumours*," Matt listed.

"Not laughing. I totally agree with all but would substitute *Cowboy Carter* for Radiohead."

"That's legit—what about live music?"

"What about it?"

"Your first concert?

"My parents took me and Jason to JazzFest in New Orleans, 2007. We went because Rod Stewart was playing, and they were desperate for me to hear 'Maggie May' live."

"That must have been awesome."

"It was. You?"

"I usually say Flo Rida at Madeline Schwartz's bat mitzvah, for the laugh, but truth is it was the Jingle Ball, also 2007, at the Garden—you're jealous, right?"

"I am!"

"You should be, Jonas Brothers and Backstreet Boys!"

"Stop! Who do you wish you could have seen? I'll go first—Prince."

"That I get. My dad saw him in DC, says it was his best ever. I wish I could have seen The Clash."

"You never talk about your dad. Are you close? Is he into music too?"

"Not really into music and close enough, for someone I have little respect for. He cheated on my mom, and even though she has clearly ended up in a better place, I still resent him for hurting her. But we get along fine. I've learned to compartmentalize."

"Wow, you seem so in touch with your feelings."

"Yeah, well, ten years of therapy will do that."

"I only went a few times, in college."

"Everyone on the Upper East Side has been in therapy for ten years. It's like a requirement once you pass 59th Street."

Maggie laughed. She was starting to see how all the clichés of New York City life were based on fact.

"I have a bootleg of Brittany Howard at Webster Hall. Want to hear it?" Matt asked.

"Yes, *Live at Sound Emporium* got me through Covid!"

They sang along for the next ninety minutes and pulled into the parking lot of the ferry terminal just as they finished belting out the final encore.

The boat was packed, and since they only just made it, there were no more seats up top. It was better actually. They

slipped onto a bench in the back, securing the cakes underneath, and fell asleep, once again, before the ferry even picked
up speed. At twenty-eight minutes, the ride was the perfect
amount of time for a disco nap. Matt leaned on the window,
and Maggie leaned on him, amazed at how comfortable she
felt doing so. She pondered the extent to which their fake-
dating scenario had contributed to their rapid connection.

She opened her eyes as the island appeared in the near
distance. It was so unlike the first time she had arrived, looking out at the unknown in fear. Now, she breathed a sigh of
relief, the way you do when you recognize that you're close to
home.

To their surprise, Dylan was at the ferry dock on the
other side when they arrived. As they exited the boat, they
saw her sending off Steve.

"What happened?" Matt asked.

"How can I be with someone who burns so easily?" she
said, laughing.

"Aw." Matt wrapped his arms around her and brought her
in for a big hug.

"At least now we don't have to pay to have him photo-
shopped out of the pictures!" he offered in consolation. Not
that she seemed to need much consoling. She handled it in
that "no skin off my back" way she seemed to handle everything. Unlike Maggie, Dylan seemed impervious to drama.

"Do you have the wagon?" he asked upon breaking away
from their hug.

"I do."

"Can you bring back the cake?"

"I can." She smiled.

"Cool. I'm gonna take Maggie back to the *Hotel, Motel, Holiday Inn*," he rapped.

Maggie laughed; Dylan rolled her eyes.

"OK. *Mamma Mia!* is playing at twenty hundred hours, sharp, I've been told—six times. My dad always speaks in army time," she added for Maggie's sake.

"Be there by eight." Matt smiled and saluted before leading them in the direction of town.

"Best hip-hop album—on three," Matt queried a few steps later. "One, two, three."

"*To Pimp a Butterfly*, Kendrick Lamar!" they both shouted in unison.

"Wow. You're so old-school—I thought you would say *Rapper's Delight*, especially after your hotel-motel joke."

"Nope, but I can do that one from start to finish," he laughed.

"Me too."

"No way."

"Way."

They walked into town to a duet of "Rapper's Delight": both claiming to know all three thousand words.

"*I said a hip-hop, the hippie, the hippie to the hip, hip-hop and you don't stop the rockin' to the bang-bang boogie, say up jump the boogie to the rhythm of the boogie, the beat.*"

Laughing uncontrollably, they made their way up the steps to Maggie's room, singing the final refrain of "Hotel, Motel, Holiday Inn," only to be startled by the presence of a man camped out in front of her door.

Rapper's Delight

♩♫♪

Maggie

MAGGIE TOOK TWO steps back and then one forward upon recognizing the man curled up on the floor in front of her door.

"Jason?" she gasped, with a mixture of shock and confusion. "You came!" she added, as he looked up at her.

"Yes, I came!" he answered, in a tone that indicated he wasn't there to happily surprise her.

"I called you a hundred times," he continued, while rising to his feet. "I thought you were dead!"

"The theme of the week!" Matt joked inappropriately.

Maggie let out a strained laugh before narrowing her eyes at Matt, silently telling him to just stand there and be quiet. He rolled his lips under and pressed them together to indicate that he got it.

"Excuse me?" Jason responded.

"I thought my grandfather was dead, and then also my aunt."

"You have a grandfather and an aunt?"

"I do." She smiled about that, maybe for the first time.

"Is this your cousin?"

They had been lying so much that, for a second, she thought to say yes, in the hope of putting Jason at ease. But she had never lied to him before, and she wasn't about to start now. The kiss at the bakery ran through her mind. She pushed it away for now and answered him best she could.

"No, it's a very long story."

"Well, I've come a very long way."

She pulled her key from her pocket and let them both into the room.

"I know you're mad, J, but I'm so happy to see you!" She threw her arms around him—she was lit up. "Now you can meet everyone!"

Her enthusiasm dimmed as she suggested to Matt, "Maybe it's time to tell Bea?" Before quickly reversing with, "But that's not really fair to your mom and Jake."

She knew she had a habit of debating with herself, but this was next level, even for her. Jason looked confused. She paused and attempted to clarify.

"Matt's mother, Renee, is the one getting married. Revealing that I'm her matron of honor's long-lost daughter would surely take away from the bride's big day."

She turned back to Matt.

"Don't you agree? The whole thing with Veronica 'drowning' was enough!"

"Who's Veronica?" Jason asked.

"My aunt."

"Your aunt drowned?"

"Only in alcohol," Matt joked, trying once more to lighten things up. It didn't work. He and Maggie laughed without Jason again, whose expression conveyed more hurt than amusement.

"So, no one drowned, and no one is dead?"

She had never seen him so angry, and rightfully so. Still, she tried to take it down a notch.

"Nope, just my phone."

"OK, 'cause if you don't mind me saying, you're weirdly, for lack of a better word . . . giddy."

"I'm not giddy," she objected with a blushing giggle that only bolstered his argument.

Get it together, Maggie, she scolded herself.

She looked back at Matt again, feeling she needed to defend Jason's atypical anger. She explained the egregiousness of her actions.

"My phone is always charged. This may literally be the first time it had been left to die. So, Jason was legit scared that something happened to me."

She put her hand on Jason's arm. "I'm so sorry, but I did call you from his phone; you didn't get my rambling message?"

"From some random unknown number? No."

He pulled out his phone to look. There it was. In the middle of a long string of text messages and calls to Maggie's dead phone.

"I should have tried again," Maggie apologized, "but with everything to see in Manhattan, you can imagine I was completely distracted."

"Manhattan?" He doubled down on his crestfallen expression.

"Yes, we went to the city to pick up the wedding cake. Anyway"—she changed the subject in a big way—"I'm so happy that you're here! I missed you so much."

As she said the words, she realized that she kind of hadn't.

"Matt Tucker, this is my fiancé, Jason Miller. Jason, this is my new friend Matt. I'm sure you will be fast friends *too*."

She emphasized "too" in a stern, factual way. As if she was clarifying her and Matt's relationship status for both men.

They shook hands. Jason was now smiling, and it was Matt's turn to look crestfallen. Maggie had already had about as much of this little threesome as she could handle. It felt as if the tiny room were shrinking before her eyes. She pulled open the rickety window, desperately needing air, and inhaled a few big gulps.

Seeing Jason felt like a jolt of reality. Like she had spent the past three days in a bubble and Jason had swooped in and popped it.

"I'm gonna walk Matt out," she said, taking him by the elbow and nudging him out the door. She stood in the narrow hallway and did the best she could to dismiss him.

"You know what? Now that Sunburn Steve left, I know the perfect way to end this. Go back and tell everyone we broke up and I'm going home. Then you can enjoy the wedding with Dylan and your family, without my complicated agenda taking center stage."

She hoped he would jump at her plan, but he didn't look enthused. In fact, he looked even more dejected.

"What about Beatrix?" he asked.

"I'll email her."

"That will be some email."

"I'll figure it out. Go, have fun. You have been an amazing friend to me. Thank you!"

She hugged him goodbye. He hugged her back. As he broke away, she held him a little tighter.

"Bye," he said, the single word caught in his throat.

"Bye," she said, barely audibly.

Even though every second away from Jason waiting alone in the room felt cruel, she took a beat to watch Matt descend the stairs. Her stomach dropped as he left her sight, and it plummeted further when she realized she might never see him again.

Jason, who could read her better than anyone, sensed her melancholy on her return. Maggie, as she reminded herself, would never do anything to hurt him, and she doubled down on making sure they were good before explaining everything that had happened. She told him the basics, including a very G-rated version of the bakery scene. She responded to his uneasy look, promising, "It was nothing, Jason, absolutely nothing."

Who am I trying to convince, him or me?

"OK, but how would you feel if the tables were reversed here?" Jason asked, employing his trademark calm and logical debating tactics.

"Awful"—she touched his cheek with the back of her hand—"but luckily you are not me."

Jason was the most cool-headed, pragmatic person she'd ever known. Even so, it was a lot to take in. He quickly dismissed the whole fake-dating thing as a means to an end and homed in on his greatest concern after hearing the goings-on over the past few days, which was:

"No offense, Maggie, but your family is fucked up beyond comprehension."

She laughed. It was better than crying.

"You must be starving," she said.

"I am."

"Let's get out of here. There's a place with good fish tacos down the block."

"You're sure you don't want to try something new?"

They exchanged a knowing smile.

She never wanted to try something new. She had miso soup and a California roll from the Japanese restaurant next to the record shop nearly every day for lunch. Maggie was a creature of habit.

For the first time, as they walked to the Salty Pelican, she questioned why that was.

TRACK 34

Ocean Eyes

♩♫♪

The Lifeguard

IT ONLY TOOK a few seconds after the dark-haired girl with his blue eyes had left the bar with Matthew Tucker, two nights earlier, for Chase to realize the missed opportunity. He'd only needed to ask to see her ID, and date of birth, to have the proof he needed. He had never been one to think on his feet, unless there was a surfboard under them, but he was really kicking himself for missing that one.

And asking Beatrix Silver about her only confused him more. It was as if she didn't know their daughter was on the island. He was beginning to think he had imagined the whole thing until she walked in again, with another guy.

This girl takes after me in more ways than just eye color, he thought, laughing to himself.

"Two menus, please, and two tequila and sodas with lime," the guy ordered for them both.

"ID?" he asked, as he placed two menus in front of them.

They both complied. He barely looked at the guy's, but studied the woman's.

"Date of birth?" he quizzed her, as he did when someone

looked underage. This time he was just stalling, committing it all to memory.

"Really," she laughed. "I'm thirty, and I was here the other night, drinking."

He raised his eyes at her in an "Answer the question, please" way.

"May fifth, 1987."

He repeated her info out loud.

"Maggie May Wheeler. May fifth, 1987. Chagrin Falls, Ohio."

He realized it might look odd for him to be reading off the details like that, and was happily interrupted by a regular, who called out on the way to the dartboard, "Hey, Chase—the usual, please!"

He nodded, and then returned their IDs.

She must have found the interaction odd as well, because the girl, his daughter, was staring at him strangely when he handed them back. He could swear she did a double take when she looked him in the eyes. There was no denying that their unusual color—almost violet—was the same as her own. When he went into the kitchen to place their dinner order, he saw her whisper to the guy she was with.

Chase questioned whether he was being paranoid as he returned to the bar and set down their drinks.

"What's to do around here?" bachelor number two asked.

"It's early, but we get a good crowd here on Friday nights."

"OK, cool, you been tending bar here long?"

"Not too long," he answered.

"We're new around here too," the guy said, fishing.

Chase fell for it. He knew he'd fallen for it but couldn't help himself.

"New? I've been here every summer since I was born, my first gig was a lifeguard, but now I mostly tend bar."

"Oh."

His daughter, Maggie May Wheeler from Chagrin Falls, Ohio, picked up her tequila and soda and downed it like it was a shot. She handed him back the menus and said:

"Actually, we're gonna go."

She knew too. He knew she knew.

At least she didn't ask to borrow his bike.

Gimme! Gimme! Gimme!

♩ ♫ ♪

Maggie

AS MAGGIE MADE her way from Ocean Beach to Bay Harbor, her anger toward Matt grew with each tequila-fueled step. She was certain he had been withholding the truth from her—that the bartender was the lifeguard, and the lifeguard was her father. He had to have known. Why didn't he tell her? Was there something sinister about her father's side of the family? Did she come from a long line of ax murderers or something? She knew she was being irrational, but she just felt so confused and betrayed.

The words Matt spoke when she entered his house that first night—*You can trust me*—echoed in her mind, making her even more furious that she had let him in. It was further proof that the high shelf was where she should remain. On top of being hangry, she had never felt so double-crossed in her life.

"Don't jump to conclusions," Jason urged, wrapping his arm around her to offer solace. She wiggled away.

"I can't right now," she said in her typical "Maggie will console herself" fashion. And yes, she was fully aware that she had, let Matt console her the other night. She became angrier still.

They arrived at the Bay Beach to a setting that, in other circumstances, would have warmed their small-town hearts. Everyone was cozied up on a sea of blankets and beach chairs. The Great South Bay was glistening in the background, and Amanda Seyfried and Stellan Skarsgård were glistening on the big screen. It was the scene in *Mamma Mia!* where they were trying to determine Amanda's paternity.

The absurdity of their timing was only matched by the absurdity of the circumstances.

"*Are you my father?*" Seyfried asks.

"*Yes, I think so, yes,*" Skarsgård replies.

"*What comes next?*" Seyfried asks.

"Good question!" Jason joked.

Maggie didn't find it funny. She instructed him to wait in the back as she navigated her way through the crowd, carefully avoiding blankets and limbs. From that point in the movie, she knew she had less than a minute until the crowd would burst into song. *Mamma Mia!* came out her senior year of high school and she couldn't count the times she'd seen it. She had played the soundtrack in the shop so often after school that her father forbade her doing so ever again.

She found Matt up front, asleep next to Dylan. People were waving their hands at her, and she looked down to see the film playing across her chest.

"Ugh," she mumbled as she scrunched down onto their blanket.

"He's sleeping," Dylan said, stating the obvious.

"I don't care."

She shook his shoulder, and he opened his eyes. She didn't wait for him to get his bearings.

"Why didn't you tell me that the bartender was my father?"

The crowd united in song.

> Gimme, gimme, gimme a man after midnight.
> Won't somebody help me chase the shadows away?

"Not here," Matt managed, above the Greek chorus.

The three of them slithered through the crowd, picking up Jason on the way out. No one spoke till they got to Matt's house.

As soon as they were safely inside his bedroom, Maggie repeated the question.

"Why didn't you tell me that the bartender was my father?"

"Because you were already soured on Beatrix. If I told you that the bartender was your father, I worried you would have been on the first ferry out. Plus, I was following your lead. You were looking for your mother."

"Her mother?" Dylan asked.

They both shushed her. She took a step back. Jason whispered in her ear, "Beatrix is Maggie's birth mother."

"Oh my God!" Dylan said, before repeating it again in a tempered volume. "Oh my God."

"You told me to trust you and you lied to me," Maggie continued.

"I didn't lie. You read that chapter in the book and didn't say a thing. I wasn't about to force him on you."

Now Jason looked confused. Dylan grabbed the copy of

On Fire Island from Matt's shelf, tapped on the cover, and handed it to him.

"C'mon, Maggie. You didn't ask me one question about him," Matt continued.

"What question should I have asked?"

"The obvious one—do you know who my father is?"

"OK, Matt. I didn't know you needed so much direction. Do you know who my father is?"

"Yes."

"Then who?!"

"Chase Logan. The lifeguard turned bartender at the Salty Pelican—ergo why I was worried he would hit on you."

"Ergo?" said Maggie, at a loss for a comeback.

"Yuck," said Dylan. They all turned her way for an explanation.

"The yuck was about him hitting on her. Chase Logan gets a bad rap, but he's not a bad person. Really. He once saved my dog from drowning in the ocean."

"So, I'm not from a family of ax murderers?"

"No!" Dylan laughed.

Maggie sat on the bottom bunk and put her head in her hands. Matt swiftly took a seat beside her and wrapped his arm around her.

"I'm sorry. I swear you *can* trust me. I thought I was doing what was best for you. I'll never withhold anything from you again."

She leaned right into him and cried, realizing, beyond all of it, that there was no part of her that had accepted she would never see this man again.

"Now what do I do?" she asked, unsure of what she was even referring to.

Jason knelt in front of her, placing his hands on her knees. "What do you want to do?" he asked kindly.

Maggie quickly saw that she was leaning, more like burying herself, into Matt. She sat straight up. Matt, suddenly aware of the awkwardness too, stood up as if the bed were on fire while Dylan looked straight through him, as presumably only she could.

To put it mildly, the dynamics were strange.

"What do you think I should do?" Maggie asked Jason, pulling herself together.

"You came here to meet your mother; I think you should meet your mother."

"I did meet her."

"But she doesn't know that," Dylan piped in. "Can I tell you something, Maggie?"

"Sure."

"My mother walked out on me when I was little. She never really wanted me—never gave much thought to the fact that she had a daughter. Beatrix has been thinking about you every day for thirty years. I think you'd be lucky to have her."

"But there's so much to unravel," Maggie cried.

"Not really. I never got the chance to tell anyone but Dylan that you were leaving. We can figure the rest out," Matt assured her. "How about we get through the wedding fake dating, if that's OK with you, Jason, and we can tell Bea on Sunday?"

"Jason?" Maggie conferred.

"It's fine, as long as no one asks me to outwardly lie."

"Jason is an ethics professor," Maggie added.

They all nodded in agreement.

As they did, the bedroom door burst open, and Jake

stood towering in the doorway. Dylan and Matt jumped, as if they forgot they were adults who could come and go as they pleased. It was amusing.

"What are you guys doing here?"

"Just talking, Daddy," Dylan said, with extra sweetness.

"OK, don't tell your mother I was here, Matt. I need some peace and quiet. I still haven't written my vows."

He shut the door and quickly opened it again, staring Jason down.

"Who are you?"

"I'm Jason, Maggie's, um, brother."

"Oh." Jake held out his hand. "Nice to meet you, Jason. Feel free to come to the wedding tomorrow; there's plenty of room." He turned to Matt and added, "We got a bunch of Covid cancellations. Your mother is going to be redoing those tables up until we walk down the gangplank." He winked.

Once he was out of earshot, they all pointed to the ethics professor and laughed. He laughed too.

Oh, what a tangled web they'd woven.

Love You for a Long Time

♩♫♪

Jake

THE DELAY IN Jake Finley writing his vows was not because he didn't know what to say; it was because he had too much to say.

He could remember the very first time he and Renee had spoken.

She was fourteen, boarding the boat with her parents. He was fifteen, and it was his first summer as an official deckhand, though he had been a fixture on the ferry since he could walk.

She was wearing a sundress, and her hair was teased high on top of her head, the way teenage girls wore it then.

"Ticket, please," he'd asked, wondering if the sudden burning in his cheeks was visible to her piercing green eyes.

"My dad has it." She smiled coyly, like she already knew the power that her smile held.

Now he pulled out a piece of paper and wrote.

> *Renee, you are as beautiful today as you were the day
> I met you.*

Two years later, at sixteen, they were at a house party together over in Point O' Woods. Jake didn't go to many parties. Summer, for him, meant rising before the sun and
working long hours on the ferry. While most other kids had
cushy jobs scooping ice cream or working at the day camp,
Jake's job was his priority. His father was the ferry captain
back then, and his father's father was the ferry captain before
that. He had a lot to live up to.

That night thirty-plus years ago, sometime after midnight,
Renee was heading back to Bay Harbor, alone. Not unlike
what happened this weekend, Bea, who she had come to the
party with, had to leave on account of Veronica's antics. Jake
watched from the back deck as Renee walked down the beach
stairs. He could see her reticence as she reached the bottom,
so he took a few steps down himself. A rowdy group walking
on the beach called out to her, clearly making her uncomfort-
able. She took a step back. Jake took ten forward.

"Want me to walk you home?" he asked.

"Thanks, Jake, that would be nice."

She knew his name. He did his best to hide a massive grin.

It was a chilly night, and he took off his prized Fire Island
Ferries Crew sweatshirt and handed it to her without even
asking. It was a good move, he thought, as she silently slipped
it over her head. They talked about the regular stuff, mostly
what it was like living on the island all year long. It was a
common question, and he did his best to impress her with
tales of riding his bike across the frozen bay and ski jumping
off snow-covered roofs. When they got to her street, she took
off the sweatshirt and handed it back to him. He badly wanted
her to keep it and toyed with telling her so when she leaned
in and kissed him gently on the lips.

"Thanks for walking me," she said softly.

He kissed her back and their tongues touched, igniting a sweet exploration of each other's mouths. She was standing on her tippy-toes in the sand. He was bent forward, not unlike a giraffe. It was over quickly, but he thought about it forever. He still thought about it. It was his first kiss.

He continued with his vows.

You were my first kiss, and you will be my last.

Renee's parents divorced soon afterward and sold the house at the beach. And that kiss became a core childhood memory—as much as riding his bike across the frozen bay or ski jumping off a snow-covered roof. Until many years later, when Renee and her then husband, Arthur, bought a summer home in Bay Harbor and their son, Matty, and his daughter, Dylan, became the best of friends.

Since Jake was a single father, Renee had helped with Dylan often over the years. Aside from feeding her many a meal while he worked the long summer shifts, she took it upon herself to teach her girly things—like how to shave her legs and use a tampon. For years, nearly every interaction between married Renee and Jake involved the kids.

You have been there for me and Dylan over the years in ways I could never repay.

Until about a year and a half ago, when Jake got a frantic phone call from Renee in the middle of the night. He ran over in his pajamas.

"It came from in there." She pointed to her sunken bathtub

and they both listened intently for the sound of the mad scratching that she had heard.

"It stopped," she cried. "I'm sorry."

"Don't be sorry. Living here in the off-season requires a certain amount of courage."

"I wish you'd told me that before I decided to do it."

"That's OK. Call me whenever you need me. I can be brave for the both of us."

The next night at 1 a.m. he was right back there, listening for the sound, again. And again, it stopped when he arrived. Truth was, he was pretty confident that he knew what she'd been hearing. There was most likely a raccoon, or a whole family of them, living below the house and sleeping in the under basin of her tub. But the truth also was he loved this knight-in-shining-armor/damsel-in-distress thing they had going on.

"How about this?" he suggested. "I'll just come over at midnight tomorrow and we can sit and wait for it?"

"How about I make us a late dinner and you can stay till then?"

"Sounds good. What can I bring? I have a nice bottle of Sicilian red."

"Perfect."

The next night they sat on Renee's bed and waited—and waited and waited—for the sound to come from the bathroom. While waiting, they finished off the bottle of wine, reminisced about the past, and confessed to how lonely they both felt without their kids in the house. Somehow, after a while, Renee was brave enough to voice the question that she had always wanted to ask.

"Do you remember when I kissed you on the beach?"

If I close my eyes right now, I can still picture that kiss.

"Like it was yesterday. That's what happens when you play something over and over again in your head," Jake bravely admitted. He may not have feared raccoons, but beautiful women were a different story.

They had both blushed at his surprisingly tender confession.

"You do? I always thought you'd forgotten. I barely remember it," she said with a small pout.

"Maybe I can remind you," he said, in possibly the coolest comeback of his life.

And they kissed.

She never heard the raccoon again, but Jake had slept over every night since, just in case.

Initially, Jake doubted that the woman in his arms could stay aloft on the pedestal he had placed her on, but his teenage infatuation soon evolved into adult love. He envied her wild combination of vulnerability and strength, the way she could quote all three *Die Hard* movies on call but would also tear up bingeing *This Is Us*. The way she took to the winter vibe on the beach, relishing the mahi-mahi sandwich at CJ's like she was dining on pâté at a Paris café, and the way she rolled over when he woke up in the morning and kissed him gently on the lips before rolling back over to sleep some more.

For his whole life, Jake had lived for being out on the water. The sea air filled his soul and helped him breathe easy. But now he breathed easiest on land, specifically the land that held the house that held the bedroom that held the bed where he laid his head every night next to his beloved, Renee.

> *You are my port in the storm, and I will be by your side for as long as we both shall live.*

A tear fell from Jake's eye onto the paper, smudging the page. He didn't remember the last time he'd cried. Better to get it out now than during the ceremony.

He would read it over and over until it didn't break him.

Wildflowers

♩♫♪

Matt

ON THE MORNING of the wedding, Matt woke Dylan up the same way he had on hundreds of occasions growing up. When they were kids, he was always up before her and would let himself into the back door of her house, slip into her room, and jump on her bed, to the tune of her begging him to stop—no matter that he was now six foot one and had to shield his bent head with his arms to avoid a concussion.

Today was no different.

"Stop it, Matty, I'll drown you in the Great South Bay, I swear."

He stopped and pulled a wishing weed from behind his back, presenting it to her. Half the petals had flown off during the storming of the bed, but she smiled just the same.

"Aw, thank you. I'm glad to see you've matured over the years."

"Maybe," he said with a smirk, lying down next to her on the queen-size bed.

"You know we're both walking down the aisle tonight. Should we practice?"

"I think we can handle it—where's Maggie?"

"She slept in town last night with Jason."

"Do you miss her?"

"No, I don't miss her."

"I call BS, Matthew Tucker."

Matt wet his finger and stuck it in Dylan's ear, shouting "Wet willy" as he did so.

"I guess my analysis was premature—or immature. Get out, I have to get dressed."

Matt headed for the kitchen, where he found his mother standing by the counter with her head in her hands.

"What's wrong?" he joked. "Cold feet?"

"The florist has Covid."

Jake rubbed her back. "Who needs flowers?"

Wrong answer.

"I need flowers," the bride cried.

The groom looked at Matt in desperate need of assistance.

"Maybe I should go fetch the matron of honor."

"Yes, reinforcements!" Jake nodded and put his hands to prayer. He wasn't a praying man.

Matt could tell that as much as this poor guy wanted to please his mother, he was truly in over his head. He and Dylan never even used place mats on their table, let alone floral centerpieces.

"I'm on it," Matt said, grabbing a fistful of Lucky Charms from the open box on the counter and heading across the street for help, where, of course, the door was unlocked.

"Where's Maggie?"

The fact that those were the first words out of Bea's mouth when he entered gave him pause. But he had no time to think of the repercussions of their lies and the shock that this poor woman was in for, not to mention the betrayal. Bea and betrayal didn't mix well. He wished he could just rip off the Band-Aid right there and then. *"Bea—Maggie is your daughter."* It was so obvious to him now; he was shocked that no one else could see it. He guessed it was because the idea was so out of left field, plus they would never have expected Matt to lie to them all.

Why was he lying to them all?

He pushed the unpleasant thoughts away.

"She's in town with her brother. The florist has Covid. There are no flowers, and my mother is a mess."

"We've got this," Bea declared without hesitation before calling upstairs to her sister. "Veronica, I need you!"

"She needs her." Shep peeked above his newspaper from the kitchen table, a prideful smile plastered across his face.

"Veronica is a master at flower arranging," Bea assured Matt.

"I don't think you understand. The florist is from the mainland. We have no flowers. There is nothing to arrange," he said as Veronica descended the stairs.

"But we have gardens!" Veronica proclaimed, hands in the air, descending the stairs like a bony version of Auntie Mame.

"Can you ask your mother how many tables there are and how many bouquets she needs?"

"I know the bouquets—it's Renee, Dylan, Maisie, and Juno, and two buccaneers."

"Boutonnieres," Veronica laughed, until her next realization doused it.

"The chuppah! That's gonna be tough."

"The chuppah is all set. Jake made it himself out of drift-wood and seashells."

"So beautiful, great, OK. Tell her we're on this and come right back—with Dylan," Veronica barked, her face lit with purpose.

"Do you need anything else?"

"We have baskets, white spray paint. Daddy, do you still have those boxes of mason jars in the attic, from Mom's blue-berry jam phase?"

There was a time when wild blueberry bushes were pro-lific on the island. Moms would send their offspring out to collect them in the mornings before it got too hot, and they'd return with full pails and purple-stained lips. They'd all but vanished over the years, along with little bunnies that were once as common a sight as the deer. Matt had no idea why.

During one particularly prolific blueberry summer, after baking muffins and pies and crumbles, Caroline had tried her hand at preserves.

"They're probably in the attic," Shep informed his daugh-ters, referring to their neighbors' house across the street.

They all looked at him suspiciously.

"What?"

"It's been over ten years now; it's not our house anymore. This is our house now," Veronica preached.

Shep smiled again.

"You have no idea how long I have been waiting for you to say that."

Into the Mystic

♩♫♪

Ben

"DADDY, DADDY," MAISIE cried, "please fix my bow like that one."

Little Maisie Morse pointed to a small sculpture of a pair of flower girls dressed in dresses that matched her own, their entirety made from clay except for two pale yellow satin bows tied behind them, not unlike a Degas ballerina. Ben's wife, Addison, was a sculptor. A critically acclaimed one, actually. She had created clay replicas of the flower girls as a wedding gift.

Ben did his darndest to tie the satin bow on the back of Maisie's precious flower girl dress in the same fashion as the sculpture. He did a pretty good job except for the fact that he tied his finger into it as well.

"I guess I have to walk down the aisle with you!" he joked, before carefully wiggling it out.

"No way, Daddy!" Maisie objected, taking a step forward when freed and proudly twirling around in circles as if it were her job.

The two little girls collected their baskets of petals. Just one piece of the lovely floral creations that Veronica had managed to throw together in a few hours' time.

The family of four, his family of four, traveled up the block, where Maisie and Juno stopped to ooh and aah over the bride. Renee looked ethereal in an ivory satin sheath, holding a bouquet of local wildflowers tied in the same color ribbon as the one on the dresses of the girls. It was remarkable how a last-minute cry out to the community for flowers had produced such perfection.

"You guys know what to do?" Addison asked her daughters confidently. Of course they did. Since learning they would be flower girls, they had treated every corridor, path, and hallway as an aisle.

Maisie nodded her head, yes, but her sister's hand went right to her mouth, chomping on her nail like it was lunch. Her dad gently placed it back at her side, but once she got a hold of his, she wouldn't let it go.

"You got this, Juno, just like we practiced."

Her eyes filled with fear.

"You can walk with her," Renee said before bringing Ben in for a hug.

"I feel her too," she whispered in his ear.

She was referring to Ben's first wife, her best friend, Julia. Her physical absence was palpable today, but he was comforted by the fact that Renee felt her spirit as he did.

Juno breathed an audible sigh of relief, causing their serious mood to shift to laughter. Together, they peeked out at the beach.

It felt as if the whole town had come out to see the two lifelong Fire Islanders tie the knot. Aside from the invited guests seated in rows of chairs on the sand, the beach stairs of the surrounding blocks were covered with onlookers, as was the length of sand in front of the dunes. Everyone stood close enough to see, but far enough away not to intrude.

Renee motioned that it was time to begin, and a trio of musicians played the first notes of Van Morrison's musical voyage "Into the Mystic."

A perfect blend of nostalgia and hope, as if the words were written for this exact occasion. The crowd settled soon after the music began, the tune blending beautifully with the crashing waves.

Jake and Dylan walked barefoot across the sand first, their fingers intertwined as tightly as their hearts. It wasn't lost on anybody there that these two had a bond beyond most fathers and daughters. For thirty years they had been each other's person, with no one to come between them. Of course, it was time for them both. They held their warm embrace at the end of the aisle before Jake took his spot under the chuppah.

Ben sent Maisie on her way, spinning down the aisle, dropping petals in her wake, before escorting Juno on his arm. He had a hard time controlling the boyish grin that sprung right from his heart.

Next, Matt reached out his hand to his mother. The two embraced at the top of the stairs, inspiring another collective "aw" from the crowd. They walked, barefoot and hand in hand, to the groom, who was doing his best to fight off tears. It was both shocking and heartwarming to see Jake so verklempt.

Matt and Renee embraced. Matt kissed his mother on the cheek and whispered "I love you" before meeting Dylan under the chuppah. Jake took two steps forward and gathered his bride close and the two did an impromptu dance in the sand, inspiring laughter and happy tears from all the onlookers.

There was something so special about it, as if no one had done this exact dance before.

The rabbi's words of welcome that followed were carried away by the breeze, causing everyone to take a few steps closer to hear them. He spoke about the beauty surrounding them, matching the beauty in Jake and Renee's hearts. The two sweetly spoke the vows they had written themselves to the soundtrack of waves crashing to the shore, before repeating after the rabbi in Hebrew.

Ani L'dodi, v'dodi li.

I am my beloved's, and my beloved is mine.

They exchanged rings and one long passionate kiss under the warm glow of the setting sun. Matt and Dylan joined them, basking in the glow of their new family. Well, three of them were basking; Matt seemed to be somewhere else. Ben followed his eyes to the row behind him, where he was not surprised to find the object of Matt's mystic gaze—Maggie.

TRACK 39

Champagne Problems

♩♫♪

The Dinner Hour According to Chase Logan

CHASE WAS NERVOUS. Not because he was tasked with pouring a hundred glasses of champagne into tall, fragile stemware lined up like soldiers at the exact right time, since nobody likes warm champagne. And not because the caterer, with his unplaceable accent, gave a ten-minute lecture on the subject of pouring said champagne as if they were aboard a fancy yacht in the south of a fancy country Chase had never visited.

"Hold the bottle by the bottom, like a bowling ball, your thumb in the divot, your other four fingers splayed around it. Wet the glass with just a splash of champagne, allowing the bubbles to settle first."

And Chase was not nervous because the Silver sisters would be at the wedding, though judging from the other night at the Salty Pelican, Veronica might become a frequent, and eventually sloppy, visitor to the bar.

Chase was nervous because of Maggie. He had lain awake all night thinking about their interactions before begging his buddy to get him the last-minute position. He wanted to see his daughter again and he had something for her, something that had been burning a hole in his pocket for over thirty years.

Chase could see the throngs of partygoers approaching the dock, each one greeted by the familiar deckhands from the ferry unfamiliarly cleaned up and dressed in white button-down shirts and jackets. He knew 90 percent of the people at the wedding but wouldn't be making much small talk with them because, as the caterer specified, he was not fond of chatty help. The pay was generous, and Chase knew that the more he made in the summers, the longer he could spend surfing in Costa Rica in the winters.

He saw Maggie through the window, walking between Matt and the other guy she had been with at the bar. She was a pretty girl. She carried herself with confidence, and he wondered what her life had been like, whether she had always known she was adopted, and whether she liked her adoptive parents or felt like an alien. Hell, Chase had felt like an alien half the time in his own house while growing up, and he wasn't adopted.

He was surprised that seeing the girl in person had elicited thoughts he had never considered before.

In any case, from the little they had spoken, she seemed very together, educated, and even poised. She was lucky to have grown up without him as a father. That thought made him feel like crap about himself and his lack of accomplishments in life. Who knows, maybe if he had been a father raising a child, he would have risen to the occasion and made something of himself. He hadn't felt this bad since the days of running around with some of the people at this party. They had all gone to schools with fancy names like Skidmore and Swarthmore and I Know More Than You Do, while his future at the time had been predicated on whether or not his uncle could get him into the welders' union.

"It's showtime," the caterer barked.

Chase pushed away his thoughts and took up his position behind the bar.

Float On

♩♫♪

The Dinner Hour According to Renee

JAKE AND RENEE were the last ones to board the wedding ferry, just as the sun took its final bow. Following the ceremony, they had gone for a stroll on the beach, receiving kisses and well-wishes from what seemed like the entire island. It had been challenging to draw the line on who to invite to the party and who to exclude. Miraculously, they had agreed on everyone. Though, as usual, Jake may have agreed to all of Renee's guests if only to bring a smile to her face. While her first marriage had been filled with petty arguments, life with Jake was blissful. He was the definition of a gentle giant.

Renee's face lit up as she took it all in. It was hard to believe they were aboard the *We're Here*, the oldest and largest ferry in the fleet. She had ridden it countless times since she was a child. Jake's crew had spent the entire day decorating every rail and pole with tiny white Christmas lights as a gift to them. The result was magical. White linen cloths were spread on long rectangular tables, and a stunning selection of local spring flowers in borrowed vases and jam jars brought her heart pure joy. She was almost happy it had turned out as it did with the florist; Veronica had done a fabulous job and the community's contribution was far more meaningful.

They headed to the bar for a glass of champagne. With over a hundred people on the boat, Jake's gaze locked on hers as he raised his glass and toasted them, making her feel like they were alone. Except for the bartender, that is. Renee caught sight of him and immediately found his presence distracting. While she had never inquired who would be on the caterer's waitstaff, she was surprised to see Chase Logan. She was happy that Veronica was back on the wagon and hopeful that Paul would fetch Bea's drinks for her, in any case feeling certain that the three of them wouldn't create a disturbance at her wedding over something that happened thirty years ago.

Almost certain.

She dismissed the thought and directed her attention to the present. She knew the night would go by in the blink of an eye.

The first level of the ferry would host dinner and speeches, while dancing and dessert would take place upstairs. According to the party planner, that way of doing things was considered the European style. In truth, there was no other way to configure it, given they were having their party on a ferryboat. It had never been done before on Fire Island and required ingenuity and flexibility.

She was excited for the evening's events, especially the first dance.

Since they had picked the song, she and Jake had practiced almost every night, dancing barefoot on the kitchen floor. In no time, Jake had transformed himself from clumsy and awkward to as smooth as Etta James singing "I Want a Sunday Kind of Love."

Renee's heart expanded as she anticipated taking the floor with the unlikely love of her life, who had been waiting in the wings for half a lifetime.

Landslide

♩♫♪

The Dinner Hour According to Maggie

MAGGIE WAS OVER juggling her real boyfriend and her fake boyfriend. Between that and the weight of tomorrow's revelation, she needed a little liquid courage, until she saw who the bartender was. She didn't need it that badly.

She'd never expected that a New York town, even a beach town, would feel as small as Chagrin Falls. But it did. In just four days, she already felt acquainted with half the people in the room.

"Hi, Maggie!"

"Hey, girl."

"Save me a dance, Maggie."

That one came from her grandfather. Her mind immediately drifted to the thought of dancing with him, arm in arm. She would control herself from taking off her shoes and climbing atop his feet, just one in a host of things she imagined she had missed by not growing up with him. She was still caught up in that image in her head when Matt arrived with two shots in each hand. He held out one each to Jason and Maggie while calling out to Dylan, who came running.

Dylan grabbed her shot and downed it before anyone even had a chance to toast.

"This is gonna be a long night," she laughed, post-shot.

"Don't drink any more until after our speech, please. I don't want a recurrence of the 2013 Labor Day Bar-B-Q."

He turned to Maggie and Jason, eager to relay the coming-of-age story.

"The Labor Day Bar-B-Q here is BYOB, and Dylan got the big idea to collect all the leftover cups with remnants of vodka and gin and wine and mix them together like a milkshake. She ended up swimming out to the dock in her clothes and vomiting into the bay while the whole town looked on."

"Every time we drink, you manage to work in that story. I swear it's the last time I threw up from drinking."

They already sounded like brother and sister.

"Maggie has a worse story," Jason cut in.

"I do not."

"Do too."

"Do not," she said, her lips turning downward, indicating he should keep it to himself.

They sounded like brother and sister too.

"You two are doing the toast?" Jason asked, kindly changing the subject.

"Yes, together. We practiced last night."

"Luckily, it is happening soon, very soon," Matt said.

"Yeah, I can never relax until after something like that is done," Maggie agreed.

Dylan saw a tray of champagne flutes pass by and followed it as Beatrix approached. Maggie's chest burned with heat. Her plan was to steer clear of Bea for one more day until the big reveal. Not one for scenes, she knew that leaving a letter for her would be the best approach, giving her space to reflect, and hopefully, forgive their subterfuge. Also, she was a wimp when it came to confrontation. She once dated an annoying guy in college for a year because he lived across the hall from her and she couldn't bear the thought of the awkward interactions she would face if she broke it off.

"Hi, Maggie, you look beautiful," Bea said, before leaning in for a hug.

"You look beautiful too," Maggie said. She loved the way Bea dressed, smart and classic but not buttoned up. She still wasn't used to seeing so much of herself in someone else. This was an everyday phenomenon she'd completely missed out on growing up, and she was surprised at what a punch it packed now.

"You know, ever since Maggie showed up, I get no love from you," Matt joked.

Bea hugged Matt before looking up at him and sweetly declaring, "You look beautiful too, Matty."

Maggie noted again that the older generation called him Matty. It was endearing to her. Matty was not a name for a grown man in the way that Maggie was for a grown woman. And it wasn't even a nickname, since her parents had named her Maggie, not Margaret. She was happy about that. She was not a Margaret.

Again, thinking of her parents made her feel guilty about the situation that was about to unfold. She uncharacteristically linked her arm through Jason's. He smiled at her gratefully. Maggie knew that she was a little too big on autonomy for Jason's taste; he had a real need to be needed.

"Let's get our table cards," she suggested, yearning for an escape. As they walked away, she let out a huge sigh.

"You'll be fine. Just go with the flow," Jason whispered in her ear.

The flow felt more like a landslide.

"They would want you to have family, Maggie."

Of course he read her mind.

"You're my family," she replied, and meant it.

Family Affair

♩♪♪

The Dinner Hour According to Matt

"IS THAT CHASE Logan tending bar?" Bea whispered to Matt discreetly.

"The one and only." He looked at Bea knowingly as Paul walked over and slipped his arm around her waist.

"Perfect timing, honey. Can you get us cocktails?"

"Of course. Want anything, Matt?" Paul asked on his way.

"No thanks. I'm holding off till after Dylan and I make our toast."

"You're doing it together? That's sweet. Is it funny or serious?" Bea asked.

"Serious enough. We tried to write a funny one, but couldn't stop laughing, so we went in a more traditional direction."

"You ChatGPT'ed it, didn't you?"

"I'm a journalist, you know!"

"C'mon, Matty, you wouldn't lie to me, would you?"

He turned ten shades of green.

"Oooh," she laughed, "it's written all over your face."

"You got me," he said. "Just don't tell my mom."

He did not use AI to write the speech, but probably would have copped to murder to cover for his guilt-ridden appearance when she'd joked about the possibility of him lying to her.

Lucky for him, she changed the subject.

"You know I always thought you and Dylan—"

"You're not the only one."

"I'm sure, but let me finish—after meeting Maggie, well, I've never seen such chemistry. You're like Nick and Nora; you light each other up."

"Nick and Nora? That's an old-school reference."

"Not to me. I teach English lit, remember? I could have referenced Beatrice and Benedick from *Much Ado About Nothing*."

Matt laughed.

Shep approached and handed Matt a drink.

"I'm legal now, Shep," he said, smiling. "No need to sneak me drinks anymore."

"Says the empty-handed man. It's an open bar, you know, my favorite kind."

Matt gave up on his inclination to hold off on drinking and clinked Shep's glass before taking a hefty gulp. And he thought the toast would be the hardest part of the night. The deception around hiding Maggie's identity, and worrying about what everyone would think of him once they found out, was getting to him. Moreover, he was starting to believe that their loving couple ruse was actually the truth; on more than one occasion he had to remind himself that it wasn't. He felt like one of those undercover cops who got in too deep. He needed his handler to grab him by the shoulders and shake him out of it.

"What were you two hobnobbing about?" Shep asked, bringing a smile to both their faces with his Shep-like turn of phrase.

"Were we hobnobbing?" Matt asked Bea with amusement.

"We were just chatting about how wonderful Maggie is, and her brother! Paul and I had a long talk with him about sabbaticals and traveling the world. He has a great career ahead of him. It's a good life, being a professor."

"I don't know the brother, but that girl. There's something about that girl. She warms my old heart," Shep declared. "You did good, Matty."

Dylan came running over, unknowingly saving him. "It's time."

The DJ asked everyone to be seated for dinner before announcing the newly minted brother and sister. They took their place at the front of the boat. It was difficult to get everyone's attention, even with the clinking of glasses and a few ineffective shushes. Finally, Jake stood up, put his pointer fingers in his mouth, and whistled. Of course he could whistle like that. It was impressive. The sounds in the room fell away, and all you could hear was the light clanging of forks and plates as the two new siblings began their toast.

"Good evening, everyone. For the very few who don't know us, I'm Dylan, and this is Matt, and our parents got married today."

The room erupted in applause and laughter.

"That was easy," Dylan whispered to Matt before he chimed in.

"To be honest, when we first learned of our parents' romance, we were more than a little surprised."

"Surprised is a nice way to put it. Matt called me sobbing."

"That's an exaggeration—there were a few tears, maybe one sob," Matt corrected, to more laughter. "Truthfully, though, we had always known that our parents were friends, but to see their friendship blossom into something deeper was, well, nauseating at first, then somewhat tolerable, and now it is honestly pure joy for us both.

"Dylan and I grew up together on Fire Island, and like most of you, it has a strong hold on our hearts. Our parents' love story is intertwined with the fabric of this magical place. They found solace, strength, and love in each other, as we've all found solace, strength, and love in the embrace of this community over the years."

They held up their glasses and spoke in unison.

"So let us raise our glasses to Renee and Jake. May your marriage be as enduring as the lighthouse that guides us home. *L'chaim!*"

"*L'chaim!*" the crowd responded in unison.

It was really something, their parents getting married and knowing their own lives would be intertwined forever. They were truly family now. Matt reached for Dylan's hand and together they took a moment to soak in the love and warmth of the room, or the ferry, in this case, before their parents joined them to thank them for their beautiful words.

Something Good

♩♫♪

The Party According to Dylan

IT WAS DYLAN who switched on the ignition, threw the first punch, fired the shot heard round the world, or around Fire Island at least.

Things had been going swimmingly on the *We're Here*. After dinner, and their killer toast, everyone was invited upstairs for dancing, dessert, and the big surprise—fireworks.

The bride and groom made their grand entrance to the usual, "Let's welcome the happy couple for their first dance as husband and wife."

All eyes were fixed on Renee and Jake as they moved across the dance floor to Etta James crooning their song, "A Sunday Kind of Love." Dylan suddenly found her view blurred by tears. As she'd said in the toast, at first it had seemed bizarre to think of her dad and Matt's mom being together, but she soon saw it as a wonderful thing. She was no longer concerned about Jake's loneliness or his winter diet of canned soup. However, it went beyond that, far beyond. Seeing him glide around the floor as if he were auditioning for *Dancing with the Stars*, gazing into the eyes of his wife, was extraordinary.

Just like the lyrics described, her dad was in love—*a love to last past Saturday night, a love that's more than love at first sight.*

Observing their togetherness in the days leading up to the wedding was inspiring—so much so that it had inspired her to end her relationship with Sunburn Steve—not that it had been much of a relationship to begin with. She was done wasting time on meh. She, too, wanted a Sunday Kind of Love.

Soon, the DJ called the bridal party to the dance floor and Matt asked Dylan to dance. Ben and Addison joined in with their little flower girls. It was an excellent twirling opportunity, and both Maisie and Juno took full advantage of it. Soon, the rest of the guests joined in as well, and despite the more adorable distractions, many eyes were focused on Matt and Dylan, who were clearly the crowd favorites when it came to coupling conjecture. Whispers and wishful speculation around them ran deep. In fact, it wasn't all whispers. On more than one occasion over the long weekend, someone said some variation of "We always thought it would be you two getting hitched."

Dylan knew that they were looking in the wrong direction. Matt was really into Maggie. She could tell by the way he looked at her. She should know. He had looked at her that same way for most of her life and she had been grateful for it. The love and attention he showed her growing up as a motherless island-dwelling weirdo had gone a long way to shape who she was today.

She wondered if Maggie felt the same about Jason. She craned her neck over Matt's shoulder, scanning the crowd for them. She saw Beatrix and Paul swing by, her head resting on his shoulder, Little Les from the market and his beautiful wife looking like they should get a room, and Shep proudly spinning his redheaded younger daughter around the dance floor, both with so much love in their eyes. Everyone was feeling the song, feeling the moment.

And then she saw Maggie and Jason. They were dancing, and they were smiling, but they were deep in conversation. She'd seen it before. Hell, she'd even done it before. That awkward slow dance with a friend, where small talk substituted for passion:

Isn't it a beautiful night?

Could that lady's dress be any uglier?

I was hoping for pigs in the blanket.

Maggie and Jason did not share a Sunday Kind of Love.

She caught Maggie looking in their direction. She quickly looked away, but not before Dylan witnessed the longing look in her eyes.

Dylan's favorite line from *The Sound of Music* popped into her head, and she smiled to herself. She and Matty would watch it on rainy days when they were kids. Back when the totality of their movie choices came from a milk crate brimming with VHS tapes. *The Sound of Music*, along with *The Wizard of Oz*, *Drop Dead Fred*, and *Jumanji*, were played on repeat until they could both recite every line.

"What's funny?" he asked.

She whispered in his ear in her best Austrian baroness accent:

"Somewhere out there is a young lady who I think will never be a nun."

Before Matt even got it, before he could deny it, Dylan made her move. She steered them in the direction of Maggie and Jason, took a step in between them, and said, "May I cut in?"

Maggie's reaction further gave her away. She blushed, her eyes widened, and a telling grin formed on her face. Though she quickly tucked away her emotions, it was too late. It was obvious that Maggie very much wanted to dance with Matt.

And Dylan was left to make small talk with a reluctant dance partner.

"Isn't it a beautiful night?" she asked Jason.

As Matt and Maggie sashayed by, clearly lost in the music and each other's eyes, Jason was barely listening to her. His gaze was fixed on his fiancée and Matt, who were dancing as if they had been dancing together all their lives.

"Wow, they're really laying it on thick for the crowd," Dylan noted.

Jason shook his head in the way one does when one's mind is elsewhere.

Time was running out for Matt and Maggie to realize what was so obvious to Dylan—but she hadn't taken poor Jason's feelings into account when manipulating the situation. He was a nice guy. She felt badly about it.

"Maggie's a good actress," she added, hoping to ease his pain.

"Actually, she's not. Like really not."

Maggie and Matt sashayed by again. The boat could have sunk beneath them, and they wouldn't have noticed.

"Will you excuse me?" Jason asked. "I don't feel much like dancing. I'm going to go down for a drink. Want anything?"

"I'm fine, thanks."

Dylan stood and watched for a bit more while Matt sang the last verse in Maggie's ear, "A Sunday, Sunday, Sunday kind of love," and though she knew that this corny old song and the woman who was singing it were probably one of his old-school favorites, she also knew that his display was spurred by more than loving Etta James. Matt was loving Maggie.

The song ended and the two of them came flying off the dance floor in Dylan's direction, still hand in hand.

"Where's J?" Maggie asked, quickly enough. She abruptly dropped Matt's hand.

It was obvious that Maggie loved Jason deeply. But Dylan loved Matt deeply, so she knew the deal. It wasn't enough.

"He went downstairs, to the bar," she answered.

Maggie's face fell. Not quickly and all at once, more like a pinpricked pool float slowly losing air.

"I'm going to go and find him," she stated, and headed for the steps.

She was no longer sashaying.

Flowers

♩♫♪

The Party According to Veronica

ALL THE ROMANCE and coupling around her had Veronica surprisingly pining for her husband. She had hardly been in touch with him since her arrival, partially to torture him a little, and partially because of the Fire Island effect: stepping off the ferry and immediately forgetting the rest of the world's existence.

Now she found herself not only longing to hear his voice but longing to share the story of how she had saved the day—florally speaking. It had been a long time since Veronica had longed for anything more than the weekly cigarette she poached from her pool guy.

As if reading her mind, Renee approached.

"Veronica," she gushed, "how can I ever thank you. The arrangements are stunning! I'm so happy you are here!"

Veronica's smile was so big, it almost cracked her Botox.

Renee moved on through the crowd, and Veronica headed downstairs to the back of the boat to get away from the music and make a phone call, snapping pictures of her floral center-pieces along the way. She felt like a million bucks from being needed and creating the arrangements, and two million bucks after hearing the guests' and Renee's reactions to her creations. They looked magnificent, if she said so herself, beachy and bright. She was on more than one planning committee for charity benefits in LA, all in need of centerpieces and whatnot. They would probably be thrilled to have her do the flowers.

Flowers by Veronica, she thought with a "dare she dream" type of grin. She repeated it again, but it wasn't quite right.

Fleurs par V, she thought, brushing her hand across the air as if it were on a marquee.

Her grin exploded. She swallowed it and headed sternward.

Veronica the florist whisked past the bar, trying to avoid the venomous gaze of the bartender. From what she remembered of the other night, Veronica the drunk had made quite a scene at the Salty Pelican. It was a good thing she didn't care what Chase Logan thought of her.

Who was she kidding? She cared what everyone thought of her.

She stopped to order a seltzer, intent on making a sober second impression to counter Thursday's train wreck. Maybe she could change Chase's narrative from Veronica-Silver-still-has-issues to Veronica-Silver-had-one-very-unfortunate-night.

As she approached the bar, she caught sight of Maggie and her brother having words in the foreground, before storming off. It left her curious.

"A seltzer with a splash of cranberry and a lime, please," Veronica ordered, as if Chase were a stranger.

He seemed happy to play it that way too. But curiosity got the better of her, or was it nosiness?

"Sibling squabble?" she asked Chase, gesturing to Maggie and Jason in the distance as he mixed her drink.

She had come at the right time. A line was forming behind her.

"More like a lovers' quarrel. She's two-timing him."

"How do you know?"

"I'm a bartender. I know everything."

"Yeah, well, you don't know this. That's her brother."

Veronica took her drink and continued on her way. She slipped out to the open back deck and rummaged for her phone. It was a beautiful night with a full moon rising over the water. Maybe she would FaceTime Larry. Since noticing the appearance of fine lines around her eyes and those threatening jowls, moonlight had become her best filter. Two guests from the party were kissing in the corner, making the prospect of FaceTime feel voyeuristic. Then the couple broke apart.

It was Maggie and Jason.

"*Oh my God!*" Veronica blurted out, loud enough to wake the fishes.

Poker Face

♩♫♪

The Party According to Matt

"THAT DOESN'T SOUND good!" Matt reacted to the loud "*Oh my God!*" coming from the bow of the boat.

He had been fielding a lengthy inquisition from Dylan that had begun on the dance floor and ended up at the bar. He was happy for a subject change. The subject had been Maggie.

"What's wrong?" Dylan had prodded.

"Nothing's wrong. I'm good," he'd told her with a smile.

"A good liar," Dylan rebutted.

"Stop. Let's just get through the night, send Maggie and Jason off on the ten a.m. ferry, and be done with this whole charade."

"About that. She's going to leave a letter for Beatrix and take off?"

"Yes. We thought it would be better that way. Let Bea digest it all and then they could meet up another time in Ohio, if Bea's even still interested."

"If she's even still interested? She's been dreaming of this day for thirty years, and now Maggie is leaving you to hold the bag."

"Wow. That big sister pill you swallowed was fast-acting!" Not that Dylan had ever needed a pill to be protective of Matt, or him of her.

"I'm serious, Matty."

"It's OK. I'll handle it. Let's please drop it tonight and enjoy our parents' wedding." He laughed as he said it, before adding, "This is all so much bigger than me and my crush."

"I knew it. Did you—you know?"

"Of course not. She's engaged. You know how I feel about cheating."

He didn't count their dramatic kiss at the bakery. That was for the children.

"Yeah, it's just—I don't see it with those two."

"It's not for us to see. Clearly, we are looking for different things than they are."

It was all so complicated.

"Let's get drunk," he said, grabbing her hand and pulling her along.

The bar was empty when they reached it. No takers and no servers. Dylan went to help herself, and that's when they heard someone scream, "*Oh my God!*" in a high-pitched tone.

Dylan left the glass and grabbed the bottle.

They followed the sound of the ruckus to the back of the boat, where they found Chase handing a cell phone to Veronica. Maggie and Jason were standing with their backs pressed up against the rails. Maggie was looking over her shoulder, as if she were considering jumping. Even without knowing what had happened, you could feel the tension in the air.

"You left this at the bar," Chase snarked at Veronica, handing her back her phone.

"Thank you," she barely managed.

He looked like he had more to say, but turned, practically slamming into Matt and Dylan.

"Matt!" Veronica stepped up. "I'm sorry to tell you this, but Jason is not Maggie's brother. At least I hope not."

She looked back at Jason and Maggie, who both shook their heads in vigorous confirmation.

"I just saw them kissing," V added, in a softer tone.

Dylan piped in, "I'm sure it was just brotherly love. Look!" she said, before planting a big smooch on Matt's lips, trying her best to defuse the bomb.

"He's not my son, is he?" Chase steadied himself while Jason and Maggie shook their heads even more vigorously.

"We're the couple," Maggie said, motioning to Jason, before adding, "Not me and Matt."

"Why would you think he's your son?" Veronica asked Chase.

"Well, she's my daughter, and you said they were siblings." Chase got right in Veronica's face, primed to give her a piece of his mind. "You know what, Veronica, I may not be well educated and live at a fancy address, but I'm a good person. I take care of my mom, and I rescued a dog last year. An old dog that they were gonna put down 'cause no one wanted him. You and Bea could have told me my daughter was in town. I would have liked to let her decide about me for herself, regardless of whatever you two poisoned her with."

"Wait, what?" Veronica was gobsmacked. She turned slowly and approached Maggie, taking her face into her hands, and staring into her eyes until her own threatened tears.

"Oh my God. I knew you felt familiar to me. I just

couldn't . . ." And then she snapped, "Wait, what the hell is going on here? Is this some kind of fleece job?"

Maggie froze. Matt stepped forward.

"Not at all. Just tell her, Maggie."

Again, Maggie looked over her shoulder like she was going to jump, before turning to face the music.

"It's complicated, but I don't want anything from anyone, if that's what you're thinking. I just wanted to meet my birth mother. And things got very out of hand."

She smiled and reached out her hand to her aunt.

"It's nice to meet you, Aunt Veronica."

"Aunt Veronica," V repeated in awe, before her tears escaped.

Chase handed V a cocktail napkin from his pocket and stepped between them, putting his hands on Maggie's shoulders—just short of a hug.

"I want you to know that I didn't know you existed until recently, and only figured out who you were on your second visit to the bar."

Maggie nodded, while Chase continued, "I hope your parents were good to you, and you had a happy childhood," as if he had rehearsed it. He probably had.

"They were, they were the best, and I did, very happy," she assured him.

"If you want to talk more, or if you ever need anything, my bike, or even a kidney, you know where to find me," he added, choking back tears of his own.

Both Matt and Jason watched carefully, ready to intervene at any moment—though it didn't seem to be going in a bad direction, and clearly Maggie could take care of herself.

Maybe Dylan was right about Chase. Maybe he wasn't a bad guy.

As if reading Matt's mind, Chase reached into his pocket, placed something in Maggie's hand, and shut her fingers tight around it. He held her closed fist in his while he continued.

"Bea was right to be upset by what happened back then. Now that I'm older, I realize that she meant something to me. More than I knew when I was an idiot kid." He squeezed her hand again before releasing it.

"I kept this the whole time and I want you to have it. Just so you know it wasn't all bad."

Maggie opened her fist to reveal the surfboard necklace with Chase and Bea's initials inscribed on it that her bio-mother had thrown at her bio-father on that infamous night a lifetime ago. Her lifetime ago.

Now Maggie's eyes began to prickle with tears. Chase handed her a cocktail napkin too, along with a smile and a quick, "I gotta go," before heading back to his station.

At this point, Dylan was the only one thinking straight. She took control.

"If that teary scene didn't prove that we should wait to tell your sister until after the party, I don't know what does," Dylan said to Veronica, urgency in her voice.

Matt was glad she did. Their parents deserved this night.

Veronica nodded in agreement.

"You promise?" Maggie asked, already quite aware of her aunt's self-serving tendencies.

"I promise," Veronica repeated.

Maggie warmly laid her hand on her aunt's arm and continued, "I was going to tell her tomorrow in a letter, but I won't put you in the position of lying to her. I know you just got over all of that. I'll tell her tonight, after the party."

Matt did his best stay on top of the situation—even with how much he cared for Maggie, his mother's big night was still top of mind.

He recapped for the group, "OK. We'll explain everything later. Let's go enjoy the rest of the wedding and keep the fireworks in the sky, where they belong."

Firework

♩♫♪

The Party According to Beatrix

"HOW FRIZZY IS my hair?" Bea asked Paul, as she tried to tame the curls with her fingertips.

"You look beautiful."

She hadn't been looking for a compliment, but she took it graciously. It was so nice to be loved as a wife, to be stuck together through fat and frizz. She glanced again at the untended bar.

"So typical that this guy is MIA."

"Here he comes," Paul said, pointing to Chase approaching.

"Never thought I'd be happy to see you," Bea quipped on his arrival, before immediately regretting it. She had promised herself on the short walk downstairs that she wouldn't engage, that it was beneath her and would make it appear that she was still bothered by the past. But she had never had self-control in that way. With her, it was always: in her head, out her mouth.

He looked oddly hurt by her words, almost as if he was about to cry.

They ordered two glasses of white wine and headed back upstairs. It was time for the fireworks. As Bea turned the corner, she saw Veronica hit the bar. She paused, double-checking that her sober sister was ordering plain seltzer. What she witnessed next was possibly more concerning.

Were the two having words?

"What was that about?" she asked when V had reached the top of the stairs, without a beverage in hand.

"Nothing, I'll tell you later."

"Tell me now," she insisted, with adamant older sister authority.

Veronica stood motionless, unable to speak. It was clearly not nothing, Bea thought, as others began to ascend the stairs toward them. She put her hand on her sister's shoulder and gently shook it.

"What is it?"

In the foreground, Renee and Jake gestured upward, prompting the crowd to erupt in applause. Fireworks boisterously lit the night sky, casting bursts of color on the calm bay and the upturned faces of the wedding guests.

All but two.

"Maggie is your daughter," Veronica managed above the racket.

On the outside Bea looked expressionless, as if Veronica had said nothing of any importance. She felt lightheaded and her ears seemed clogged. She could see the fireworks lighting up the sky, but she could barely hear them.

She had never felt so confused in all her life.

Maggie was not close enough to hear the words that came out of Veronica's mouth, but from Bea's head, cocked to the side and covered in shock, it was easy to figure out what they were. There was no denying the expression on Bea's face. For whatever reason, Veronica had told her.

"Oh boy," Matt said out loud. Jason just shook his head, while reaching for Maggie. She stepped forward, unsurprisingly pushing aside both Matt and Jason to go it alone.

Maggie stepped between the sisters, looked into her mother's tear-filled eyes, and squeezed her own tight, trying to keep her composure.

"Is it true?" Bea asked, rendering Maggie speechless.

Maggie let out a sob and nodded her head.

The color drained from Bea's skin, and her eyes grew wide and intense. They scrutinized Maggie's face, as if she were an alien from another planet. Maggie must have mistaken her expression for anger, because she pleaded:

"Please, don't be angry, Matt is not really my boyfriend, he was just helping me. I came here to find you. I was going to tell you after the wedding, tonight," she had to shout it over the oohs and aahs the fireworks were prompting from the wedding guests.

Bea felt her shock dissipate, replaced with a feeling she would later describe as pure joy. She leaned in and took her daughter's face in her hands.

"My baby?" she said, mouthing the words more than speaking them.

"Yes, I'm your baby," Maggie managed before her mother opened her arms and pulled her into what may have been the sweetest, most welcome embrace either of them had ever experienced.

And it all fell away: the pain, the betrayal, the longing, all instantly replaced by love. They held each other so tightly that Bea felt like she would shatter into a million pieces if Maggie were to let go.

Those who understood what was happening cried too, and in Veronica's case all-out weeping, miraculously paying no mind to her makeup. Matt and Jason found themselves embracing in a giant bear hug. When they broke away, Jason explained the basics to Paul, whose eyes immediately welled with happiness as Matt panned the crowd for Shep to do the same. He barely got the words out when the old man rushed over and threw his arms around his daughter and granddaughter. The two women broke away, laughing through their tears.

"Can you believe this, Daddy?" Bea managed.

Shep squeezed Maggie's face, absorbing every inch of it.

"How did I not know?"

He hugged her again just as the explosive grand finale faded in the night sky, followed by a round of applause and then . . . silence.

"I see my mamma in you, like I see her in Bea," Shep cried. Which set everyone off again, especially Maggie. Shep wiped a tear from her face as the iconic first notes of Donna Summer's "Last Dance" echoed from the speakers.

"May I have the last dance with my granddaughter, please?"

"I would love that," Maggie said, collecting herself.

Beatrix and Veronica watched, arm in arm, along with Paul and the others, as grandfather and granddaughter spun around the dance floor. When the tempo picked up, they all joined in, the celebration turning back to the bride and groom, or so they thought.

When the party was over, Beatrix watched Maggie quietly make her way to the lifeguard / bartender / devil-may-care ejaculator. As much as it annoyed her, she was happy that her daughter had been raised to be such a decent person.

Maggie returned with his number scribbled on a cocktail napkin.

"One thing," Bea asked, careful not to begin their relationship by prying about the conversation with Chase. "You and Matt?"

"I'll tell you everything on the way home."

"It seems like we need more time than that. Do you really have to leave tomorrow?" Bea asked, putting her hands to prayer.

"I really should get back to the store. And Jason definitely needs to go back to work."

She knew Phoebe Buffay would be happy to cover for her, but she also knew she should be heading home with Jason.

"Can you come to the house for a bit? We have so much to catch up on."

"Of course," Maggie said, adding, "There's plenty of time to sleep when I'm dead," in her best Shep imitation. Bea laughed, before linking her arm through her daughter's.

"Good. Let's go home!"

Mother and Child Reunion

♩♫♪

Maggie

MAGGIE AND BEATRIX led the barefoot procession home, arm in arm, their party shoes dangling at their sides. Maggie marveled at the ease she felt with her birth mother. The four days when only one of them was aware of the weight of their connection helped. There was none of the awkwardness and tiptoeing she imagined would have occurred if she had straight up introduced herself. This was not a normal mother and child reunion.

Her brain cued up the Paul Simon song of the same name and she did her best not to hum the first notes.

Beatrix suggested they walk on the beach and Maggie was happy to. She would miss the beach. She would miss this magical island, and Shep and her birth mother, of course. Even Veronica had grown on her. But if she was being true to herself and completely honest about what she had felt over the past four days, she would miss Matt most of all.

She turned to see him walking a few steps behind with Jason and Dylan. She caught Jason's eye, and he shook his head in a "Can you believe it?" way. He loved her so much, it was as if this was happening to him as much as her. Maggie decided against being true to herself and went with her old standby, being true to Jason. It had worked for her thus far and she wasn't about to jeopardize it for some guy who had slipped into her heart just when it was cracked wide open.

Dylan hiked her dress up to her knees and dashed in and out of the ocean's edge while Matt and Jason spoke about who knew what. Ben and Addison also tagged along, towing their wagon of sleeping flower girls over the packed sand at the shoreline. Paul and Shep were standing between them, Shep clearly talking their ears off.

The bride and groom, far in the distance, were bringing up the rear.

When they reached their block, Beatrix asked Maggie if she'd like to hang back a bit so they could be alone, sit on the steps, and catch up. It was a beautiful night and there was certainly a lot to catch up on.

"I hope you'll be returning next summer, Maggie," Shep said before pulling her in for an old-man bear hug. When he finally let go, he climbed up a few stairs and announced:

"I have something to say."

"What a surprise," Ben ribbed. "You know, Shep, you should really consider doing a TED Talk."

Even Maggie knew this was their schtick. She had been using a lot of Yiddish lately, dipping her toe into the vernacular of the tribe without even meaning to.

"I think this night is worthy of some old-man wisdom," Shep declared, and launched ahead.

"You know, I've spent near sixty years on this glorified

sandbar. No matter where I go or what I do, all roads lead me back to this narrow spit of sand." He pointed to Matt and Dylan. "It's why these two whippersnappers always return, no matter where life takes them, and it's where Ben and I escaped to when Caroline and Julia went and left us. It's where beautiful Addison came for seven weeks and stayed for seven years. All roads lead us here. This is our Rome. I hope it becomes your Rome too, Maggie. I know you must leave in the morning, but I want you to know you are always welcome. I think I can speak for everyone here when I say—you stole our hearts."

"Veni, vidi, vici," Ben proclaimed, keeping with the Roman theme, before loosely translating it for the few confused faces in the group.

"She came, she saw, she conquered."

"She certainly did," Dylan added in a knowing tone.

"What's going on here?" Renee asked, showing up late to the party.

"I'll explain it all at home," Matt assured her, wrapping his arm around his mother's shoulders, and pulling her in for a hug. Renee bent his head down and kissed the top of it.

"My sweet boy," she said, effusive with love.

"Whatever you have to say, you better make it quick, Matty. It's our wedding night," Jake warned.

"Ewwww, gross, Daddy," Dylan laughed as they all helped Ben and Addison lift their precious cargo up and over the stairs.

Paul gave his wife a quick peck on the lips. "You OK?" he asked quietly.

"More than OK."

Jason did the same to Maggie. And Bea and Maggie watched them all go before getting comfortable on the second-to-bottom step, both happily wiggling their toes in the cold night sand. There was so much ground to cover.

"I really wish you weren't leaving in the morning."

"Wow, didn't take you long to tap into that Jewish Mom guilt, huh?"

They laughed a little too hard. They must have both needed it. But when the laughter had subsided, Beatrix quickly took it in another direction.

"Seriously, though, Maggie, I'm so sorry."

"I'm the one who should be sorry. For deceiving you all week."

"Oh my goodness, don't give that another thought. It was brilliant to try to get to know me before committing. I'm surprised you even stuck around after seeing that horrible scene between Veronica and me."

"We have Matt to thank for that—he convinced me to stay, that you were worth it. Wait," Maggie added. "Why are you sorry?"

"Because I gave you up without any idea of where you would end up."

"Never be sorry for that. I am endlessly grateful for what you did, really. I had the most wonderful parents and a childhood in a beautiful place."

"You can't imagine what it means to me to know that. I hoped and prayed that was the case, but sometimes my mind would take me to awful places."

Beatrix took off her pashmina wrap, spread it out on the sand, and patted it.

"Let's get comfortable."

The two women lay next to each other, heads on the blanket, eyes on the stars.

"Tell me everything!" Beatrix said.

"I'll try," Maggie replied.

For the next hour or so she did just that. There was so much to say, so much Bea had missed. Her questions were endless; Maggie did her best to answer each one before another popped out of Bea's mouth. When she felt satisfied with their coverage of the past, Bea moved on to the future.

By now, she had turned on her side, staring at her daughter.

"You know, it's funny. This weekend, I didn't doubt any of it. Even for a second. You and Matt seem made for each other, and you and Jason really do seem like brother and sister."

Bea laughed until it was obvious that Maggie wasn't joining in. She somewhat changed the subject.

"Oh my God, Jason! I forgot about Jason."

"Don't worry. Paul took him back to the house. I'm sure they're both sound asleep on the couch by now."

Maggie looked at her phone. There was a text from Matt, but she didn't read it.

"It's almost three a.m.! We should go. I'm leaving on the ten o'clock boat."

They grabbed their stuff and headed home to collect Jason. Maggie stopped in her tracks in front of Matt's house. The lights were out. The whole street seemed to be asleep.

"It's so quiet and dark," she remarked.

"I used to love that when I was a teenager. Coming home late at night when the entire street was sleeping. I would picture everyone cozy in their beds."

"This place is unbelievable," Maggie said quietly.

"It truly is."

"Is every block like this?"

"You mean close?"

"I mean like family."

"Some are, for sure. But I like to think ours is special."

Maggie read Matt's text.

> Come by when you're done.

Along with a selfie they took on the dance floor.

When she looked at the photo, her heart dropped to her stomach and an enormous smile crept across her face.

"What?" Bea asked. "What does it say?"

Maggie did her best to rein in her smile, but as soon as she flashed the picture to Bea, it escaped again.

Bea silently raised her eyebrows.

"Don't," Maggie said.

"I'm not," Bea replied.

Their dynamic was already familial.

She texted Matt back.

> Sorry it's so late. I'm sure you are sound
> asleep.

Before she could walk away, the light in his bedroom flicked on.

"Damn," she said under her breath.

"I'll leave you be," Beatrix offered, and headed home.

Matt opened his window and shout-whispered, "Come up."

Maggie shook her head and pointed to her watch.

"I'll come down."

"Don't," she said, her eyes immediately filled with tears. She collected herself as best she could and added, "Come see us off in the morning?"

"OK, I will. And, Maggie . . ."

"What?"

He took a beat.

"Nothing. It can wait till morning."

Growin' Up

♩♫♪

Maggie

MAGGIE LOOKED AT the clock at the Inn in the way one does when calculating how many (or few) hours of sleep are possible if one were to fall asleep that very second. It was the fourth time she had done so. Maggie couldn't sleep.

"What's wrong?" Jason asked, similarly restless.

"Nothing. Just processing the weekend."

"You sure that's it, Maggie?"

She tried to speak, to say, "Yes, I'm sure," but she felt physically ill. All she could manage was a grunt.

Jason leaned over and switched on the lamp.

"Look, Mags, I was going to wait till we got home to tell you this, but I think maybe now is better. You know I would do anything to make you happy, right?"

Her lips pressed firmly together, she nodded again.

"Well, after watching you the past few days—I'm having doubts."

"What kind of doubts?"

"Doubts that I can make you happy."

"That's ridiculous. You make me happy."

He listened and she rolled over and closed her eyes, before rolling back to face him.

"Do I make you happy?" she asked.

"Yes."

It was the weakest *yes* she'd ever heard.

"What is it, Jason?"

"I just think maybe we want different things."

"Like what?"

"Do you mind if I turn the light out?" he asked sheepishly. She didn't blame him. This conversation was hard to face head-on.

She smiled at him. "You're the one who turned it on."

He switched it off.

"Well, for starters, you want to spend your life above your record shop, rarely leaving the town we grew up in. And I get that you're deeply connected to it, and that you long to be surrounded by memories of your mom and dad, but—"

"Stop. You're only saying all of this because you saw something between Matt and me—I have been lying here thinking about it too, and I know it was just the excitement of the weekend that you saw. You're my person. You always have been." Even in the dark, she looked deep into his eyes.

"You're my anchor," she added, touching his cheek with the back of her hand. He rolled over on his back, speaking straight up toward the ceiling, without having to look at her.

"About that, Maggie. I don't really want to be an anchor. I want to see the world. I want to study abroad and teach abroad. My favorite part of this weekend was talking to Paul and Bea about their travels and sabbaticals. It's one of the main reasons I became a professor."

Maggie wondered where this was coming from, his true feelings or, as she suspected, an elaborate invention. "This isn't working, J," she said. "I know you're making this up to set me free."

He switched the light back on, got out of bed, unzipped his backpack, and handed her a printed form.

"What's this?"

"A frequent flyer credit card application."

"This is your proof? We shouldn't get married because you applied for a new credit card on the airplane? I need a little more than that, sorry."

"I love you, Maggie, but I think I've been living your adventures for too long. I want to have some of my own."

"You're just saying all this because you think I like Matt."

"I don't think, Maggie, I know. It's all right there in your eyes. You don't look at me the way you look at him."

"How do I look at him?"

"You look at him like a new album that comes into the shop, when you can't wait to rip off the wrapper, place it on the turntable, and soak up every track before playing it over and over again. And you look at me like your worn-out copy of 'Big Yellow Taxi' that you put on when you're feeling blue and sentimental. They're both love, don't get me wrong, but there's a difference."

His eyes were on the ceiling through this whole speech, but now he turned to her.

"I want to be looked at like that, Maggie. But not right now. Right now, I want to see the world."

"But I belong with you, Jason. I—I always have," she stammered.

"And you always will. You'll always be my best friend. But

I think you may belong with Matt now. It's obvious to everyone."

"It's so late, and I'm so tired, I can't think straight."

He placed his hand lovingly on her head and whispered:

"Go to sleep."

A few minutes later Maggie whispered:

"Are you still up?"

"Yes."

She swallowed the lump in her throat, before asking, quite
painfully:

"Do you think this is our last sleepover?"

"I do."

Her eyes filled with tears, and he pulled her close. While
she lay in his arms, a stunning thing happened. She felt as if
she were being unfaithful, to her heart.

TRACK 49

Real Love

♩♫♪

Matt

LATE THAT NIGHT, after Matt had watched Maggie walk away in the moonlight through his bedroom window, he had fought the overwhelming desire to run downstairs, sweep her off her bare feet, and confess everything he had been feeling since the first moment she'd smiled at him.

Meeting Jason had only made matters worse. Matt had scrutinized and evaluated him, searching for faults, but found none. He may have been the nicest guy Matt had ever met. Plus, their bond seemed unbreakable. Not unlike his and Dylan's. But his feelings for Maggie were completely different from his feelings for Dylan, or anyone else for that matter. Even though they had only just met, he worried he might never stop thinking about her.

When she had walked out of the shower the other day, completely enveloped in his big old bathrobe, he went weak at the knees. The only other time he remembered feeling that sensation was when he was a kid at Yankee Stadium. Ben had hung a set of press credentials around his neck and taken him into the locker room to meet his hero, Derek Jeter. Jeter went to shake Matt's hand, and Matt had to press his knees to-gether to keep them from buckling. He couldn't even speak, hardly able to wrangle himself enough to get his ball signed. Matt begged Ben not to share the incident with the guys on the Bay Harbor ball field but Ben couldn't resist. Matt had barely survived the ribbing he got that summer.

How would he get it together to say goodbye to Maggie at the boat in a few hours, when looking at her out the window, for possibly the last time, made him want to vomit?

All the possible scenarios ran through his head, and none were good.

He canceled his alarm and drifted off, composing different versions of banal texts in his head: Sorry I overslept, it was great to meet you. Good luck with everything.

Turned out his alarm went off anyway—in the form of Dylan clanging two pots in his ear.

"Wake up, Romeo!"

"Stop," he whined, burying his head under his pillow.

"I heard you last night promising that girl you would see her off. If you want to brush those rancid teeth first, you'd better get out of bed."

"I'm not going. Leave me alone."

"What do you mean you're not going?"

"I'm not going. What's the point?"

"My point is you are clearly crazy about her."

"Not your point—I know your point. What's the point of me going?" he groused, with the sourest of expressions. "Don't answer. I don't need you to be my cheerleader here; just leave me be." He rolled over to face the wall.

Dylan climbed over him and wedged herself between the wall and his face, demanding his attention.

"I can't. I can't leave you be. The last time I saw that *holy crap* look on your face was when that guy from Scoops gave us a five-gallon vat of birthday cake ice cream to take home on Tumbleweed Tuesday."

"And I was sick to my stomach for a week after."

"Yeah, well, my bet is it will be two weeks this time. Maybe longer."

"Leave me alone. I mean it, Dylan. I'm hungover and not doing this."

The newlyweds stuck their heads in the door.

"Not doing what?" Renee asked.

"He's not going to the boat to tell Maggie how he really feels about her."

"I told you!" Jake swatted Renee's arm.

"This whole conversation is moot. It's too late." Matt tapped on the decades-old alarm clock next to his bed. "Look: nine fifty-eight. The boat leaves at ten."

"Well, it's a good thing your new dad is the one person on this island who can hold a ferry," said Jake.

"Oh my God, that's the first time you said that," Renee gushed.

"I love you, Jake, really I do, but even if you do stop the boat, I'm not calling you Dad."

"Does that mean I should stop the boat?"

Matt paused. Dylan screamed, "Nine fifty-nine!"

"Fine," Matt conceded.

Jake whipped out his cell and dialed a crew member. When the call was answered, he commanded, "Hold the boat!"

Two seconds later, he held the phone out to his side and addressed the three anxious faces in front of him.

"It already left."

"No!" Dylan and Renee shouted.

"Oh well, you tried," Matt conceded—clearly relieved.

Jake put his phone back to his mouth.

"Turn the boat around!" he ordered. "Of course I'm serious. Have you ever heard me make a joke?"

He put his phone aside again, this time with a big smile.

"It's done. Go get her."

Dylan licked her fingers, wiped down Matt's cowlick, and took her gum out of her mouth.

"Here," she said, popping it in his mouth, "it still has lots of flavor in it."

Aside from the chewing, he froze.

"I don't know what to say to her," he bemoaned.

"Just say anything," Dylan advised.

Matt's face lit up at her suggestion. He grabbed his old boom box from on top of his desk and bolted, stopping only to warn the three of them:

"Don't follow me."

Obviously, they didn't listen.

TRACK 50

In Your Eyes

♩♫♪

Maggie

MAGGIE SAT ON the ferry, staring off at the bay. She had spent the morning imagining what she would say to Matt—and what he would say to her. A scenario where he didn't show up at all was not among the choices she had envisioned. She composed a text but didn't bother sending it. It had been a late night, to say the least. Maybe he had overslept. She went with that.

Maggie's feelings about the last five days hadn't even begun to catch up to her. Even with the crazy winding road she had taken to get there, she knew that her life would forever be divided in two, like a line in the sand—before Fire Island, and after.

She was happy to be leaving, though. The island had a way of swallowing you up and making you forget that anything existed outside of it. She wanted to go home, plant her feet firmly on the ground of her landlocked town, and unpack all that had happened.

But as the boat pulled away, quite unceremoniously, she felt an aching pain deep in her soul, as if she had left something behind. She twisted her mood ring on her finger. It was black.

"I'm sorry he didn't show," Jason said consolingly.

"It's fine. It's better for me not to go from one lifeboat to the next. You know, stand on my own two feet for a bit."

"You stand on your own two feet all the time."

"Yes, but you are always there to catch me when I fall."

"That will never change, Maggie. I'll always be here for you."

"Me too," she said, squeezing his knee for reassurance.

Suddenly, the boat began to turn.

"What's going on? Is this normal?" Jason asked the couple in front of them.

"Not in the fifty years I've been here," the older gentleman replied, before standing to face the shore.

"I see a man on the edge of the dock, holding something high over his head," the man reported.

Jason stood too, and squinted at the distant sight.

"I see him too." He looked down at Maggie. "There's a guy holding something in the air with both hands." He squinted more, and then opened his eyes wide, trying to focus on the image in the distance. "He looks like . . ."

"John Cusack in *Say Anything*?" Maggie asked, still facing sternward, her butt flat on the bench.

"Exactly!" the older man said.

"Yes," Jason concurred with a mixture of happiness and wistfulness. "This guy is a little corny, Mags. Are you sure about him?"

A single tear rolled down her cheek.

"I'm not sure at all, Jason. I love you. So much."

He sat back down next to her.

"I love you so much too, Mags. That's not changing."

She wiped her cheek and kissed him goodbye.

"I'll see you back home," she whispered, the words getting caught in her throat. "And Jason?"

"Yes, Maggie?"

"Thank you for knowing me better than I know myself."

The boat pulled into the harbor. Some people on board stood and waved at the small crowd who had gathered on the dock: Shep, Beatrix, Veronica, Dylan, Renee, and Jake. And some just sat, checking their watches, calculating the time lost, or questioning the crew, trying to make heads or tails of the unusual ferry ride.

But only one, Maggie May Wheeler, grabbed her bag and flew down the steps, her feet barely touching the ground, her heart clenching in her chest so tightly that she could barely breathe.

She arrived at the gate before the ferry landed and shuffled her feet in place until a crew member finally pulled it open.

And there he was. Just Matt. Standing away from the others, boom box now at his feet.

"You came to say goodbye?" Maggie asked breathlessly after stepping off the boat.

"I came to say hello," Matt said, wrapping his arms around her.

As the ferry pulled away again, the Matty and Maggie Fan Club waited patiently in the background. Matt held Maggie's face in his hands and looked into her eyes, before kissing her with five days of pent-up longing. It felt more like five years' worth. Everything she had always thought to be make-believe suddenly came true—her stomach dropped to her toes, her knees shook, and a tingling sensation traveled up and down her spine. She reached her hands around Matt's neck to steady herself. Looking deep into his eyes, she basked in their reflection of a wonder and certainty that matched her own. It was almost too much. She held his gaze until she had to look away, burying her head in his chest, wiping errant tears on his T-shirt.

The peanut gallery couldn't take it any longer. With wide arms and even wider hearts, they stormed the party of two, enveloping them in a group hug.

As Maggie's wobbly legs grew strong, her breath light, and her heart full, fuller than it had ever felt before, she caught sight of her mood ring on her hand. It was bright violet, to match her eyes and her heart. Violet signals romance, abundance, and clarity. She had never felt so abundantly clear in all her life.

The group finally broke apart, and Maggie stood in the center as seven sets of eyes she'd never seen a week ago beamed in on her. Seven sets of eyes filled with love. She looked back at them, at a complete loss for what she could possibly say at such a monumental moment.

"Anyone up for a bacon, egg, and cheese with salt, pepper, and catsup?" she asked.

"Catsup?" they all laughed.

Matt put his arm around his girl and explained.

"It's ketchup around here, not catsup. You were so close, though!"

He took her hand and led her off the dock. The whole group walked in silence to the Bay Harbor Market, wrapped in their thoughts.

It had been some week.

Unwritten

♩♫♪

Maggie

FROM THE MOMENT Maggie stepped off the ferry, everything felt surreal. On the one hand, she felt completely comfortable. Since she and Matt had been faking a relationship for days, it was just more of the same. But on the other, for the first time in her life, her future felt unwritten. Her belly was brimming with butterflies at the thought of being alone, truly alone, with Matt. When she pictured it, she couldn't stop smiling—and blushing. She pressed her lips together, worried that she looked like a loon, until she glanced over at Matt, who had an even bigger grin on his face. She relaxed and smiled some more.

As much as being alone with Matt was all she could think about, she was happy that it wouldn't occur for hours. The day was still celebratory, wedding-wise, and would be until the six o'clock ferry when the newlyweds would receive their grand send-off, along with Dylan, Bea, Paul, and Veronica, who were all headed to the airport.

Between now and then, she found herself waiting with bated breath for Matt's every touch. His hand on the small of

her back when holding open the door for her, his finger glid-
ing over her lip where a bit of errant catsup, excuse me,
ketchup, lay. Right now, his foot was entwined with hers on
the beach. Pinkies linked as well, they lay on a blanket surrounded by his family—and hers, she remembered, hers too.
How had her life changed so dramatically in a week?

She thought of Jason and felt guilty for having not reached
out since he left. She sat up and checked her phone. He was
already in the air, but she texted anyway.

You are the very best. I'll love you, always.

She sent it feeling awful that she had nearly forgotten
about him over the last few hours, even though those had
been his instructions.

"You're starting to burn," Dylan warned, eyeing Maggie
over the cover of the novel she was engrossed in. She tossed
a can of spray sunscreen at Matt to do the honors.

"I got you." Matt smiled, holding her ponytail out of the
way. She arched her back as the cool spray shocked her. He
began rubbing it in, gently and methodically. She tried her
very best to play it cool.

In hindsight, she had been extremely conscious of Matt's
touch since they'd first met, although she hadn't allowed herself to entertain thoughts beyond kissing him. Which, thanks
to the bratty girls at the bakery, was behind them. Now his
touch had a domino effect that went way farther than her lips.

If the thought of it was too much to bear, what would the
reality be? She took the can from him.

"I got it from here, thanks," she managed—barely.

"You OK?" Matt asked quietly.

"Yes, yes." Even with the two yeses, she wasn't very convincing.

He softly brushed a wayward curl aside and whispered in her ear, "I know this is weird. We'll take it slow," thinking he was reading her mind. If he only knew that her mind was ripping his clothes off.

In the hour before the evening ferry, she and Matt sat on the back deck drinking cold lemonade and playing gin while everyone else flew by in a mad rush of packing and showering. Matt had won three games in a row, and she didn't even care. She was completely in her head.

"Maggie! I just picked up a jack, and you threw another one down—gin."

She barely reacted.

"What are you thinking about?"

"Later," she confessed, not knowing if he would understand what she meant. It could have been, *I'll tell you later*— or, *I'm thinking about later.*

"I know we have put this all out of order."

He got it.

He took her face in his hands and kissed her gently on the lips.

"We can just do more of this . . . later."

He kissed her again, pushing the cards to the floor and pulling her close to him. His lips tasted salty from the ocean air, his tongue cold and sweet from his last sip of lemonade. Her breath caught in her chest, and she could swear her heart skipped a beat.

"It's time," Jake's voice bellowed from the house, and they both jumped to attention, whichever cards had survived the kiss now flying to the ground.

The goodbyes at the ferry dock were chaotic and touching. Matt bounced around between everyone—receiving last-minute instructions from his mother and unsolicited advice from Dylan—while Maggie spent most of her time saying goodbye to her mom.

"It looks like rain," Bea said, pulling a zip-up from her tote, adding, "Do you want to take my jacket?"

And they both laughed at how her maternal instincts had kicked right in. Maggie was glad for the laughter. She didn't want a long, heavy goodbye.

Matt and Maggie stood on the dock, dramatically waving as the ferry pulled out of the basin. A giant JUST MARRIED sign was draped across the back of the boat, along with a cacophony of cans clanging in the wind. It was storybook stuff until a few drops of rain landed on their faces, snapping them out of the moment.

As they jumped on their bikes, the light drizzle quickly escalated to a deluge, the rain falling in relentless sheets and soaking through every layer of their clothing. Their hair stuck to their foreheads and necks; fat droplets streamed down their faces, outrunning their legs. They pedaled home at double speed, laughing at the turn of events.

On their arrival, Maggie shouted above the noise of the storm, "This is like that scene in *The Notebook!*"

"Well, that's a lot of fucking pressure," Matt yelled back, pulling her into his arms and attempting to outdo Ryan Gosling's iconic rain kiss with Rachel McAdams.

"How'd I do?" he asked afterward, running his fingers through her wet hair. She grinned and kissed him again until a bolt of thunder sent them running for the house.

Maggie kicked off her sandals and watched Matt peel off

his sneakers and socks before following him upstairs. He playfully jumped up and down on both feet when he reached the second-to-last step, where the squeak rang out for no one to hear but them.

They were alone.

In the bedroom, they stood and faced each other. Dripping and cold. Their clothes plastered to them like, well, plaster. Maggie reached her hands straight up over her head for Matt to peel off her dress. He did, and she stood, nearly naked, shivering. He pulled the quilt from the bed and wrapped it around her. Peeling off his clothes too, she opened the blanket wide like the wings of an eagle to let him in. And there they were, skin to skin, slippery and cold, pushing back against heat and desire. A chill sent shivers up both their spines. They laughed before looking into each other's eyes, taking in each other's desire, letting it breathe and build in intensity for a long minute.

"Matt?" Maggie whispered, cautious of breaking the spell.

"Ye—" he said, his answer jumbled in his throat.

"Can we maybe forgo the bunk beds tonight?"

A huge and mischievous smile crossed his face before he scooped her up and carried her to the guest room. Kissing him along the way, Maggie kicked closed the door behind them.

"You're sure about this?" Matt asked, the wild desire in his eyes fading, replaced with something far deeper—an intensity that felt undeniable. Like it had always been there. Like it was written in stone.

I've never been more sure of anything, she thought, but only managed one word.

"Yes!"

I'm Gonna Be (500 Miles)

♩ ♫ ♪

May 4, 2026

MAGGIE MAY WHEELER fastened a strip of Scotch tape onto the yellow vintage Maggie May Records wrapping paper just as the reindeer bells rang on the front door of her shop. She looked up and smiled as Jason strolled in. A matching smile lit his face.

"Hello, thirty-first birthday girl!" he said.

"Hello, thirty-first birthday boy," she responded.

"I just wrapped your present—but I don't think I can wait till tonight to give it to you!"

"But what about the game?"

"We can rewrap it and feign surprise," she said, handing it to him.

"That is highly unethical," he retorted, ripping off the paper.

Maggie laughed, before holding her breath to see his reaction.

A big smile crossed his face, and he made his best attempt at crooning the B-52's hit single "Roam."

"*Roam if you want to, roam around the world.* It's perfect, Maggie."

"I'm going to miss you so much, J."

"Me too."

They went in for a hug that lasted until the reindeer bells rang again. A fit man in jeans and Timberlands, bags and boxes piled high in front of his face, backed into the store, pushing the door open with his cute butt. Maggie and Jason went to assist him. Maggie was glad for the interruption. She had felt her mood shifting and had promised herself she would not go there. Jason would be leaving for Europe in a week, traveling the continent before beginning his postdoctoral studies in Leeds, and selfishly, she was sad. She would miss him terribly, though she was happy that he had waited to celebrate their birthdays together as usual before taking off.

They both grabbed boxes from the struggling man, the top one, the cake box, revealing Matt's beautiful smile. His grin disappeared when he recognized the melancholy in Maggie's eyes.

"What's wrong? You're sad that young Jason is off to see the world and you're stuck here with me?"

"Exactly."

He kissed her lips sweetly and she melted. She wondered when that would stop, this heart-jumping-at-the-sight-of-him and melting-at-his-touch thing.

"Hey, Matt." Jason shook his hand and went in for a half hug.

"Happy birthday," Matt said in return.

"Thanks, I gotta run, but I'll see you both later at the big shindig."

Everyone would be coming that night to a special birthday seating at the Maggie May Records Listening Room and

Sake Bar, which was heading into its sixth successful month. Everyone included her mother and Paul, who she was beyond excited to show it off to. She hadn't seen them since Christmas, when she and Matt had flown to England to visit them on their year abroad. It was the first stamp on her passport, and while she was happy to go, she was equally happy to return to her Chagrin Falls home on top of the record store that she now shared with Matt.

After much back and forth and meeting in the middle, mostly at concert venues, Matt had officially given up his apartment in Manhattan and moved in with Maggie that February. They were still in the honeymoon phase of their relationship, amazed by how every love song seemed to be written just for them.

Matt ponied up to the counter to check out the pile of unwrapped records that Maggie had picked out for each of tonight's guests. She had told him all about the tradition; he had never heard someone so excited to give out presents on her own birthday. He tapped on the top one—"My Way" by Frank Sinatra.

"I bet this one is for Shep."

Shep, her grandfather, was coming too. Even Aunt Veronica had enthusiastically accepted the invitation that Bea had suggested. She was bringing her husband, Larry, whom Maggie had never met and was having a hard time matching to a record album. It would be the first time that the ratio of Jason's family and Maggie's bordered on equal.

Matt began to lift the first album to peek at the rest, but Maggie stopped him.

"Wanna guess yours—without looking?"

"Sure, but it's gonna annoy you when I get it on the first try."

"It's gonna annoy you when you don't."

She knew he would go with the song that was attached to his big romantic gesture back on Fire Island. Peter Gabriel's "In Your Eyes," from *Say Anything*.

"Peter Gabriel, 'In Your Eyes,'" he said, with the confidence of Lloyd Dobler holding a boom box over his head.

"Nope, one shot only, close your eyes."

"One shot only? That's BS!"

She put her hands on his knees and planted butterfly kisses on his eyes, closing them.

"My game. My rules. Keep them shut," she instructed.

"You're very bossy on your birthday," he complained sweetly.

Maggie took the record by The Proclaimers out of its sleeve, placed it on the turntable, and dropped the needle to play. He knew it by the rousing first notes, as most people would. It was "500 Miles"—the exact distance from Fire Island to Maggie May Records in Chagrin Falls, Ohio, an homage to the fact that Matt had picked up his life and moved five hundred miles to be with her. Yes, she had calculated it as well.

He was so touched that when he opened his eyes again, she could see that they had tears in them.

Soon they were dancing around the old wooden floor of Maggie May Records and yelling the rowdy chorus at the top of their lungs, like the two Irishmen who'd made the song famous.

"But I would walk five hundred miles / And I would walk five hundred more / Just to be the man who walked a thousand / Miles to fall down at your door."

"Again," Matt requested, following the last note.

"You have to kiss me first," Maggie said, picking up the needle and gently placing it down again.

And he did.

But this time they never made it to the makeshift dance floor.

"*Da-da da da (da-da da da) / Da-da da da (da-da da da) / Da-da dum!*"

ACKNOWLEDGMENTS

As always—it takes a village to publish a book, both before and after its release. I will begin by thanking my loyal readers! Thank you for all your support, encouragement, and love of reading.

I was lucky to have many sets of editorial eyes review *Songs of Summer*. Thank you to my five-time superstar editor, Amanda Bergeron, for her years of direction and finesse; to the brilliant Sareer Khader, who is always there for me and my novels; and to new team member Randi Kramer for providing a fresh and sharp look. Also, thank you to my eagle-eyed copyeditor, Joan Matthews; and, as always, to my first and best reader, Linda Coppola.

To Eve MacSweeney, my agent and friend, endless thanks for always making me a priority. Still counting my blessings that I found you!

Much gratitude to the one and only Jin Yu and to Elisha Katz, for their marketing mojo. Thank you also to Theresa Tran for all of your help with this novel.

I took the song selections very seriously for the chapter

titles. Thank you to the daddy/daughter Juke Box Heroes, Colin and Sabrina Finkelstein, for your fabulous input! And to my personal hero, my husband, Warren Rosen, for bringing so much music and inspiration into my life. Thank you for your input on the chapter titles and your invaluable record store insight from your first job in high school.

Thank you to Vi-An Nguyen and Katharine Asher for creating another beautiful cover. And, of course, to Claire Zion and Craig Burke for continuing to support my novels.

Finally, to one of the greatest loves of my life, Fire Island. For over forty years, you've been the backdrop to my summers and the heart of my last three books. You brought me my "meet-cute" with your charmingly absurd "no drinking on the walks of town" rule, arresting my future husband for sipping a Snapple, and giving me the chance to rescue the cute guy I had just met at the beach. That same cute guy who's been rescuing me right back for thirty-five years.

You convinced me that there's no better place on earth to raise my three children, placing your sand and sea between their toes, and instilling your resilience, sense of community, and boundless freedom in their hearts. You've taught me that age is irrelevant, and you've redefined what *home* truly means.

And most importantly, you've gifted me with an incredible array of characters, comedy, and a community I've been honored to portray and share with readers around the world. Let's just hope they don't all decide to visit on the same weekend!

Songs of Summer

Jane L. Rosen

Songs of Summer Soundtrack

♩♫♪

CREATING THE SOUNDTRACK for this novel was a complete and collaborative joy. And I believe listening along while you read will bring you joy as well!

Some songs, like Chapter 16's "Indiana Jones: The Main Theme," were chosen to make you laugh, while others, like Chapter 38's "Into the Mystic," should bring a tear or two. Certain songs were selected because their titles were right on the money ("The 59th Street Bridge Song") and others were chosen because their lyrics align with the characters' thoughts ("Riptide"). A few play on one word ("Rock Lobster") or one sentence ("Something Good") while others just capture a vibe ("Good Day"). And then there's the final track, "500 Miles," which I first chose because it's a personal favorite and represents taking a journey for love. Imagine my surprise when I calculated the distance between my town on Fire Island and the fictional location of Maggie May Records in Chagrin Falls, Ohio. You guessed it, 500 miles!

Visit JaneLRosen.com to find a Spotify link to the
***Songs of Summer* Soundtrack, and listen along.**

PROLOGUE: Maggie May | Faces

TRACK 1: Put Your Records On | Corinne Bailey Rae

TRACK 2: Birthday | The Beatles

TRACK 3: I See the Moon | Nancy Sinatra

TRACK 4: Smile | Jimmy Durante

TRACK 5: Little Lies | Fleetwood Mac

TRACK 6: In My Life | The Beatles

TRACK 7: Veronica | Elvis Costello

TRACK 8: Rock the Boat | The Hues Corporation

TRACK 9: Ironic | Alanis Morissette

TRACK 10: Up on the Roof | Carole King/James Taylor

TRACK 11: What's Going On | Marvin Gaye

TRACK 12: Should I Stay or Should I Go | The Clash

TRACK 13: Peace Train | Cat Stevens

TRACK 14: A Bar Song (Tipsy) | Shaboozey

TRACK 15: Glory Days | Bruce Springsteen & the E Street Band

TRACK 16: Indiana Jones: The Main Theme

TRACK 17: She Drives Me Crazy | Fine Young Cannibals

TRACK 18: Stay | Jackson Brown

TRACK 19: (Sittin' on) the Dock of the Bay | Otis Redding

TRACK 20: La Mer | Charles Trenet

TRACK 21: Good Day | Nappy Roots

TRACK 22: Rock Lobster | B-52's

TRACK 23: Pulling Mussels (from the Shell) | Squeeze

TRACK 24: The Joker | Steve Miller Band

TRACK 25: After Midnight | Eric Clapton

TRACK 26: SOS | ABBA

TRACK 27: Riptide | Vance Joy

TRACK 28: The House That Built Me | Miranda Lambert

TRACK 29: The Search Is Over | Survivor

TRACK 30: All | GROUPLOVE featuring Jake Clemons

TRACK 31: The 59th Street Bridge Song | Simon & Garfunkel

TRACK 32: The Shoop Shoop Song | Aretha Franklin

TRACK 33: Rapper's Delight | The Sugarhill Gang

TRACK 34: Ocean Eyes | Billie Eilish

TRACK 35: Gimme! Gimme! Gimme! | ABBA

TRACK 36: Love You for a Long Time | Maggie Rogers

TRACK 37: Wildflowers | Tom Petty

TRACK 38: Into the Mystic | Van Morrison

TRACK 39: Champagne Problems | Taylor Swift

TRACK 40: Float On | Modest Mouse

TRACK 41: Landslide | Stevie Nicks

TRACK 42: Family Affair | Sly & The Family Stone

TRACK 43: Something Good | Mima Good

TRACK 44: Flowers | Miley Cyrus

TRACK 45: Poker Face | Lady Gaga

TRACK 46: Firework | Katy Perry

TRACK 47: Mother and Child Reunion | Paul Simon

TRACK 48: Growin' Up | Bruce Springsteen

TRACK 49: Real Love | Regina Spektor

TRACK 50: In Your Eyes | Peter Gabriel

TRACK 51: Unwritten | Natasha Bedingfield

EPILOGUE: I'm Gonna Be (500 Miles) | The Proclaimers

Discussion Questions

♩♫♪

1. Thirteen-year-old Maggie writes a letter detailing her hopes for her adult life and reads that letter when she turns thirty. When you were thirteen years old, how did you think your adult life would turn out? Has it turned out like you expected?

2. Maggie's adoptive parents waited until she was in second grade to tell her that she was adopted, which Maggie believes made her become self-reliant and slow to trust others. How do you think her life would have been different if her parents had told her about the adoption from the beginning? Do you think she would have approached the events in the book differently?

3. How do you feel Bea's mother Caroline handled Bea's pregnancy and the adoption? Do you think Shep may have handled it differently? How does the novel portray the emotional complexity of adoption for both the mother and the child?

4. With the increasing accessibility of DNA testing, more people are discovering unexpected family connections.

How do you think *Songs of Summer* reflects the real-life complexities and consequences of this modern phenomenon? Would you consider taking a DNA test after reading the novel?

5. Beatrix and Veronica were very close as children but have been mostly estranged for thirty years. Would you have forgiven Veronica for what she did to Beatrix? Do you think Veronica was totally at fault? Do you have a contentious family relationship you wish you could repair?

6. Maggie and Matt take a day trip to New York City and Matt gives her a personalized tour of the city in which he grew up. What would your perfect day in New York City (or your hometown) look like?

7. Maggie is torn between her growing feelings for Matt and her longtime love for Jason. Do you agree with her choice? What would you have done in her position?

8. If you have read *On Fire Island*, you were probably rooting for Matt and Dylan to end up together. How do you feel about how it all turned out? Did you have an *if we're not married by thirty or forty* person growing up?

9. Letting go of anger and fear in order to move forward is a big theme in this novel. Do you think the risk was worth the reward for Maggie? How about for Beatrix and Veronica? How do you envision their relationships in the future?

10. Music is as powerful a medium as words in conveying emotion. How does the author use music to describe a character or a situation? Did you listen along? Did you discover any new artists or songs from the selections?

Photo © Captain W.

JANE L. ROSEN is the author of six novels: *Nine Women, One Dress*; *Eliza Starts a Rumor*; *A Shoe Story*; *On Fire Island*; *Seven Summer Weekends*; and *Songs of Summer*. She lives in the Hudson Valley and on Fire Island with her husband; their rescue pup, Rosalita; and, on her happiest of occasions, their three grown daughters.

VISIT JANE L. ROSEN ONLINE

JaneLRosen.com
⊙ JaneLRosen
❶ JaneLRosenAuthor
𝕏 JaneLRosen1

Ready to find
your next great read?

Let us help.

Visit prh.com/nextread